Against All Odds

Against All Odds

Michael Faunce-Brown

iUniverse, Inc.
Bloomington

Against All Odds

iUniverse books may be ordered through booksellers or by contacting:

iUniverse
1663 Liberty Drive
Bloomington, IN 47403
www.iuniverse.com
1-800-Authors (1-800-288-4677)

ISBN: 978-1-4759-3732-9 (sc)
ISBN: 978-1-4759-3733-6 (ebk)

Printed in the United States of America

iUniverse rev. date: 07/12/2012

Front Illustration
by Little Cloud

Back Illustration
thanks to Jake

PART 1

CHAPTER 1

An almost clear blue sky in Queensland, Australia showed no hint of storms to come. Storms to wreak havoc on the cattle property of Greg and Mary Hartley and storms in the life of their fine young son, Tom, aged seventeen, who rode his bay mare among the sparse gum trees checking for dingoes.

Tom fingered his rifle in its saddle holster as he saw the remains of a young cow, ripped apart by the feral dogs and probably still alive as they ate their fill. The blond headed lad could never forgive the ferocity of the dingoes, but he was to face almost as harsh a treatment himself before he was not much older, but not from four legged creatures.

"Better get back to the homestead. They'll be long gone."

The mare shied at a brown snake lazily zigzagging across their path and nearly threw Tom onto it. He just managed to regain his seat and calmed the startled beast some fifty yards further on. A kookaburra cackled at their discomfort and brought a grin to Tom's brown face.

Only an hour later, rain clouds fluffed across the sky and soaked him to the skin. It was a welcome break from the stifling heat.

As he rode up to the horse paddock by their weather-boarded Queenslander house, its paint peeling off it, he wondered if Mum and Dad had sorted out their differences? Mum, once a quiet American, had just about enough of living ten miles from their nearest neighbour and three hours from town, if that's what Kilacoy could be called, all of one street and five hundred inhabitants. There was a chemist and a surgery, staffed by one nurse on and one off.

The police station had a sergeant and occasionally a visiting copper getting a taste of keeping the law in the outback. There was a pie shop and judging by the texture, they had a kangaroo culler on their supply chain. A hardware shop also sold second hand paperbacks and mended the occasional lawnmower. A chemist, doubling as a greengrocer, as they shared the double fronted shop, just about completed the shopping section. Not a place to set Mrs. Hartley, Tom's mum, on fire.

The saddle seemed heavier than ever as he released the girth and carried it inside the tack hut. The mare enjoyed a bundle of hay and a drink from the trough. She even found time to nuzzle Tom with her velvety nose.

As Tom passed the car shed, he noticed Mum's car was missing. Only the battered old model-T Ford remained.

"Dad," he called, dreading what might have happened. There was no answer.

He strode into the living room and found his dad sitting, gazing into space.

"Dad, where's Mum?"

Dad turned as if seeing a stranger. For a moment he didn't focus.

"Dad, it's me, Tom. Where's Mum gone?"

Dad rose stiffly, looking ten years older and hugged Tom.

"She's gone, son. Said she's leaving us for good this time."

Tom broke away. "No! Without a goodbye!" He struggled to contain his tears.

"Said she's had living out here, drought or flood. She's going home to the States."

Tom gulped. "This is home . . . Our home. All we've got."

"Gone back to her rich rellies across the sea."

"Don't we mean anything? Nothing?" cried Tom, desperately.

Dad looked at him, shaking his head slowly. "Apparently not . . . Still we've got each other. We'll make do."

* * *

CHAPTER 2

The rain machine gunned on the tin roof, just to bring them back to matters in hand.

"We'll have to move the cattle to higher ground if it goes on all night. You're too young to remember the floods we had twelve years ago. Lost lots of stock then. Could happen again."

"I'll throw some grub together, Dad," said Tom, hiding his feelings in action. He dived into the kitchen to inspect the larder. There was a hunk of meat behind the fly screen. "Better eat it before it goes off," he thought. But his appetite seemed to have shrunk.

The party line phone rang six times and Dad answered. He listened. "Yeah, thanks for the warning . . . Will do. Take care."

"Who's that?" asked Tom, hoping it might be Mum had changed her mind.

"Just Jack Benyon on the next property but one. They've heard there's heavy rain up north and the creek's ten feet high already. Reckons it'll hit us early morning."

"Be up at first light?" asked Tom.

"Yeah, around four thirty rise, grab a bite and get after those cows by five. Be light enough to find 'em."

Tom peeled some spuds and paused to check the logs in the stove. They were glowing nicely. There was never any shortage of eucalyptus, so koalas were also plentiful.

Next morning Tom awoke to Dad shaking him. He switched on his torch and looked at his watch: 4:15.

"What's the matter, Dad? Couldn't you sleep?"

"Come on son. No, I didn't sleep a wink; the thought of not waking up in time and all the cattle drowning. Get your skids on."

Dad left to snatch some corn flakes while Tom had a quick dunk in the water trough to kick start his protesting body.

As Tom entered the kitchen he saw Dad leaving in his raincoat. "I'll saddle the horses," he called as he strode into the relentless rain. The odd flash of lightning didn't bode well for their controlling the frightened cattle. "Well Mum, you're well out of it," thought Tom as he bolted his breakfast. A pang of resentment nevertheless intruded.

"You might've taken us with you," he thought. Plenty of people had just walked off their property and left them to the banks. He stood, clattered his plate into the sink and donned his raincoat and leggings.

A dash through to the barn and Tom found Dad ready with his gelding and Tom's mare waiting patiently for their baptism. They mounted their steeds and made for the distant paddock where most of the cattle should be, including that expensive bull that Dad bought only last month. The rain pattered steadily on their oil—skins, leggings and sou'westers. There was no sign of it giving up as light strengthened through lowering clouds. They cantered on in silence, both worried that the river might burst its banks any moment.

As they reached the trees, a mile from the homestead, they found most of the cattle sheltering from the wind, under the lea of some gum trees. A possum ran up a tree seeking refuge in its top branches.

"The bull's not here. Have a search round the far side, while I move this mob through the gate and up the hill, Tom," said Dad.

"Right on," said Tom, wheeling his horse in that direction. The ground was boggy and he settled for a fast trot. In minutes he found the bull with his harem of heifers where Dad indicated.

He pulled out his whip from its saddle clasp and cracked it. The bull reluctantly moved, followed by his admirers. Tom cracked the whip again and again, suddenly conscious of a flow of water from the river likely to cut them off. He barked like a dog and the cattle surged towards the open gate. They jostled through and the water was already a foot deep as Tom closed the gate behind them.

"Hiyah! Crack! Woof! Woof!" It would have been funny if not for the water flooding close behind them.

Dad felt mightily relieved as he saw the mob of cattle plus bull stomping up the hill. There was sufficient grass in the higher paddock for a week, and no shortage of water!

"We'd better get home or we'll be up here with them for God knows how long," said Dad, turning to canter away.

"Yeah. I hope these are good swimmers," said Tom, following him close behind.

They reached the water, which had cut them off and was flowing fast around the hillock the house was built on. No way could they walk their horses across.

"We'll have to swim them across," shouted Dad over the wind.

"You first," said Tom, thinking he would be able to see if Dad got into difficulties.

Dad plunged his horse into the water, with a sharp prod of his heels, staying in the saddle. All went well till half way across, when the horse's head went under. Dad slid off his saddle and swam after the horse, grabbing its tail to be towed to safety. Tom breathed a sigh of relief and entered the flowing current. He stayed in his saddle and with a lighter load his horse swam strongly to the other side.

They changed into dry clothes, and put through the wringer and hung out their wet garments to steam in front of the fire. Dad tried the phone to check how Jack had fared but the line was dead.

"Well it looks like we're on our own Tom, so I'll check the accounts. Must keep on top of things," said Dad. "Make sure to keep the fire going."

"Will do," replied Tom, and he searched for a good book to read from their copious collection. Little did he guess what troubles were about to hit him.

* * *

CHAPTER 3

Next morning never came, least not for Dad. In the middle of the night Tom woke to the sound of water running through the house and rending timbers. As he gained consciousness he realized what was happening and shouted, "Dad!"

There was no reply. He flung on a shirt and trousers and felt for his boots, about to float away. He waded through water already up to his chest and into his dad's room. It was pitch black but he could see the light of a cloud swept moon through the shattered end of the house. In panic he felt for his dad's body and dived down to his bed. A beam had fallen across him, pinning him into his bed and he had no chance in Hell of surviving. Tom felt the cold body and pulled the beam away before surfacing for air. He dived again and managed to pull the body to the surface but then let go as something snagged his own trousers, sucking him under the current. When he finally struggled free, gasping for air, Dad's body had floated away out of sight.

For a moment Tom was too puffed and devastated to think what to do. No way could he find Dad in the dark and tempestuous water raging past. The horses! He could hear their petrified neighs from the stable. He swam across the current and forged his way to the stable which was already part loose from its foundation and threatening to float away. With Herculean effort Tom pulled open the door and swam across to his dad's horse. There was no question of finding saddle or reins. He undid the bolt and heaved open the door against the flow of water.

"Swim for it boy," Tom shouted and as the frightened beast hesitated, he smacked its rump and it swam out of the doorway.

Bad luck had to end and he saw reins hanging on a nail, about to be dragged off by floating debris. He threw them over his horse's head and pulled out the door bolt. "Let's go, girl," he shouted, and inspired by her master and her companion's example she dragged Tom out of the building just before it filled with water.

By now Tom was exhausted and he just allowed her to tow him along in the current. After a mile or so, her hooves felt land and they hauled themselves dripping, out of the torrent. Horse and rider just lay where they were and eventually watched the sun come up.

Tom saw the water was beginning to recede and before he knew it, was fast asleep. Somewhere near midday he awoke, nuzzled by his mare, and looking around him he was amazed by the devastation. Fences had been swept away. Pieces of houses, some whole walls had caught on the higher ground, while others still floated past. In the distance he did not need to look to find the empty space where the tractor shed had once stood. The reality of the past night hit Tom like a falling tree. He could not contain his tears. Dad gone. No one to help him or be a companion. Totally alone but with the responsibility of maybe two thousand head of cattle, for what?

Suddenly hunger overcame exhaustion and self-pity. He would have to ride into town, if the road was passable. It would take him a couple of days, if all went well. Then what? Would he be able to take from Dad's bank account? Could he rebuild? Never on his own. Tom stood up unsteadily and approached his precious horse. She was eating from the water flattened grass.

"All right for you, old girl. But we're on our way."

Tom put on her bridle and vaulted onto her back, after two unsuccessful attempts, where he just slid over to land on his rump. They waded through the still fast flowing water and looked for the road, what was left of it. The rain water had gouged out many gullies and no vehicle was going to get along there for a while. As he reached the road, Tom thought of searching for his dad but on his own, it could take weeks and he was already weak from hunger and lack of sleep; he too could die so he set off for town.

It was after about three hours in the saddle, frequently having to wade his horse through new gullies, that Tom was wondering if he would make it. Ironically, with all this water flowing, he was parched for the want of drinkable water. He had reached the boundary of their property and saw the fence had been washed away. Bodies of sheep and cattle plus the occasional kangaroo or wallaby lay in abundance. Suddenly he saw a young child, a girl of about eight spread-eagled, caught in a bush. He heaved himself out of the saddle and ran across to her, but she was dead. He felt a twinge of pity for the bedraggled little girl. He could not leave her there for the dingoes and crows. He hoisted her across his saddle and walked with the reins in his hands.

An hour or so later Tom was stumbling along, wondering whether he might be feeding the crows himself before nightfall. The creek followed the road for a while, still flowing as a wide river. Large trees and pieces of houses floated past. Suddenly a fish caught Tom's eye. It was trapped in the roots of a bush.

"Stay there," he mouthed to his horse and he ran back to the fish. It wasn't quite dead, flipping its tail weakly. At least it would be fresh. He carefully lifted it out of the water and dropped it in his haste. It flipped towards the river but he caught it and bashed its head on the ground. Taking his skinning knife from its sheath, he cut off the fish's head and gutted it. Then he washed it clean in the river, taking care not to fall in.

Everything was soaking wet so there was no chance of a fire. He cut off a small portion and tasted it. "Not bad. Could do with some salt," he grinned but this would keep him going for a few hours yet. Suddenly things were not quite so drastic after all. He put the remainder in his saddlebag, thinking it would make it smell when it warmed up.

"Dad, where was he?" he wondered sorrowfully as they plodded on. How was he to manage the place on his own? The question reared its ugly head again. Eventually he reached the remains of the next property. There were no signs of life, nor was the old model T-Ford around, so with some luck they had escaped the flood. The end of the house had been sucked out and the roof was in danger of collapsing, as it sagged inwards.

"I can't take her all the way to town. Better bury her here and ask the police to trace her parents," Tom thought, searching for a spade. Luckily the out buildings were still standing, the door flapping in the wind. He looked inside and found a variety of tools including a spade.

Tom dug a hole round the back easily in the wet soil and carried the body to it. He carefully laid her to rest and then filled in the earth. He looked around for something to mark the spot and found some wooden struts inside. He banged one into the earth near her head and cut a shorter piece with a rusty saw. He tied this tightly to form a cross to the upright with a piece of wire. Then he felt the urge to say something in keeping with her burial. "Take good care of her, God, if you've room for another after this flood. I've done my best." He struggled against tears, as he felt all alone, and mounting his mare, rode off towards town.

How Tom kept riding and how the mare kept carrying him he never knew. Mind you, he was a light enough burden. Skinny to start with and only a fish that was finished a day ago. He rode into Kilacoy late afternoon, swaying in the saddle and slid off by the pub entrance to the concerned astonishment of potential customers. A stranger gathered him up and carried him inside, while Patrick the hardware owner took his mare and looked after her as if she were his own, with a good feed of bran and oats and a rub down with a fist of straw. He was amazed how much water she drank.

*   *   *

Chapter 4

nside the pub, the tall stranger had placed Tom on a settle and was equally amazed by this kid's thirst. He drank pint after pint of water and then had to be wakened for a feed of sausages, beans and mashed potatoes. Blearily he thanked the stranger, who he learnt was a Mr. Kit Rivers, who was just passing through.

"Give the kid a room and put it on my bill," instructed Kit Rivers, "and I'll pay for whatever he eats for the next couple of days."

Publican Jack O'Leary nodded, glad to be helping the Hartley boy, whose Dad had often bought a pint or two when in town at the cattle mart. He was concerned how way-out Tom was and helped him up to his bedroom as he threatened to fall asleep as soon as he had finished his meal.

Late next morning, refreshed by sleep and food, Tom carefully descended the stairs and looked to thank his benefactor. "Think nothing of it, kiddo," said Kit. "Anyone'd do it. I was just first on the scene."

Suddenly Tom remembered the child he had buried. "Excuse me," he said to Kit. "I've got to report a death, no, two to the police. Little girl drowned and my dad was washed away."

"Sorry to hear that," exclaimed Kit, as Tom approached the door. "How's your mum taking it?"

"She left for the States," said Tom, biting his lip. "Must go. See you later and thanks again. You're a real mate." He left the pub.

At the police station Sergeant Holmes listened attentively as Tom recalled his experiences.

"So your dad could still be alive?"

"I don't think anyone could have survived that rush of water," said Tom. "Besides . . ."

"Besides what?" asked the sergeant, gently.

"Dad was sinking when I last saw him and cold to the touch." Tom blinked rapidly, trying to control and hide his feelings.

"We'll mount a search immediately," said the sergeant, rising from his chair. "But why Tom, why didn't you tell us as soon as you got to town?"

"I was only part conscious," said Tom, and I'm sure he's dead." He just knew it in his heart. His shoulders shook.

Sergeant Holmes patted him on the back. "Well, I guess you're right, but we must do our best to find him and dig up the little girl. It's good you marked her grave well."

"Her folk will want her buried properly and will be relieved to know, however upset," said Tom.

"There was only her grannie, we heard and she was drowned up river," said the sergeant. "They were looking for the girl."

"Oh," said Tom, looking despondent.

The sergeant told him to stay in town while the search for his dad was on. He was in no fit state to ride back, as with the road cut, horses were the only alternative. He got Tom to draw him a map of where he had last seen his dad and where the current had been flowing. The sergeant warned him that some bodies had been recovered as far as thirty miles from where they had perished.

*   *   *

CHAPTER 5

When he left the police station, Tom felt a weight off his mind. He was surprised and pleased to see Kit sitting on a bench near the Police Station.

"That all over?" asked Kit.

"Yeah. Thank God," said Tom. "He said I wasn't fit to ride with the searchers for my dad."

"Quite right," agreed Kit. "By the look of you, you'll need a day or two to recover . . . But how are you going to manage on your own? While you were eating last night, you were rambling on about a large herd of cattle and fences down. It'll take time to repair them."

"Oh, I'll manage somehow on my own. I've got to visit the bank now to see if I've got enough to pay someone."

"Oh right," said Kit. "I guess you'll be okay. Your dad'll be solvent . . . will have been," he corrected himself quickly. "See you later, then."

Tom nodded. "Thanks for all you've done for me." He turned and strode off to the bank.

The manager, Mr. Granger, hardly kept him waiting; just enough time for a kind girl to bring him a coffee and a biscuit.

"Well young Hartley, I am so sorry for your loss. You'll need someone to care for you. Your dad was a fine man."

"Yes," said Tom. Suddenly he wanted to be through the business and out. The bank felt stifling and claustrophobic. The manager treated him like a boy just when he needed to be a man. "Could you tell me how much he has in the bank?"

"Normally I could not reveal this but since you are the only one left in your family, I'll make an exception."

"Big of you," thought Tom.

The manager pulled out a brown cardboard file and studied it for a moment.

"You have fifty thousand pounds, and a little more in shares. Your dad sold his fat cattle well last year."

"Wow!" said Tom, greatly relieved. "Can I have a cheque book so I can pay someone to mend the fences? They need doing right away or we . . . I'll lose all my cattle."

"Good thinking, but I"ll have to countersign them, till we can find you a guardian."

"A guardian? I don't need a guardian. I've been working like a man since I left school nearly two years back."

"The Law will decree you must have a guardian, I'm sure. You'll need legal advice and a magistrate will sit to hear your situation. Of course, I could be your guardian?"

Tom did not like that idea one bit. He did not trust or like Mr. Granger. He had a handshake like a wet fish and looked at Tom as if he wanted to take him over. Better not show his true feelings. "That's very kind of you, but I wouldn't want to take up your time. I'll consult the magistrate. Thanks Sir."

"How much money do you need right now, to survive and maybe get your home right?" said Mr. Granger, thinking: "Damn! An opportunity wasted."

Tom thought for a moment. "£1000 should keep me going for a few weeks. I'm going to need a lot of fencing wire, posts and nails plus some tools."

"Take this to the counter and we'll give you a loan on what you have coming." The manager quickly filled in a form and presented it to Tom.

"What interest?" asked Tom.

"3% per month," said the manager. "You should be free to pay it off in a couple, when the paper work is through."

"Thanks for your time and advice," Tom shook his hand and left as quickly as he could politely.

"That's a bright kid, and wealthy," thought the manager. "He'll go far, if he doesn't go under. There has to be a way."

The magistrate's hearing was not till next month, giving Tom a chance to show he could cope on his own—he hoped.

A week later the search had not found Tom's dad and an exhausted party returned to town. He was resigned to the fact that Dad had drowned when he saw him sinking, and must be buried under a pile of debris somewhere. He preferred not to dwell on it, tears not far away. Tom rented a flat-deck, or "ute" and was loading it up with coils of wire, nails, a hammer, a bow saw, a spade and crowbar plus two wire strainers and fencing pliers. There were also boxes of tinned food and a sleeping bag. As he had just about finished, Kit sauntered up to him. He eyed the load and offered, "You look as if you could do with some help. What about it, if you just feed me till you get your finances right?"

His ready smile won Tom over. Kit was friendly and looked easy to get along with. He would be able to get those fences up twice as fast and having someone to talk to would be great. Ten minutes later Kit had fetched his swag and thrown it in the back of the vehicle. Tom put it into gear and drove out of town, his spirits high.

Kit asked about the size of the property and how many stock he had. "I need to know how long I'm to stay," he explained. "I don't want to leave you until you've got everything under control."

Tom answered his questions and thought how lucky he was to have found a willing helper so easily.

"I'll pay you when the money comes through," said Tom. "Don't need any charity, but thanks a million for helping me out."

"That's okay. Could hardly leave a youngster in the lurch," smiled Kit.

*   *   *

Chapter 6

They travelled slowly because although the flood water had subsided and the search party had filled in some large pot holes on their return, the vehicle slid from rut to rut and threatened to overturn in one hole.

They had been going very slowly for many hours when Tom noticed the fuel gauge was low. "We'd better re-fuel," he said and drew in some yards from the creek.

Kit lifted down a jerry-can of petrol and Tom pulled out the funnel from under his seat. They filled up the Model-T and Kit placed the jerry can in the back.

"Time for a break," said Kit.

"Yeah," agreed Tom who was pretty tired after hours of driving.

They sat down under a tree and Tom handed Kit an apple he'd bought in town. As they sat, each one with his thoughts, the mare started acting up. She whinnied and became increasingly fretful.

"Jeez! What the Hell's got into her?" said Kit as they both stood up.

"A hornet or . . ." started Tom, "oh fuck!"

A fifteen foot crocodile was scrambling up the bank towards them. It made for Tom, who froze. Kit picked up a stone and bounced it off the creature's head, making not the slightest impact.

"Run!" shouted Kit as he picked up a branch and advanced on the croc. It stopped for a moment and then decided Kit was tastier. Kit fumbled behind him and drew out a pistol.

Tom jumped into the car and started the engine. Kit took careful aim at the croc's eye and fired. He hit the eye and it snapped wildly, just missing Kit's feet. He jumped to the other side and fired hitting the other eye. Blinded, the monster came to a halt.

Kit raced round the other side of the vehicle and jumped in. "Go!" he shouted as the croc charged blindly in their direction.

"Hey! That was lucky you were carrying that." said Tom as they surged forward. "You saved my life. I don't know why I froze."

"I do," laughed Kit, replacing the gun in his belt.

"Why do you carry . . . ?" started Tom, and then stopped as he realized how silly the question sounded. "I can't ever repay you."

"Just say you owe me," said Kit, grinning.

The mare trotted behind on a long rope and whinnied when she saw familiar territory.

When at last Tom drove up to what remained of his home, his spirits fell as he saw the enormity of their task. He went inside and Kit let him be considerately while he explored.

The heavy wood stove was still there and one bedroom was habitable. Debris and mud covered the floor. The roof sagged and needed urgent attention before the next Westerly blew. Outside an axe was imbedded in a large log, snagged by the water trough.

Tom strode to the pump and worked the handle. Water gushed up, brown at first but it soon cleared. He gave a thumbs-up to Kit, who looked relieved.

"We'd better have a bite to eat and then look for the cattle," said Tom.

"That's right by me," replied Kit, as he hauled his swag into the house.

"There's a room still habitable," said Tom, pointing to the bedroom, "as long as you don't mind sharing."

"Beats the verandah any day," joked Kit, as he dropped his swag in the bedroom.

Tom found a tin opener and they feasted off corned beef and beans from the tins.

The meal over, Tom tied up his mare near the barn, which had survived miraculously, where she could reach the water trough and eat the grass sprouting above the mud. Then they drove off up the paddock, searching for cattle. They did not have to go far. Some of the best grass was near the creek and at least a thousand head of cattle were grazing happily. Tom was exhilarated to see the precious bull surrounded by his harem and a smaller rival.

"We'd better take a look at the top end," said Tom. "See how the boundary has fared."

"Okay by me," said Kit, as helpful as ever.

Tom drove carefully over the bumps and eventually reached the paddock's northern boundary. He was relieved to see the fence posts were still upright but many wires were snapped or snagged with debris ranging from a wooden bedstead to a china doll. He wondered whether its young owner had survived. Perhaps he had met her. Oh God!

"It looks like you're in luck," observed Kit, as they came to a halt by the corner strainer, a larger post supporting the whole fence line in two directions. "We'd better check out this fellow."

"Yeah, it looks okay," agreed Tom. He strode over to the strainer and pulled at it. There was no movement. "Firm as a rock." He tested its two supporting timbers and was relieved to find them also stable.

Kit was already unloading a roll of number eight wire. Tom walked the line to the next strainer some two hundred yards distant and tested that. It also seemed to have stood the test pretty well. Kit watched Tom pulling a broken wire tight and making figure of eight knots to join the two ends with a wire strainer. "He's almost a man," he thought, "yet so vulnerable."

*   *   *

Chapter 7

They worked all week till the north boundary was secure. The two lateral fences were pretty sound as unaffected directly by the water flow. Their companionship had grown, Kit letting Tom make all decisions and just questioning gently if Tom appeared to be taking a short cut like hanging a gate, which really ought to be repaired more effectively.

Once the southern boundary fence was complete and the livestock secure, they started on the house. It would have been quite impossible without Kit's help. Their relationship was almost like a younger to an elder brother.

"Do you ever have school friends to visit you?" asked Kit breaking a long silence as they worked, hammering back loose boards.

"No, we're too far out," said Tom, regretfully. "No one ever comes to see us, since Mum left the first time." He sounded a bit choked. "That's why it's good to have you here. It'd be Hell on my own." Kit put his hand on Tom's shoulder and gave it a friendly squeeze.

Again at the homestead next day, they inspected the state of the house. It was a proper mess.

"We'd better stay the corner timber," said Tom. For the first time, Kit showed authority. Tom was surprised when he said, "No, we must prop that roof timber. It could fall on us."

He was right of course and Tom quickly agreed. They found a long strut and levered the doubtful piece of wood so it was safe. They worked together, Tom holding while Kit hammered in fresh nails. By "smoko" time, Tom was fairly "bushed" while Kit still seemed fresh.

"Anyone can hammer in nails," thought Tom. He nearly suggested that they swap tasks, after they had eaten, but did not want to rock the boat. They were making such fast progress, he had better continue with the tiring task. By dinner time, Tom was ready for bed. Kit rustled up a hash, lighting the stove till it glowed. He had suggested Tom saw up some old fence posts, while he prepared the meal.

"Grub up," said Kit and Tom hauled himself into the house and to the table.

"You've done really well," said Kit, making Tom feel better. At the same time he felt Kit was acting like his dad, even becoming the boss. "We should do the back wall next," continued Kit. "You're whacked aren't you? I'll do the dishes, while you get some shut-eye."

Tom needed no persuasion. He stumped into the bedroom, stripped to his underpants and was immediately fast asleep under a sheet.

Sometime later, Kit came in and looked at his young employer with a smile. Things were going smoothly. He too was soon asleep.

Next morning Kit was already up as Tom washed himself in the trough. Kit had breakfast ready and Tom was grateful for his endless sausages and beans. Anything to keep his ribs apart. They got the back wall into place without too much trouble. The damage was less and practice made them into a formidable team. Tomorrow Tom would have to be at the magistrate's court to learn his fate. He had decided that come what may, he'd stay on his property and no one was going to stop him.

"I'll be rooting for you all the way," said Kit, as they drove into town.

"Thanks," said Tom and meant it. The route into town was far easier as the mud had dried hard and they were there by mid-day.

The court room was empty save for the magistrate, the bank manager, a social worker, Tom and Kit. They sat round a polished table in upright chairs with the magistrate at the head.

"G'day. I am Mr. McPherson, the town magistrate. I call upon Mr. Granger from our local bank to affirm Master Tom Hartley's financial position, so we can ascertain whether he is capable of existing free of State help.

Mr. Granger looked up from a set of figures he'd been studying. "Master Tom Hartley is in a sound financial position. He has £48, 599 in the bank, £40,000 being on deposit at 2% per annum. He has no taxes owing and if his cattle are all complete . . . ."

"They are, including the bulls," interjected Tom.

"Please do not interrupt, young man," admonished the magistrate, sternly. "You'll have your chance later."

Tom tried to look suitably abashed, while inwardly simmering at the man's patronizing attitude.

"Please continue, Mr. Granger."

Mr. Granger continued, with a look at Tom, as if he were a little boy, "The cattle can be valued at £40 apiece, if in good condition. And there is the receipt valuing a bull at £300. I understand that the house is a write off and will have to be replaced, costing . . ."

Tom raised his hand.

The magistrate looked at him. "Well?"

"There are a thousand and five good cattle there and some in—calf, and the house is almost repaired" said Tom, looking at Kit for support. He nodded.

"So forty thousand odd dollars there," said Mr. Granger, "and the cattle, a wealthy young man."

Kit smiled to himself, pretending he was blowing his nose.

"So the boy is financially independent. That part is settled," said the magistrate.

Tom only just contained himself, being talked about as if not there.

"Now we come to the tricky bit," continued Mr. McPherson. "Who is to take care of him? He has no relations and no friends. We can't leave him unprotected, out on his own in the bush."

Tom was fuming.

The social worker raised her hand.

"Well, Miss Smith?"

"At his age, he should be put into Care. We have places to cater for children like him. I might even find a foster home. Nice looking kid. And fit." She looked at Tom like a hungry piranha.

"Would you like that?" asked the magistrate, already anticipating Tom's reply.

"No, I would not," he said hotly. "I'm not a kid. I'm seventeen and have worked for my dad after leaving school over a year ago, and I was top of my class! And I've got a gun and I can use it!"

"It's not up to him," said Miss Smith. "He needs protection and we can provide it till he's old enough to fend for himself. He might have an accident with the gun."

"I'm not sure he's the one who needs protection," smiled the magistrate.

"He is vulnerable," said Mr. Granger, siding with the social worker, "having all that money makes him the more so."

Tom gave him a dirty look, enough to fry an egg. He turned hopelessly to Kit.

On cue, Kit raised his hand.

"And you are . . . ?" asked the magistrate.

"Mr. Kit Rivers," said Kit. He passed his driver's licence to the magistrate, who looked at it closely and then returned it.

"And where are you from and what do you do for a living, Mr. Rivers?"

"I'm a farmer, who lost his farm to the Bank in Western Territory, after a drought."

"And he's helped me repair the fences and the house," added Tom, incurring a frown from the magistrate. He continued: "He's my mate. I couldn't do without him."

"A fortunate meeting," said the magistrate. "I'm prepared to let you take care of the boy for a trial period . . ."

"You can't!" exploded Miss Smith. "You know nothing about the man. He could be an escaped convict, or a p . . ."

"Have a care, Miss Smith. "I'll have you evicted from court if you don't mind your manners. You are wrong. By the powers invested in me by the Crown, I can award the boy to anyone I feel confident will look after his interests well, and I like the look of Mr. Rivers and what he has already done for Tom. I allow you, Mr. Rivers, to take care of Tom for a period of three months, to be increased to a year, if it goes satisfactorily. Would you be happy with that, Tom?"

Tom flashed a smile of gratitude to Kit. "Oh yes please, Sir. We get on corker."

Miss Smith looked daggers at the magistrate and stormed out. Mr. Granger appeared completely satisfied.

"Well, that's that. All seems to be on an even keel. He's all yours till three months from now, Mr . . . Rivers. Take good care of him as I am sure you will." The magistrate stood and everyone else followed suit as he walked out.

"Oh thanks, Kit. I hated her. You saved my bacon," said Tom.

Granger smiled at Kit and exited. Kit put his arm round Tom's shoulders and they followed the others out of court.

* * *

CHAPTER 8

R epairing the front, the roof and verandah went well. Kit held the ladder while Tom knocked in nails to hold the corrugated iron in place and enjoyed taking the more important part. He had complete faith in Kit and the ladder was steady as a rock. It made most sense for him to be on top, being lighter, as Kit said. It was satisfying to know that when it rained again, the roof would not leak like a colander. As Tom slid down the ladder, the task complete, Kit slapped him on the back: "Well done kiddo. You've done a champion job." Tom glowed with pride.

The fences all complete and the house sound, Kit came back from town one day with sandpaper, paint and brushes and Tom helped carry them to the verandah. "I've got you a new task," said Kit. "You prepare the walls and then paint them. Have the front finished in a week, and I'll give you a present."

Tom, always keen to complete a worthwhile task, was soon hard at work. He was sweating in no time, as the sun beat down on his back, and the dust raised from sandpapering, blew around in eddies of wind. He had a job keeping it out of his eyes. Kit came out with a handkerchief and tied it round Tom's nose. "We don't want you breathing that stuff in." Then he returned to the house. As Tom worked, he wondered what Kit was up to. He stopped for a breather and washed off the dust in the trough. The ceasing of scrubbing sound brought Kit out to investigate. He looked at Tom's progress and paused. "You'll need to go faster than that if you're to finish it in a week," he said, smiling to take the sting out of his words.

Tom said nothing but returned to his task determined to show what he was made of. Another hour of arm breaking work and he stopped again for a rest. He quickly went inside to find Kit reading through a mass of papers. "What are you reading?" asked Tom.

"Just checking through the title deeds to make sure all your land is included," said Kit. "I've got to look after your interests as your legal guardian. How's the work going?"

"Slowly," said Tom. "I'm tired." This was an understatement. He was well and truly "bushed".

"Let's have a look," said Kit, getting up from the table and carefully folding up the documents. Tom peered at them but could not see what they were. Kit placed them in the heavy iron safe and locked it, pocketing the key.

"Can't I have a look at them?" asked Tom, realizing that he was no longer in control.

"Man's work," said Kit, smiling. "When you're eighteen. Don't worry. They're safe with me, kiddo."

Tom didn't like being called "kiddo". It somehow forced him back into childhood, making him subservient to Kit, but he could not afford to offend his saviour. But for Kit, he would be in Care and forced to obey that grouchy woman. The house would still be a ruin and the cattle scattered all over the country. He could smell an appetizing aroma from whatever Kit was cooking for smoko and that soon resolved him to earn his tucker. His good humour quickly returned.

They sat down to their meal after Kit had told him to wash his hands and face. It was all falling into a pattern. At least Tom knew where he was. Regular meals and the property under control; Kit's control, maybe, but only till he was eighteen in nine months' time. In a way it was nice not having to take responsibility; more relaxing and no more worries.

After the meal, Kit allowed him half an hour rest and then pointed out to the verandah. Without a word, Tom returned to his task. He scrubbed away with the sandpaper and brushed away the dust. By the end of the day, he had prepared a third of the front. He looked at what remained to be done and washed his aching arms in the trough.

Kit came out and told him to wash himself all over. "Can't stand the smell of sweat in the house," he said over his shoulder as Tom stripped off, and he returned to the house.

Next morning Kit was looking at the sky as Tom surfaced from his dreams. "Looks like rain by afternoon. You'd better get some paint on that part you prepared yesterday, kiddo; otherwise it'll be too wet for a week. Grab some breakfast and get cracking."

"Can't you help me?" asked Tom, wondering what Kit would be doing otherwise.

"Sorry. That's you job," said Kit. "I'm working out a breeding schedule for the cattle and where to graze them next."

"That's easy," said Tom, "in the un-cleared bush paddock. It's good for shelter and there's a dam up there. No chance of flooding, too"

"Uh,uh. Leave the organizing to me," said Kit. "You need me in many respects. Just be patient."

"Hell!" thought Tom. "He's got me properly cornered. Just have to grin and bear it."

"Yes Sir," said Tom, masking the sarcasm.

"'Sir.' I like that. It shows due respect," said Kit. "Nice you know your place, kiddo. Now get stirring that paint, well and truly, for five minutes. Then dip your brush into the paint and scrape off the surplus. Every drop on the floor is a waste as well as a mess. Start up the top with the ladder. Here, I'll help you." Kit lifted the ladder and propped it against the front of the house.

Tom stirred the paint with a clean stick as he was told, while Kit watched approving, and then poured some into a smaller tin with a wire handle. Kit bent a piece of number eight wire into an S shape and showed Tom how to hook the tin onto the ladder rungs. He watched Tom painting for a moment and then went inside. Before long, Tom's chest was spattered with tiny drops of paint but he had made a good job of an area about four feet wide by the same in height. He looked at it proudly.

Tom descended the ladder and called for Kit to help him move it as it was too heavy for him on his own. He quickly ran to the trough to wash off the paint but most of it had dried on him.

Kit laughed as he saw his spotted worker. "Don't worry, kiddo. It'll peel off in a few days. It shows you've been working."

"No one else to see it," said Tom, grinning as Kit moved the ladder for him.

"Coming this way," said Kit, gazing at black clouds over distant hills. "You'd better get a move on. Otherwise you'll have to prepare it all again." He paused. "Does anyone ever come out to visit you?"

"No, not since Mum left us," said Tom, choked. "Funny," he thought. "Kit had asked a similar question before."

Tom's heart sank as he thought of wasted effort and future sweating. "Must get this finished."

He almost ran up the ladder and only just avoided upsetting the paint tin.

*   *   *

Chapter 9

In a couple of hours Tom had finished, working at double speed as he got used to the routine. He was relieved to find the paint had dried as fast as on his chest. It had not all been for nothing. Apart from the paint splodges, his body was turning a light brown. In a week or two, he might be taken for an Aborigine. He smiled at the thought. On the other hand his hair was bleached even fairer.

The threatening rain passed over and the heat returned remorselessly.

Next day Kit announced he was going to town to get food, petrol and even some new trainers for Tom, as his were splitting with the ladder work.

"What about my present?" asked Tom.

"I'm going to give you pocket money since you're working so well," said Kit, "ten shillings a week."

"But it's my money already," said Tom, reasonably.

"Ah yes, but I'm responsible to the court for looking after it, and if they found I was neglecting my duties, they'd sack me and you'd be in Care, just like that."

Tom nodded glumly. Every which way, Kit had him corralled. Perhaps he could run away while Kit was in town? But where would he go to? And he did not want to make him angry. He had never seen him angry. What would that be like? It was better to go on slaving away and keep on the right side of him.

"When I get back, I expect to see the rest of this side prepared," said Kit. "And don't fall off the ladder." He showed Tom how to turn the ladder along the side of the house without it sliding.

"I'll try," said Tom, thinking this was almost impossible. He set to immediately and soon his arms began to ache again.

At least without Kit overseeing him, Tom was free to dip in the trough frequently. He opted to wear a torn old shirt to keep the worst of the sun off him. By lunch time nearly half his task was completed but he wondered whether he would ever be able to rouse himself again to his sandpapering, having stopped.

In town Kit visited Mr. Granger in the bank. The manager was in terrific form. They both joked and enjoyed a couple of cold beers. Kit came out looking very pleased with himself, and why shouldn't he? Kit measured a pair of trainers for Tom, and even bought him a new shearer's vest. He visited the gun shop among others.

By dusk, Tom was again worn out and he staggered down to the trough for a bath. As he was pulling up his shorts, he was astonished to see a brand new Ford ute approaching. At last a contact with the outside world! His face fell when it stopped by the barn and Kit jumped out. "Like it?" asked Kit.

"Crikey!" said Tom, nearly collapsing with astonishment. "Did you buy that . . . with my money?"

"Sir," corrected Kit. "Yes, kiddo, I'm entitled to proper transport while looking after such a splendid property, and if you're good, you can sit in it with me."

"Bloody Hell!" exploded Tom. "You can't go spending all my money without asking me."

"That's where you're wrong, kiddo," said Kit. "I have complete control of your money and this property, till you're eighteen. And you will call me Sir. I insist on everything being correct." Kit reached inside the car and brought out a whip, which he cracked, its knot coming perilously close to Tom's legs.

"Yes, Sir," said Tom, swallowing his pride. "Oh my god, what now?" he thought. "I should have taken the mare and escaped."

His precarious situation suddenly hit him. He was totally under Kit's control with no witnesses to intervene, come what may.

"Let's see what work you've done," said Kit and he strode over to the house.

Tom took a quick look inside the car and saw that the keys were no longer in it.

"Hm. Not bad," said Kit. "As a reward, I've bought you these, out of the kindness of my heart." He threw the trainers and vest to Tom, who put on his most grateful face.

There was a bulky object in the back and some smaller boxes. Kit backed the ute up to the front door, while Tom wondered what it was all about.

Kit got down from the vehicle. Tom looked at him, enquiring.

"Just give me a hand with this inside, kiddo. Careful. It'll be heavy."

Tom obeyed and lifted with both his hands under the large package. Kit was dead right. It was all Tom could manage. They struggled inside with Tom nearly dropping it as soon as it was through the door.

"Right, you can unpack it and satisfy your curiosity," said Kit, smiling. He passed Tom a little penknife. Tom cut the binding twine and pulled off the cardboard revealing a large white metal chest.

"A deep-freeze. Now we can kill a beast and have plenty of meat any time we want it," said Kit.

Tom refrained from commenting on more of his money being spent. "But how do we get electricity, Sir?" he asked.

"Easy," said Kit. "In those packages you can also unpack, there's a windmill and a generator, plus twelve car batteries. We'll have all the power we need."

Tom could not contain his admiration. No more candles or paraffin lamps to bed or in the long dark evenings of winter.

"You're a genius, K . . . Sir," said Tom.

"Learning," said Kit. "Yes, I'm improving life in the outback in many ways."

There were some other packages, which Tom wondered about, as he unpacked the power plant, while Kit watched and then started to put them together. After an hour or so, the windmill was ready for action. "Hold the ladder, kiddo. I'll fix the windmill to the apex of the roof, so make sure it's steady."

As Kit stretched and drilled screw holes in the apex timber, Tom had a terrible thought. "Just suppose he let the ladder slip. He could blame the wind which was just getting up, and making the ladder hard to hold steady. That would be the end of Kit and he would be free. But free for what. He couldn't manage the place on his own and Kit seemed to have an answer for every problem. While he was pondering, Kit was already descending the ladder and it was too late. Tom's thoughts may have been portrayed on his face as Kit gave him a long, hard look as he reached the bottom rungs.

"Jeez! Can he read my mind?" wondered Tom as he struggled to lower the ladder with Kit.

*   *   *

Chapter 10

B y evening the cable from the windmill was connected to the generator and that to the batteries. A lead led from a battery to a double plug on the wall and Kit plugged the freezer lead into it. Immediately the freezer started to hum. Kit opened the lid and beckoned Tom over. "Feel how it's cooling already," said Kit, smiling with pride.

Tom bent down to place his hand inside. Like a flash, Kit upended him and he slid into the huge freezer. As Tom wondered what was happening, Kit slammed the lid and slipped the bolt, trapping him inside.

"Hey what . . .".? yelled Tom.

"Nice and cool?" asked Kit.

"Let me out," yelled Tom.

"Sir," said Kit.

"Sir," said Tom.

"Please Sir" said Kit.

"Please Sir," said Tom, beginning to shiver. It was very efficient, this coffin.

"I'll just make a cup of tea," said Kit.

Tom said nothing, not wanting to annoy his master. He sat for about ten minutes, getting steadily colder, and wondered what lesson Kit was teaching him now? Suppose he just left him there? Was he to be the next meal? He leant away from the side of the deep freeze as his skin was sticking to it.

Kit opened the lid and lifted Tom out. He slumped to the floor, shivering violently.

"My little joke. Just another way of teaching you who's Boss here," laughed Kit. "Have a cup of tea."

Tom drank his tea in a gulp, enjoying the warmth coasting down his throat.

"What are the other packages, Sir?" asked Tom.

"There are some locks for the doors. We are so vulnerable out here on our own at night and the tack room and stable need locking. Aboriginals might steal things."

"Our local Aboriginals don't steal, Sir," said Tom hotly. "Only white men steal! They're my friends."

"Are they indeed? We'll have to watch that," said Kit grimly. "Well, no one's stealing our stuff. All will be secure."

Tom nodded as Kit pointed to yet more packages. "There's a new fork and spade and some young plants and a watering can. We can be self-sufficient. You can dig the garden and grow veggies. No need to waste petrol and wear out tires going into town once a week."

Tom nodded, having learnt that it was best to agree to everything. Kit noted this and smiled to himself. The conditioning was happening even more rapidly than he had imagined. The boy had learnt his place, trained like an obedient dog. That whip was a nice touch. Just a sign of what could happen.

"Well, I've done all the work and now it's your turn. You can go and mark out the rows in the veggie patch. You'll need to clear the weeds and then dig tomorrow. Better be up early as it'll be hot later."

Tom nodded. "Yes, Sir," insisted Kit.

Tom obediently and meekly said, "Yes Sir." He picked up the tools and went outside. It was getting dark but light enough to dig away a straight line of weeds. Even in the cool of the evening, it was hard work.

Kit came out and watched. "That's not straight enough. Do I have to show you everything?"

It was the first time Kit's good humour evaporated.

"Yes Sir," said Tom, quickly.

"Use this binder twine," said Kit, handing him a roll. "Drive a stick in each end and tie the twine tight as a marker."

Tom quickly did as he was told, under the approving eye of his master.

When it was too dark to see what he was doing, Kit let Tom into the house, where he was glad to sit and recover from his painting, his unpacking and his first steps in gardening.

"It'll be your first job in the morning and last at night to water all the plants and seeds, kiddo," said Kit.

"Yes Sir."

"Then you can bring me a cup of tea before I get up, and prepare breakfast."

"Yes Sir," said Tom, realizing what a strait jacket he was in. There was no alternative but to work hard and do as he was told till he was released on his eighteenth birthday. But suppose he was not released? Well that would have to be faced if it arose. Not likely. The magistrate seemed a fair minded man. He would guard Tom's interests.

As Tom made for his bedroom, he noticed there was already a lock on his door. Well, at least it gave him privacy. But Kit had the key and he heard it turn in the lock as he lay on his bed. Another chain around his ankle! Surely Kit would have to go to town sometime. Then he might be able to hide in the Bush.

* * *

Chapter 11

Kit had his own ideas. The boy was his now, the house was rapidly becoming smart, and comfortable. He watched the electric table lamp gradually shining brighter as the batteries charged. He had five months plus to establish himself as the new owner in town. With the bank manager already on his side, thanks to a small share in the property, it should be easy enough. He could explain Tom's disappearance as having gone to Further Education in Brisbane and after a couple of years there, he had opted to take a gap year abroad. People did not always return from them, finding the bright lights of London or Paris much more alluring. And all the time, Tom would be locked in by night and working his heart out during the day. It was lucky that the mail bus only passed the end of their mile long drive once a month and no aircraft had a route overhead.

Next morning Tom tried his door. It was unlocked. He opened the draught on the wood burner and then saw the electric kettle. Well having Kit here wasn't all bad. He poured him a mug of tea and one for himself, and set the pan going on the stove with some eggs Kit had brought from town, and slices of bacon. The smell was appetizing.

Something more sinister had arrived from town in the rear of the ute . . . Just another parcel that Kit had bought from the blacksmith. Patiently listening to the old craftsman's tales of the history of the town, how it had gradually progressed, to a guided tour of historical tools and artifacts, Kit had managed to steer the conversation round to the early convict days. Eventually he had walked out with a brown hessian sack containing rusty shackles, which when oiled, miraculously worked a treat, and should come in very useful one day.

While Tom was having a quick wash in the trough, he noticed the tack room was locked. That meant he could not ride his mare without Kit's permission, another tether to the property.

Tom knocked on Kit's door expecting to find him up but he was lying in bed obviously enjoying being waited on. "Put the mug there, kiddo." He pointed to an upright chair beside his bed. "Look more cheerful about it."

"Yes Sir," said Tom dutifully, pulling a fake smile.

"And get more painting done, first. I expect all the top front finished by smoko time. Then you can get cracking on the veggie garden."

"Yes Sir," said Tom, practising his smile. He left Kit, who was looking thoughtful.

"The boy seems as if he's still got some resistance in him. Well, I'll see what he's like after another hard day's work. And by God, it will be hard." Kit's smile was genuine.

Tom was scorching as the sun beat into his back. He just wore shorts to let whatever breeze there was cool him. He had completed the top half and was parched. Kit had been sitting watching him in an old rocking chair for the last hour. Being the only one working made it all the harder to take. He climbed down the ladder and made for the pump to have a drink of water.

"Where do you think you're going?" shouted Kit in a stern voice.

"I'm only having a drink," said Tom. "I can't work without water. I'll collapse."

"You stop when I say," said Kit, "and not a moment before. Understand?"

Tom suddenly exploded. He had had enough, working his guts out while Kit lazed around, watching him for any mistakes. "You sit there like a lazy dog, and I'm slaving away. I've had it up to here." He faced up to Kit, but suddenly dizzy with the heat, he swayed and nearly fell.

Kit rose quickly from his seat. "Sir! . . . You owe me everything. I saved your life from the crocodile. I saved your cattle. If it wasn't for me, you'd have walked off the property or be dead. You're my property. I own you. You do as I say, when I say, and work till I decide you can stop."

Kit picked up the whip he had beside his chair and cracked it.

Tom staggered and leant against the ladder. He hadn't the energy to fight or even contest Kit.

Kit whipped Tom across his shoulders. Tom crumpled to the ground, trying to hold back his tears. Kit whipped him again. "Well?"

"Please stop it, Sir . . . I can't take any more." The weals were already rising and stinging.

"Broken his spirit at last," thought Kit. "Keep him down. My slave for life, well, his life."

Kit filled a bucket of water and threw it over Tom, who showed no sign of resistance.

"Okay, you can have a drink, but then you work till I tell you to stop."

"Yes Sir," mumbled Tom, too exhausted to resist or even think of it. He stumbled to the trough and using his hands, scooped up water to his face, swallowing as if his life depended upon it.

"Back to work," commanded Kit. "I'll tell you when you can finish."

By late afternoon the painting of the front was complete. "Not bad," said Kit, inspecting his handiwork carefully. "When you've done the rest of the house, you can put a second coat on. Easy. No preparation needed for that."

"Yes, Sir," muttered Tom, wishing he'd taken his chance earlier when Kit was up the ladder. It had just been the thought that he might have only broken a leg, and still had that pistol in his belt, that had kept Tom from the deed. Plus a finer feeling that he couldn't take a human life . . . or could he?

Later in the day Kit appeared on his horse, with a young steer in front of him on the end of a rope. He tied the steer to a post and took out his skinning knife. With Tom watching, he cut its throat in one swift slice and watched it kicking as it bled quickly to death. Kit enjoyed the look on Tom's face as he was disgusted Kit had not shot it first. He smiled at Tom as if to say, "You could be next." Kit quickly and efficiently jointed the beast and called Tom to help carry them to the deep freeze. Tom kept a wary eye on Kit while near the deep freeze, to Kit's amusement. "Frightened I'll joint you, kiddo? It'd not take long but you're more valuable alive."

Tom breathed a sigh of relief.

Kit allowed Tom half an hour for his dinner and then it was out to the veggie patch. The ground was hardening up and breaking through the top soil blistered his hands. Eventually Tom collapsed over his spade and when Kit came out in the dusk, he helped his slave to the trough and threw another bucket of water over him.

"You stink, boy. Wash yourself and your clothes and come in when you're clean."

Tom entered the house in his dripping underpants and staggered to his room. He had left the rest of his clothes to dry on the line. He fell on his bed and was asleep in a minute.

Kit came in and looked at Tom with a delighted smile. "That's the way I'll keep you, kiddo. You'll never think of fighting back again."

*   *   *

Chapter 12

Tom fell into the routine, until the painting was finished, and then he guessed Kit would have another task waiting for him. The veggies were growing well, thanks to his hauling water morning and evening and careful weeding that Kit inspected daily.

Kit was off to town on his monthly "business trip." Kit drove off in a cloud of dust, having shown Tom where the last tin of beans was. As soon as the cloud of dust vanished over the horizon, Tom ran to the tack room to find his precious rifle. He would hide it just in case. In case of what? He wasn't sure, but it would be comforting to know he had it for an emergency. He would hide it away in the barn. He found the tack room locked as he expected but the barn was open. Kit did not know of a route through the hay loft and down through a dusty manhole in the stable's dark ceiling. Choking from dust and keeping his ears tuned in case Kit had forgotten something and returned unexpectedly, Tom carefully made his way between the rafters to above the stable. He had a job prising up the manhole cover in the ceiling but eventually coughing from the dust, he was peering down into the stable. He waited for his eyes to adjust to the poor light from the cobweb strewn window, and looked down at his saddle. The rifle was gone from its holster, where he always stowed it. He searched around, but it was definitely not there. It was like a kick in his gut.

Damn the man! He was always a step ahead of Tom, almost as if he had anticipated his thoughts and actions. Carefully replacing the cover, he re-traced his steps, and reached ground level in one piece. He washed off the dust before returning to his painting.

As he had some sandwiches to eat, during a rest period, Tom noticed Kit had put up hooks on the walls of the living room and a towel was already hanging on one. There was also a large iron ring bracketed securely to the wall in the living room and another in his bedroom. He wondered what they might be for and then forgot about them.

Kit had a horse he had bought in town and brought home trotting on a long rein behind the ute in second gear. It was a fine beast and Tom reckoned his bank balance was significantly lower, but he dared not ask what it cost.

Early next day Kit allowed Tom to ride round the cattle with him. "We need to check on those in the Bush," he told Tom. "Dingoes could be around. I'll show you something I bet you don't know."

Tom wondered about that. He reckoned he knew all about dingoes.

They had ridden not long before they found another trace of the savage wild dogs at work. The head and tail, and bones of a young cow were lying under an iron bark tree. The traces of raw meat on the bones showed it had been killed in the past few hours.

"Bastards," said Kit. "We'll give them a surprise." He dismounted, followed by Tom and tied the horses to a nearby tree. Then Kit brought out his rifle from his saddle holster and waved Tom under some bushes. He followed Tom in and sat so he had a view of the clearing and the horses.

Kit suddenly howled like a dingo. It echoed far away. He kept this up for a few minutes and then listened. There was an answering howl. Kit repeated and was rewarded by a closer howl. Every few minutes Kit howled again and then suddenly approaching the terrified horses, pulling wildly at their reins, there arrived four fully grown dingoes in their prime. They ran towards the horses. Kit took quick aim and shot the first. As it somersaulted into the air, stone dead, he reloaded and shot another. As they froze, wondering where the shots were coming from and where to run to, he shot the third. The last bolted away.

"Great shooting Sir," said Tom, wondering at Kit's speed and accuracy.

"The last will give the rest of the pack the good news and I guess we won't be troubled again for a fair old time." Kit smiled and slid the rifle into his saddle holster.

They calmed the horses, mounted and rode away. Tom reckoned he could never match Kit's speed and accuracy in shooting.

One evening Kit let him join him on the porch, lit by the moon. Kit rocked in his chair and Tom sat at his feet, like his dog.

"What did you do when you were in your teens, Sir?" Tom dared to ask.

"I worked on my dad's property like you now." Kit replied. "My dad used to beat me if I shirked my jobs."

"And I bet not nearly so hard," thought Tom.

"And then I joined the army. I had a good two years in the infantry. Come here. I'll show you what I learned."

They both rose and Tom waited off the verandah, wondering what would happen next?

"It's called unarmed combat," said Kit, approaching Tom with a smile. "Attack me, any way you like."

"I don't want to hurt you, Sir," replied Tom, not wanting to give him an excuse to beat him.

Kit found that very funny. "Go on. Or haven't you the guts?"

Tom thought quickly. Maybe this was his chance. He seized a spade, leaning against the house and whacked Kit with it, except he sidestepped in a flash, swept Tom's legs from under him with a back kick and was kneeling on his chest, pressing the spade to choke Tom in seconds.

"Not so smart, kiddo. You really meant to hurt me, didn't you? I saw it in your eyes."

Tom was bright red, unable to breath or reply.

"So you know what I learnt in the army, and what I'm capable of. Let that be a lesson for you." Kit released the pressure and Tom started to breathe again. He gasped, lying unable to get to his feet as Kit eased off him. He tried to get up and then collapsed.

"Okay?" asked Kit, still smiling.

Tom nodded: "Yes, Sir," and gasped again.

"Come on, I'll show you a few more moves."

"Do I have to, Sir?"

"Yes, unless you want rougher treatment. Don't worry. I'll not kill you or even break anything." Kit went through a number of throws and holds, all the time showing Tom his supremacy. At last he got tired of throwing Tom around and easily blocking his punches and kicks.

"Tomorrow we brand young stock and castrate the calves. Get to bed now. You'll need to feel fit for that."

Tom nodded and staggered up the steps to his room. Shortly after the key turned in the lock, he was asleep.

*　　*　　*

Chapter 13

Next day they rode up to where the cattle were grazing and siphoned off the young stock from their mothers and the bulls, amidst much mooing. They herded them into the stock yards and Kit closed the gate. Kit set Tom to gathering fire wood and soon had a glowing fire into which he placed the branding iron. Kit put one youngster at a time through the cattle race into a smaller yard. He showed Tom how to wrap the rope round their ankles and jerk them off their feet. As they lay helpless, he quickly branded them with the red hot iron. "Mustn't hold it there more than a second or two. It'll scorch them," he said. And as Tom felt surprised at such compassion, he added, "it'd spoil their hides." Then he produced a castrating tool on which he placed a rubber ring, expanded the ring and fitted it above their testicles.

"They'll drop off in a couple of weeks or so," explained Kit. "It improves the meat and stops them impregnating their sisters and cousins."

Tom looked suitably impressed. His dad had never let Tom attend the annual activity but had a neighbour help him. Perhaps he had thought Tom would have been squeamish. The day seemed to drag as they got through over a hundred young cattle but finally they got to the end. Kit looked at Tom. "Your turn, kiddo," he said as he suddenly roped Tom's ankles and pulled him relentlessly towards him.

"No Sir, please no Sir," cried Tom.

Kit stood over him with the castrating tool in his hand. He knelt on Tom's chest, smiling.

"It'll take the sting out of you, kiddo and you'll be as meek as a lamb. Just a dull ache for a few days." Kit knelt on Tom's chest, enjoying his fear.

Tom lay there, waiting for the inevitable, his ankles looped tightly, Kit's weight preventing all movement. Suddenly inspiration. As Kit reached back with his free hand to loosen Tom's belt, his hands still free, he scooped a handful of sandy soil into Kit's eyes. He yelled and stood up, blinking and making for the water bottle.

"Right, you're for it. I'll make it quick with my knife," yelled Kit. The water was washing out his eyes and he would soon see clearly again. He bent to snatch up his rope.

Tom frantically un-roped his ankles and kicking his bonds aside, picked up the red hot branding iron and plunged it against Kit's chest. He screamed and fell over backwards, tripping into the fire. Kit scrambled off the fire but Tom plunged the iron into the hair at the back of Kit's head. It was now or never. There was a sizzle. Kit lurched away from him. Tom picked up a small piece of firewood and smashed it time and again against Kit's head. He only stopped when the man seemed unconscious. Then he roped his wrists and ankles and staggered with him to his horse. He just managed to lift Kit across the saddle, and tied him with what was left of the rope.

Panting with the effort, Tom wondered at what he had done. Then what was he to do with Kit? He could not bring himself to kill him, but if he let him go, Tom would live in fear of his life forever more and the man had shown only too clearly of what he was capable.

He decided to lock him in the stable for the night and give himself time to think things out.

Taking him to the police might not work. It was his word against Kit's and the magistrate would probably believe how Tom had suddenly had a brainstorm and attacked his kind benefactor. They always seemed to believe adults rather than children. It would be Tom put away for the rest of his life in some mental institution. Oh God, what could he do?

Reaching the stable, Tom emptied Kit's pockets, avoiding his evil stare and ignoring his groans. He found several keys, including the one he knew fitted the safe. He pocketed it and tried out them all till one fitted the stable lock. Then he untied the rope binding Kit to the saddle and let him fall on the ground.

He dragged Kit into the stable and checked his bonds. They looked secure.

"What're you going to do next?" asked Kit, groaning. "They'll put you inside for this, unless I don't tell them."

"Shut up, shut up," repeated Tom. He was at a loss what to do for the best.

"At least get me a drink of water?" asked Kit.

Tom left him and fetched him a tin mug full of water.

"Untie one hand, please?" begged Kit.

"You must be joking," said Tom, and offered the mug to his lips. Kit drank greedily.

"What now," asked Kit. "Just untie my legs. They're crucifying me."

Tom considered that and then decided Kit could not untie his hands with his feet, so he untied them.

"Thank you. That's heaps better," said Kit. "You know, I never did anything to you like you've done to me. What's got into you, kiddo?"

"Tom, not kiddo," he snapped.

"Yeah, Tom. I've looked after your interests, taught you some skills, kept the property together, helped make you quite rich instead of losing everything, saved your life and this is how you reward me? I wasn't really going to castrate you. Just a joke."

"One joke too far," snarled Tom, remembering his belt loosening and still unsure of what to do with Kit. The more he spoke, the less easy Tom felt about his attack. "You've just made me your slave. Even made me do the cooking from last week. And cleaning the house, whipping me. Just where were you going with me?"

"You'd have made someone a good wife," joked Kit.

Tom almost smiled.

"I'm going to leave you here for the night. Maybe I'll have thought of something by morning. You'd better hope it's not a visit to the police station," said Tom, making for the door.

"Oh yes, do take me there," said Kit. "They'd love what you've done to your benefactor."

Tom had enough and shut the door, locking it.

"Give me a crust of bread," yelled Kit. "Please Tom. That's all I ask."

Tom shortly returned with a plate of beans and mash that he was also having.

"Just loosen my wrists a little so I can eat," said Kit.

"So you can escape! You must be kidding." He placed the plate close to Kit on the floor.

"You treated me worse than a dog. Eat yours off the deck."

Kit hid his anger and crawled towards his plate. "Thank you Tom. You're a mate."

Tom bottled up a sarcastic reply and watched him eat for a moment, getting potato on his nose.

"Enjoy," said Tom and locked the door on him.

*　　*　　*

Chapter 14

Tom enjoyed a bathe in the trough after his meal and then sat in the rocker to consider his next move. It was true that Kit had treated him no more harshly than some tough dads. But he could see the way things were shaping. He was being conditioned by degrees to accepting complete obedience and was already at the mercy of the bank manager and Kit, who he was convinced were in collusion. It could be that they might do away with him eventually, when they had milked his property dry. The events of the day had worn him out. He soon nodded off, and slept in his chair.

Taking advantage of his legs being free, Kit worked on his bonds against the sharp edge of a stirrup. He would have no compunction about brainwashing this boy so he had no thoughts of his own, except to work him as a slave for whom the rod would no longer be spared. He eventually freed himself by one o'clock in the morning and had no trouble with the lock and a bent piece of wire. He passed Tom, sleeping soundly and returned with a large pillow slip; opening it wide, he slid it easily over Tom's head and shoulders, down to his waist, effectively creating a strait jacket.

Tom woke to wonder where he was and what was happening. He soon found out when he was bent over the chair, and the whip descended. He howled and moaned till exhaustion took over. Kit ran out of energy. He took the bloodied pillow case off Tom's crumpled body and attached the manacles to his wrists.

"You're a dangerous criminal," said Kit, "so I'll treat you like one. From now on, you'll be shackled in my absence."

Tom had nothing to say.

"Say thank you, Sir," ordered his captor.

"Thank you, Sir," whispered Tom.

"Louder," shouted Kit.

"Thank you Sir," whispered Tom as he sank to his knees and then lay face down on the earth.

"Well, I might let you live a little longer," said Kit, "You'll earn your keep." Kit picked up the whip, but Tom could not see or feel anything more. He was out cold. Kit placed the whip high on the verandah wall across two nails. He then lifted Tom and carried him into his bedroom.

As an afterthought, he re-possessed his keys from Tom's pocket.

He laid him on his bed, checked his breathing and left, locking the door behind him.

Tom lay as one, dead.

Kit washed the blood off Tom's back next morning, none too gently. He undid the shackles and surprised the boy by cooking him breakfast.

"We may have both gone a bit too far yesterday," Kit said.

"Yes, Sir," said Tom and meant it. While Kit was in a kinder frame of mind, he tested it.

"Please Sir?"

Kit smiled at him, as far as the bruises on his face let him. "Well?"

"You couldn't cut my hair, could you? I'm looking like a girl."

"A pretty one at that," laughed Kit. "No, I think you can stay like that for a while. It might stop you being so aggressive."

"Huh! Who started that?" thought Tom to himself.

"You can help me round up the cattle, kiddo. I don't think you're in a fit state to make a break for it, and you know what'll happen if you do."

Tom knew better than to ask why they were rounding up the herd again. The branded young stock had been left in a paddock by themselves, so they would not be included.

Tom eased himself painfully into the saddle and rode beside Kit up the paddock. Eventually they had enough of the fat eighteen month-olds for Kit's purpose. It was obvious what was happening. They were to be sold and Tom bet he would not see any of the money. He was manacled and left inside the living room, chained to the iron ring. So that was its purpose.

A drover arrived at the end of the drive, where Kit handed them over to him, with instructions not to hurry them. "Let them graze and keep their fat on them," Kit instructed.

"I'll give you a bonus if they arrive in prime condition."

The man looked at the bruises on Kit's face. "Had a fall when my horse bolted," explained Kit and the drover looked understanding and sympathetic.

The drover took them off at a leisurely pace, all four hundred of them.

"That'll make me £10,000," thought Kit. "Granger needn't hear about them, and even if he does, he knows if I fall, we fall together."

On Kit's return, he unshackled Tom. "Right kiddo, you can water the veggies and then early to bed."

Tom wondered what tasks he would be set tomorrow? Probably something exhausting if he was being rested. "Like cart horses before they work up the land," he thought.

*   *   *

Chapter 15

Next morning Tom was shocked to find how accurate he had been. As soon as he had finished washing up the breakfast things, Kit took him out and fitted a leather harness around his chest.

There was a single blade light plough in front of the barn.

"We'll see how strong you are, kiddo. No carthorses so you can try pulling that, beyond the veggie patch." Kit cracked his whip, stinging Tom's thigh.

"Sir, I can't pull that!"

"I've set the blade shallow, so it won't dig too deep. You'll lean forward and we'll soon find how strong you are. Yes, I've noticed you're putting on some useful muscle. A pity to waste it. I'll keep it straight and push a little too. Ready boy! Take the strain."

The plough rode forward easily until they were in the paddock. Then Kit set the bolt which governed its depth. He cracked the whip and Tom heaved forward. To his surprise the plough cut through the soil fairly easily. They turned over a couple of hundred yards and then Kit rested him, while he turned the implement in the opposite direction. Tom heaved but it was now up hill and dug in deeper. He struggled but made slow progress.

"Get your shoulders into it, slacker," yelled Kit, who was getting angry as he had to push harder himself. He cracked the whip, nicking Tom's sore back.

"Ow!" yelled Tom. "I'm doing all I can . . . Sir."

Eventually Kit saw reason and they only worked downhill. By the end of an hour, a useful patch of ground had been turned over. Tom collapsed in his harness and Kit released him from the plough. He fell forward, totally exhausted.

"That's taken the fight out of you, boy." said Kit, staring down at him.

"Sir," gasped Tom. He had nothing else to give.

Each day for a week, Tom was worked like a cart horse. Each day he was weaker and Kit saw there was no point in breaking him. He actually gave Tom Sunday off and he just lay on his bed as if in a trance.

The next day, Tom was made to pull a light chain harrow, which had less drag but wore him out almost as quickly. He fell into bed each night, miserable and too tired to think of escape.

When Kit eventually left for town to collect the cattle earnings, he still manacled Tom and fastened him to the ring by a chain, but he could see there was no fight left in the boy. He looked emptily at the wall in front of him, his mind blown.

In town, banking part of his cattle money, Kit met Granger and shouted him a meal at the pub. "You can have ten per cent," he told the fat manager. "I do all the work and you just sit here getting richer."

"I've made us both better off," said Granger. "I've invested in a gold mine and they say it's very rich. We'll retire in a year or two and you can put in a manager."

"It'd better only be a year," said Kit. "The boy won't last any longer. I'll plant him in the asparagus bed. It'll taste sweet!" They both chortled with laughter.

On leaving the pub, Kit came face to face with the magistrate. He acted calm and friendly, controlling a ripple of anxiety.

"G'day Kit," said the magistrate. "How's life on the farm and how's our young friend doing? Is he in town with you?"

"Good to see you," said Kit. "No, he's a bit shy you know. Doesn't like meeting strangers."

"So it's profitable, is it?" continued the magistrate. He had a habit of looking very straight into one's eyes that Kit found disconcerting. "You're making the boy rich?"

"Going well and he enjoys his work," said Kit. "A fine young man. I'm proud of his progress. Okay to leave things how they are for another six months?"

"Well if things are that good, it seems a pity to disturb the equilibrium. Yes, I'll support you staying with him for a further term of six months. Still one to go of the original."

"Many thanks, Sir," said Kit, controlling his exhilaration at the thought of another seven month's profits screwed out of his slave's labour. He said goodbye to the magistrate and strode down to the Ford Coupe 302. He would work the lad to the bone and pocket the money. Perhaps he could arrange for an accident and then sell the property, which would become rightfully his as Guardian and farm manager . . . A just reward for all his hard work. No, just a disappearance as he had previously planned: Tom taken off on his gap year. He liked the sound of that. He could never be blamed for Tom fading into obscurity abroad.

On his return Kit placed the money in a tin in the barn, hidden behind a rafter end, never likely to be discovered.

Tom still looked vacant but a little rested. He would be capable of planting the new patch with potatoes. Back-breaking but not totally exhausting.

In town the magistrate, no fool, was pondering over Tom's sudden avoidance of people. He had been full of the joys of spring as a youngster and readily engaged people in conversation. Of course there was no reason to doubt that smiling fellow, Kit, who was so engaging everyone liked him. Even so, he would drive out to the property one day and just check on the lad. It would have to wait a month or two as he was up to his neck in court cases. As the town grew, it attracted some wasters, who were either fighting at the first excuse, usually after too much beer, or when they had drunk away their earnings, they invaded people's property and stole their saving, which sensibly would have been in the bank. There had been a couple of cases of arson, which were disturbing in a town mostly built of wood.

Oh well, teen-agers went through funny moods as the hormones kicked in and Tom was probably no exception. The magistrate went about his business and promptly forgot about the boy. In the meantime Tom slaved away, mentally only half there. His mind came and went on the past, from happier times before his mum had walked out on them, to the various events that led up to the present. It was as if seen through a haze, and should he drift into full realization of the present and show a sign of asserting himself, the shackles were soon on.

He had now added to his duties all household chores including sweeping, dusting and laundering their clothes. Kit was increasingly particular about standards. Everything had to be spotless. The veggies grew and the potatoes in mathematical rows produced enough for Kit to take to town and sell. Some were put in a clamp and covered with straw and then earth, to keep for the next season. Inefficiency or slowness to obey were immediately rewarded by a beating. Kit found the leather belt a handy instrument. He was pleased how he had trained his slave into the perfect domestic and labourer. A slap of the whip and he was instantly at his master's bidding.

*   *   *

Chapter 16

A
t a distant hospice a sad middle aged man was being attended to by his nurse. He had been found after a terrible flood which had begun fifty miles north-west. He was wedged on the end of a house, between the rafters, fortunately head above water. Even after six months, he still could not remember his name or where he had come from. Casual enquiries had found no one unaccounted for, thirty miles up-stream.

They gave him the name of Jim. He was affable and pleasant to have around. He helped with the other patients, after his recovery and no one had the heart to put him out of their safe haven. He had been heard to call, "Tom," in his sleep but there were no clues in his washed out pockets and the hospice elders were more concerned with immediate demands on their time. "Jim" gradually grew stronger and physically was of sound health. In the flood, his head had been under water for too long, when he nearly drowned and the lack of oxygen had killed memory cells in his brain.

One day a stray horse wandered into the hospice garden. The matron in charge, well named "Miss Goodheart", a strict but kindly woman, was fearful for her charges' safety. As she was about to ring the police and the vet, Jim strolled up to the horse and breathed into its nostrils, as if a normal activity for him. Minutes later he was riding it around, with no saddle and no bridle, just using gentle pressure from his knees to direct it.

The nurses and patients watched in astonishment and Matron said to no one in particular, "Now we know something about Jim. He's either been connected to a circus or the land."

Eventually the horse's owner was traced and he gratefully tipped Jim twenty dollars, the equivalent of two weeks' wages. Jim accepted it gratefully and casually put it his pocket as if he was used to that sort of money all the time. Matron took that in, too. "I guess he's a property owner. We should extend our enquiries."

A few weeks later Kit was in town and noticed a newspaper mentioning in a tiny notice, that a farmer had been found fifty miles away, who had almost drowned in the flood. He frowned, shoved the paper in a waste paper bin and went on his way. No one else had bothered to read beyond the local cattle prices and gossip. In a week, he relaxed, realizing that no one would link the survivor with Tom's farm.

Kit had the party phone line repaired so he could keep in contact with cattle prices and Granger. He was always interested in how their shares were faring. Pretty well, considering the world slump. He always favoured breweries and food stores. People tended to drink more when depressed and they had to eat. He watched Tom ironing one of his shirts. The boy was growing into a fine specimen, his labours broadening him and building a fine display of muscles, under the whip scars.

When the men came to install the phone, Kit manacled Tom and stowed him away at the back of the barn, gagged and bound. Tom heard new voices and tried to yell through his gag, but only a faint mmm could be heard, similar to a local bird. He twisted and turned in his bonds, but with his wrists fastened around an upright prop a foot in diameter to his ankles, he was truly powerless. Tears of frustration trickled down his face. As always, Kit was in complete control. Tom gave up the pointless struggle but pondered as to how, if ever he might be freed. There was a coded number ten digits long before one could access the phone, so no hope lay in that innovation.

One day, as Kit and Tom were riding their horses, boundary checking, they came across four Aborigines seated round a fire, cooking a young wallaby. "What the Hell are you doing on my property?" shouted Kit. "His property!" thought Tom.

"Not your property, white fellow. We've owned this land for thousands of years."

The speaker, Billy, a very black man of about forty, knew Tom from way back. Tom's dad would let them camp there and even killed a small cattle beast for them on one occasion. He looked at Tom. "What's the matter, Tom? Cat got your tongue? Who's this fella?"

Tom started to reply but a look from Kit silenced him. "This property is mine now and I want you off it in ten minutes or . . ." Kit patted his rifle holster.

Billy looked at Tom again, but he shook his head. "Where's you dad, Tom?"

"He drowned," blurted Tom and Kit looked approvingly at him.

"We'll be back, white fella. I don't reckon all's well."

"I'll be waiting for you," said Kit. "Five minutes."

Billy and his three adult mates gave Kit hostile stares and kicking the fire out, walked deliberately slow to the boundary fence. Kit pulled out his rifle and fired a couple of shots into the air. The Aborigines kept strolling without even looking back.

A few months later it happened to be Tom's birthday, not that it made any difference. Kit, inspecting his dusting on the furniture with a white handkerchief, observed, "You are eighteen today, Tom. Legally you could have been in charge of this place, but I find you simple of mind and not fit to take over. I'll keep running the place for another year, out of the kindness of my heart and raise my salary in keeping with the bank, plus my share of the profits, and as I provide you with everything, we'll forget about your pocket money won't we?"

Tom nodded his head and said, "Yes Sir. Thank you Sir."

Kit swished the riding crop he had bought as handier for quick chastisement. He always felt a gleam of satisfaction as he squeezed another drop of fear out of the boy.

"It sounds as if your dad might have survived the flood. His description fits."

This was the ultimate test to see Tom's reaction.

Tom could not stem the feeling of joy, soon dashed with Kit continuing: "It seems the poor old boy has lost his mind, so no hope for you there."

Tom's face fell. The crop descended on his backside, just one stinging blow.

Kit smiled, "Aren't you pleased? I'm your only hope for ever."

Tom forced a smile to avoid another blow. "Yes, Sir." His backside was smarting once again.

In the hospice Matron Goodheart thought of Jim's position. He must belong somewhere to some family. If only she had a photo of his loved ones to jog his memory.

*   *   *

Chapter 17

Billy, the aboriginal and Bertha, his wife were worried about Tom. Something wasn't right. They could tell from Tom's subdued attitude. This new guy seemed to be in control. And had Tom's dad really died? Billy felt vibes that he was still alive. His people had this second sight that was seldom wrong. Billy told Bertha he was going to have a closer look. "Don't be seen," said Bertha, really worried. "That white fella with the rifle, I think he'd shoot you as soon as a dog."

"Don't worry Bertha. He won't see me." Billy merged with the Bush and was soon back on Tom's property. He noticed there were good fences and the two bulls were still there, but cattle numbers were well down. Perhaps Tom had sold them, or that man, the intruder. Billy felt he had no right to be there. No point going to the police. They'd just tell him to get lost.

Kit was riding in his direction well away from the trees. Brian seemed to dissolve into thin air as the evil land thief rode by. Brian shuddered. Very bad vibes. He waited till Kit had disappeared over the hill and then sprinted down to the house. He must have a word with Tom before Kit returned. Find out what was going on. See if he could help, maybe with others of his tribe. They were no match for a modern rifle but their spears were weapons of high repute.

Billy found Tom working on the veggie patch. Gone was his cheerful sunny smile. He looked as if he carried all the world's troubles on his shoulders. "Tom, what's wrong?"

"Get away, Billy. He'll shoot you if he finds you here, and beat me."

"What's the hold he's got on you, boy?"

Tom hardly paused in his work. "He's my legal guardian and can do anything he likes with me. He runs the property and keeps the profits. He beats me if I don't do as I'm told. Treats me like a slave."

"Why don't you run away?"

"He'd soon run me down on his horse. The ute keys are in his pocket. If I don't get this weeded to his liking, he'll beat me like a dog on his return."

"I'll get my tribe after him. Hunt him down like a dog," said Billy.

"It's a great idea, but I don't want to risk you losing half your people. He's got a repeater rifle and I've seen him killing dingoes. He'd shoot a dozen of you in minutes. You'd better go before he catches you out in the open. Thanks for coming, Billy. Love to Bertha and the kids. Wait a moment. Suppose you create a diversion, like a fire. If I get the opportunity to escape, I'll leave a bit of myrtle horizontal over there."

"You're on," said Billy. "We won't be far away. Take care."

Tom went on weeding and Billy faded into the landscape, like a ghost. If only Billy had a rifle too. But then he'd have to be taught to use it. A silly idea. Still it was good to know someone out there was on his side and knew he was still alive.

Another couple of months passed and in town, the mini crime wave had faded away with the incarceration of the worst offenders. The magistrate decided he would pay Kit and Tom a visit. He reckoned they would be dry with all their work and placed a dozen of beer in his car boot. He told his secretary where he was off to. He checked the local phone book and hesitated about giving Kit a ring. He did not want to disturb the farm work.

As he motored off in his car, Granger saw the road he was taking and had a sudden attack of panic. He rushed back to his office and found his secretary a job to attend to in the outside office. He shut and locked his door, before getting on the phone. He tried but got no answer. "Hell! What if he sees Tom?" Granger went white as a cotton bud. He tried again and after a long series of rings, was heartedly relieved to hear Kit's voice.

"Hello. G'day. Can I help you?" came the polite tones of Tom's master.

"Granger here. Kit where's the boy?"

"Weeding the veggies. What's the panic?"

"Hide him quick! The magistrate's taken your road out of town. He might be checking up on you."

"Good on you," exclaimed Kit. "No problem. He'll be out of sight and out of mind," said Kit. "When did he leave? ... Just? ... Plenty of time. He can't make it out here in under three hours, the state the road's in. 'Bye." He slammed down the phone and thought for a moment. The barn was out of the question. The nosey man might make an excuse for looking there first if he had any suspicion that Tom was in trouble.

His mind worked with lightning speed. There was time to hide Tom in the Bush where he would never be found. He fetched the two horses and put on their tack. Then he brought Tom away from digging potatoes and they both rode off into the nearest Bush. He carefully followed the dry paths so there would be no trace. Tom looked wondering at him but did not dare ask where they were going. Finally his apprehension got the better of him.

"You're not going to kill me, are you Sir?"

"Good heavens no," said Kit. "You're just going to sit out here for a few hours while a nosey parker looks around and then I'll bring you back in time for a feed tonight. Giving you a nice rest."

Kit stopped in a little clearing. "Come," he ordered.

Tom slid off his mare and approached Kit apprehensively. He was bound the usual way, wrists to ankles, preventing any movement. Then Kit hauled him up below a strong bough, about twenty feet off the ground. "Can't give the dingoes a free feed," laughed Kit, as Tom swung like some eagle bait. "I'll be back later," said Kit. "Enjoy your flight."

*   *   *

Chapter 18

Kit rode off homewards after tying Tom's mare with her reins securely to a sapling. Tom was both uncomfortable and nervous. Just suppose an eagle decided he would make a good meal? He was too frightened of falling such a long way to try struggling free. Just recently he had become used to and hardened to his situation. Mentally he was beginning to cope but think as he might, there seemed no way of escaping Kit. He always had every opportunity covered.

Kit had time to rub down his horse so it did not appear to have been ridden. He had left the mare under cover of the Bush so the magistrate would believe Tom had ridden off on his own to mend fences. He looked around the house and hid the shackles. He put towels through the iron rings and checked it all looked homely. As a nice touch, he brought in some flowers from the patch and placed them in a jar with water on the table. He checked there was some beer in the cooler. He spilt a few blobs of paint on his overalls and left a paintbrush out.

When Mr. McPherson eventually drove up, he was impressed by how tidy the homestead was, with its smart paintwork and veggie patch. When Kit came out acting surprised but pleased to see him, he immediately asked after Tom.

"Oh, he's ridden off to check the boundary fences," said Kit, pointing in the direction where no car could possible travel through rocks and scrub. "So keen, he is. A pleasure to have working for . . . with one."

The magistrate did not seem to notice his slip of tongue. "And is he well?" he asked, drilling Kit with his gaze.

"Oh very fit. He works hard and likes to do all the tough jobs. He's proud of his muscles. You know the age," said Kit, laughing, totally relaxed.

Mr. McPherson laughed too. "So when do you expect him back? I'd like to meet this paradigm of virtue."

"He usually likes to arrive about nine or ten, as there's a full moon tonight," responded Kit, knowing full well that the magistrate would not wish to drive back in the dark, with the risk of hitting a kangaroo miles, from anywhere. "He's so work proud, it's usually a job to stop him."

"You've done wonders to this place," said the magistrate, enjoying a cool beer on the verandah, near the paint brush.

"Well, we've both done our share," said Kit, as if generously giving Tom credit. "Do you reckon they'll ever improve the road out here?" asked Kit, eager to change the direction of their talk.

"Well it's unlikely for a few years yet. We've got to improve the town first," said the magistrate, taking a long draught of beer.

As he finished his glass, Kit was quick to fill both glasses and to drink, keeping pace.

"What are Tom's next projects?" asked the magistrate.

"I'll have to ask him. We need to clear some more bush for pasture," said Kit. "It was Tom's idea. After losing his dad, it's a question of pride to make this a first rate property."

"He's lucky to have you to help him."

"I enjoy it. Acting as mentor to the young is rewarding," said Kit, thinking he'd never go to Heaven. He had a sudden flash of Tom still swinging in the breeze, so high up. He hoped the knots were sound. "How about looking at his vegetable patch?" He emptied his glass and stood up. "Have another one?"

The magistrate declined and they sauntered round to the rear of the house.

"Good Heavens," said the visitor, suitably impressed. "Did he really do this all on his own?"

"With a little help from his friend," lied Kit with a smile. "I told you he's a good lad. Well young man now."

"Yes, eighteen," said the magistrate. "He can legally take complete control now."

They wandered round to the front and stood by his car.

"He's in control already," said Kit, thinking fast. "Every morning we discuss what the day's tasks are and once a week, we sit down and he usually leads with his ideas. Very sound they are too."

The magistrate sat in his car. "Thanks for your time, Kit. Tell him I'm sorry to have missed him but I'll warn you next time I'm coming and you can tell him I'd like to congratulate him in person. In six months or so then. Cheerio."

"Cheerio," responded Kit. He stood waving for a moment, enjoying his relief, and then walked to pick up the paint brush. It was only after the car vanished in the distance that he put it down and wiped the sweat off his brow.

"Six months! Oh what we can do in six months!" He pictured Tom grovelling at his feet, naked but for a loin cloth.

Kit had another beer and then leisurely rode up to collect Tom's mare and his "eagle's bait."

Tom was in an agony of cramps and quietly moaning. Kit lowered him and untied his bonds.

"The magistrate was so impressed by what we have done to the place. He thinks the sun shines out of you and that I'm the next best thing to sliced bread," said Kit, enjoying Tom's misery. "He says I can use you for at least another six months," continued Kit. "Hmm. What tasks can I set you next?"

Tom was quite unable to stand up so Kit had to massage his legs. Eventually he made it to his horse and they jogged slowly homewards. Tom thought he could not stand another six months with this sadist. Yet there was one dubious benefit: While he was of value to Kit, he would be kept alive. He gritted his teeth and searched for inspiration. First, he must get physically fit as possible. He had one advantage and he aimed to use it. He knew every inch of the Bush on his property; every path, clearing and thicket as he had played there when a youngster. Suddenly he knew the answer. He would only have one chance and if he blew it, Kit might well kill him. Just as well he did not know of the asparagus bed plan. It would have shot his nerves to pieces, unfit for any action.

*   *   *

Chapter 19

J ust one opportunity occurred when Tom might have escaped. One day Kit left him manacled, while he drove the cattle from the top paddock into another which had more water in its dam. As soon as Kit had ridden off, Tom shuffled to a kitchen drawer and using his teeth, managed to pull open a drawer. Inside was a knife sharpening steel, just the right diameter to fit through the manacle's key. Using his teeth again, he lifted out of the drawer the key to his freedom. He manipulated the sharpener so it dropped through the manacle's key and by degrees managed to loosen and then undo his shackles.

Delighted, he stood up and flexed his legs. Kit had the weapons with him but at least Tom could run off. Where to? That was the problem. He stumbled over to the myrtle bush, hoping Billy was still around, and ripped off a branch leaving it horizontal.

The creek hadn't enough water in it to swim down. If he took to the open range, he would still be in sight for an hour or more. That left the Bush. He hobbled off towards the Bush and gradually his legs felt stronger. As he ran, he knew what to expect from Kit, should he be re-captured. The man would show no mercy for his run-away slave, just like the Americans before their civil war. The thought made him sprint towards cover. Once there, since Kit lacked a dog, he would have to track Tom through the various paths, many of them ending in thick creepers.

Looking back, Tom saw a wisp of smoke rapidly spreading through a stand of gum trees on the top of the hill. He grinned and increased his speed. Hopefully Kit would be drawn in the wrong direction, giving Tom precious time to hide in the thick Bush.

Tom had no idea how long he had been running but he heard to his horror the sound of a cantering horse. He leapt off his path into the cover of thick scrub. He heard the horse slow and Kit shouting, "You've done it this time, slave boy. Don't think to outrun my horse."

Tom realized he had made an error. Hiding as he was, he could not move without giving away his position. He just crouched and hoped Kit could not find him. For a while Tom was safe. Kit searched around like an Aboriginal tracker. Kit had noticed a footprint and then another and then no more, confirming that Tom had not gone far. He took his time searching for Tom's brown back. Just a little piece would do.

Suddenly he called out, quite close to Tom, "Got you," and bounded over to where Tom was hiding. He grabbed Tom and pulled him over to his horse. Tom had no chance of beating him in a fight so he just accepted his fate and stood while Kit bound his wrists. Then he tied the other end of the rope to the saddle and mounted. "This is just your first lesson," smiled Kit. "I'll enjoy it more than you, I guess."

He stuck his heels into his horse and wheeled it towards home at a canter. Tom tried running to avoid being dragged along the track but soon stumbled and fell, quite unable to match the horse's speed. He was hauled along, skinning chest and back as he was twisted and turned.

As they left the Bush, Kit drove the horse into a gallop so Tom sometimes was dragged along the ground and sometimes catapulted into the air as he hit an obstruction.

By the time they reached the house, Tom was a bleeding mess and semi-conscious. Kit looked at him lying there with contempt.

"That's just the softening up, slave. You're too valuable to waste, so here's the painful bit." He stripped off what little remained of Tom's rags and doused him in the trough, time after time, making Tom think he was going to be drowned. When the blood was washed off, Kit swung him over his shoulder and entered the house. He tied Tom's wrists to the large ring and then went into the kitchen, returning with a bucket of water and a bag of salt.

"We wouldn't want your body to fester, slave boy and I'm afraid this is going to hurt."

Kit tipped the salt into the water and stirred it. Then he applied the thick solution to all parts of his body. Tom yelped in pain. It was like nothing he could have imagined. Eventually he fainted from the agony. Kit continued till he had cauterized the whole of Tom's body.

"That'll teach you slave boy not to mix it with me," Kit said, as Tom regained consciousness. "You can lie there all night. And as I don't want my beauty sleep disturbed . . ."

Kit gagged Tom, who was breathing in short pants, wondering why Kit wouldn't put him out of his misery?

Kit let Tom recover over the next four days. There was no infection, in spite of all the filth Tom had been dragged through, but his pain lasted almost a month. By the time he was fit for work, he was physically and mentally broken, with no thought of escape, but just avoiding the next beating. Very slowly, Tom's character buoyed him up and his mind healed. Someday there had to be a chance. One day he would kill Kit, if he had to wait till he was senile.

Work continued as they cleared more of the Bush. It was a slow job, hacking down trees with a crosscut saw or an axe. Then they would trim the branches and burn the debris.

Tom was conscious of Kit's pistol in his belt, as he used the axe. His master took no chances and as if to reinforce the threat, some days he would have a short target practice, knocking tins off a fence post. At twenty feet, he was a crack shot. Tom knew there was no chance of snatching the gun. As for physical combat, Kit proved his point every so often, by challenging

Tom to a wrestling match and he knew every trick in the book. Inevitably, Tom would be on his back in seconds, winded, with Kit on top of him, smiling triumphantly.

Tom bided his time, hoping it would come and it did. One morning Kit told him to saddle the horses as they were to check the cattle for condition and dingo attacks. Kit had his rifle as usual in his saddle holster. Tom waited till they were on the leg back home, facing down a gentle slope near the trees he knew so well. Suddenly he dug his heels into the mare's sides and took off at a gallop amongst the trees. Kit whirled his horse around and was in hot pursuit, gaining by degrees. He took out his lasso, whooping with the excitement of the chase and prepared to jerk Tom out of his saddle, which would certainly end with a broken limb or two. Tom rounded a corner in the track and hooked his leg over the saddle, Indian fashion, hanging down the side of his horse to avoid being swept off it by the thick overhanging branches he knew so well.

Kit was standing up in his saddle as he rounded the corner, whirling the lasso over his head, whooping and enjoying his last smile. As Tom had planned, he galloped flat out into a heavy branch and was flung to the ground with an earth shaking crunch. Tom pulled up his horse and jumping off, ran to Kit's body. He pulled the pistol out of Kit's belt and stood over him. There was no need. His tormentor's neck had snapped and his head lay twisted to one side.

Tom was shaken, trembling and then delighted. He was free, free at last! At first he could not really take it in. Life had returned. Then he approached Kit's horse, taking its reins as it shied away from the body. Free! Free! He hoisted the body across the saddle and tied it there with Kit's lasso. Then he caught his mare, which seemed to sense his exhilaration, nosing his face with her soft muzzle. Tom responded, hugging her with delight. He mounted her and led the other horse back to the homestead.

*   *   *

Chapter 20

Now for the hard bit. Tom must take Kit in to the police and tell them about the "accident". Well, he hadn't laid a hand on his master. He loaded the body into the back of the ute and removed Kit's various keys before driving off to town. It was nearly dark by the time he reached the police station. It was locked up so Tom tried the pub. Yes, the sergeant was there, laughing with his mates at a table near the bar.

There was a sudden hush as this scruffy youth, with a halo of golden hair entered tentatively, eying the policeman.

"Hey! You can't come in here, kiddo," shouted the huge barman, striding forward.

Tom winced at the familiar title but he ignored the barman and reached the policeman before his shoulders were seized prior to his eviction.

"I've got a body," Tom announced to the policeman, who had already turned back to his mates.

"You sure have, Darling," said the admiring barmaid.

The barman was forcing Tom towards the door.

"Hey, Sergeant! You need to see it." shouted Tom.

"After me," giggled the barmaid.

The sergeant turned and looked at Tom. "Were you addressing me, young . . . fellow?"

The barman had reached the door with Tom.

"A death. I've got to report it." There was a silence as all the customers were suddenly interested. Nothing as exciting had happened for months. Not since the local drunk had been knocked down by an escaping bull.

"Bring him here," commanded the sergeant. "What did you say? This had better not be a hoax. I'll tell your dad to give you a . . ."

"I've got no dad. Come outside and see for yourself."

The barman had released Tom and the bar emptied as they followed Tom and the sergeant into the street. Kit was not a pretty sight, his badly bruised head lolling to one side, spread-eagled across the tray of the ute.

"Christ! Did you run him over," said the sergeant.

"No,"gulped Tom. "His horse bolted and he hit a low bough. Come out to my property and I'll show you where it happened."

The sergeant checked the front of the ute for any damage and looked hard at Tom.

"You're the Hartley boy, aren't you, under all them locks."

Tom nodded, blinking back tears. The drama of it all was getting to him.

"I'll take care of this," said the sergeant in a kindly tone. "Go and get yourself a haircut, and then a shower and a meal, and you can sleep at my place. My missis has always had a soft spot for strays. Or if you prefer it, try the pub. Here's ten pounds. Pay me back later. Word has it you're rich." He handed Tom the note.

Tom could not prevent the odd tear and the tactful sergeant looked the other way.

In the barber's Tom had a shampoo and a neat haircut. "Jeez, you're a good looking kid under all that camouflage," joked the barber.

Then he went and booked a room at the pub and had a shower. He pinched himself. Is this real? After a meal of bangers and mash, with the locals looking at him one way and the barmaid in another, he made his way up the stairs to bed. Even the pub noises could not keep him awake. He looked around him at the fairly basic room and thought, "Ecstasy!"

Next morning Tom had breakfast of bacon and eggs and again could not believe it was not all a dream. He strode over to the police station and entered, hoping they would not find any loop-holes with his story. Well it was an accident in a way, he repeated in his mind. The sergeant sat him down saying," Now Tom, what do you know about Kit? We have no records and it's as if he had landed from outer space."

"I only know that just after my dad drowned, he appeared, as you say and offered to help me. We've worked together and improved the property no end. I'm so sorry he's gone." Tom had real trouble with that falsehood.

"Well your story checks out with his wounds and I see no point in going all the way to look at a tree. I'll arrange to have him buried and put a notice in the paper. What are your plans?"

"I'm going to see the bank manager and to get some cash to repay you among others," said Tom. "I'm eighteen and legally able to live on my own now. I can't thank you enough for your kindness." Tom swallowed. He still felt emotional after all he'd been through.

"You surely can't manage a large property on your own, and I suggest you stay in town a little longer, just to re-charge your batteries. Losing Kit must have been a great shock."

"Sure was," said Tom, thinking he ought to become an actor. "Thanks again."

He made for the bank and booked himself an appointment to see the manager in an hour's time. "I'm going to be so careful who I employ to help me," he thought. "Never again!"

He wandered around town and saw a number of men queuing for the dole. There'd be no trouble finding a worker, but the right guy? What about a girl?

Mr. Granger was all smiles when he met Tom in his smart office. No, the books would not be available for a couple of weeks. "The annual audit, you will understand, Sir." He added that by way of buttering up Tom. "But," he looked at some figures, "the price of beef was down when your cattle were sold."

"Really?" asked Tom. The figures Kit gave me were quite pleasing."

"Bugger my days," thought Granger. "What the Hell was his partner in crime giving the figures to Tom for?" "Well, that all depends upon what you compare them with," said Granger, like a slick politician and a little too quickly for Tom, who had him summed up in no time.

"A slippery eel I'd better not trust a mite," he thought.

"So sorry to hear about your guardian's demise," said Granger, trying to change the subject.

"Yeah, a pity about him," said Tom, drily.

"You'll be replacing him straight away?" said Granger. "I might be able to help you there."

"Thanks but no," replied Tom, thinking, "You louse. You want to keep your chains on me."

"I'm not in need of a guardian, any more and I'll choose my own Help, thanks all the same for your kindness." It was all he could do to refrain from sounding sarcastic. "I'll be in to see the audited accounts in two weeks' time. And a cheque for £1,000 please, now, thank you." He waited as Granger wrote out the cheque. "G'day to you, Sir." Tom shook his sweating palm and left.

"Hell! That's a bright kid and he's surfaced too darn quickly from the pressure Kit put on him. I must check the books pretty tight myself." Granger was a worried man.

Outside in the street Tom breathed a sigh of relief that all had gone smoothly. He paid the bill at the pub and for a further night plus meals and then wandered over to the police station. On the way a man, who had watched him leave the bank, after such a long time in there, accosted him.

"Give us the price of a drink, Sir." and as Tom reached in his pocket for some change, he swiveled Tom into a narrow alley and began searching his pockets. The right to the jaw from Tom laid him out cold, empty handed. Tom looked down at the unconscious thief, thinking Kit had taught him something useful, like aim for a place a foot behind your opponent's head. Then, sardonically, he left a shilling coin on the man's chest.

Rubbing his knuckles, which stung, he made for the police station and found the kind sergeant inside. As he gave him what he owed him, he offered a little more.

"No, Tom. It's a pleasure to be able to help your father's son. So very sorry about him."

Tom winced and said his farewell.

* * *

Chapter 21

That evening Tom had his meal, and sat in the bar for a while planning his next moves.

"A load on your mind, gorgeous," said the cheeky barmaid.

Tom smiled but said nothing. "You're not that bad yourself," he thought and shuffled closer to the table to hide his erection. Shortly afterwards he made for the stairs, not noticing her eyes following him up them. He stripped, showered and as it was so hot, lay nude on his bed, falling asleep almost immediately. Hours later he was having an erotic dream, where he was being explored by soft hands. They started at his nipples and quickly ran all over his body, lower by degrees. He felt an unfamiliar thrill as his dream took him into a tiny cave that he had never met before. As he began to tremble all over in ecstasy, he woke fully to the realization it was not a dream. In the low light of a street lamp, he found he was being ridden by the barmaid, also naked. "I do believe I've found a virgin," she whispered, "and isn't he enjoying it, you beautiful boy."

She was dead right there. Tom rose and fell in a wonderful part dream world, which was nothing to what she would teach him through the night. When he woke alone he wondered whether it all had been a fantastic dream, but there was a faint female aroma, which he knew was not him. He slept in that morning, exhausted but happy. So that was what men joked about in the bar. He was delighted to have discovered it.

When Tom came down to breakfast there was no sign of his companion of the night. He had his meal and then wandered around the town hoping to catch a glimpse of her as he shopped, but no luck. "So that's what they call a 'one night stand' is it?" he smiled to himself. "A week would have been better!"

Shopping for food, clothes, rifle ammunition, petrol and a lighter, he was about to get into his ute when the magistrate walked up.

"G'Day, young Hartley. How's tricks?"

"Hello Sir," replied Tom, glad to see a true supporter.

"Anything I can do for you, Tom?"

"Well Sir, if you know of any young guy who's intelligent and willing, I'd pay him well. I don't know how I can cope on my own."

"I'll look around for you. See what I can do. Got a feeling the last one wasn't right for you?"

The magistrate looked right through Tom, with a friendly smile. "By the way, were you really fencing when I called a few months back?"

"Just flying high," grinned Tom, as he recollected being trussed like a bird for the oven and hoisted twenty feet up. "I'll always be in your debt, Sir, if you can find the right mate."

They parted with a firm shake of hands and Tom drove off, while the man stood looking after him, like a favourite son. A pair of rainbow lorikeets whistled past his windscreen, their brilliant colours flashing in the sun, hopefully a symbol of happier times to come. "Hmm," thought Tom, grinning. "Last night might just be the start."

He was tired but contented when he finally drove up to the homestead and unloaded his purchases. He immediately loaded the repeater rifle and hid it above a rafter in the house. Kit's pistol was also checked for a full magazine and placed in a strategic position in the stable. No way was anyone going to take him over again.

He had thought of buying a dog in town but they need attention much of the time, feeding and exercising, no problem here, but he did not feel like any ties at this stage.

In a distant hospice Matron Goodheart showed Greg, Tom's dad pictures of families and children from old newspapers, just hoping one might jolt his memory. On one occasion she had an old paper from some fifty miles North West, which seemed much too far to be relevant. Suddenly Greg pointed to a picture of a gorgeous young boy with fair curls. "Tom," he exclaimed. "Tom".

The date was eight years ago and it was some event in a distant town, Kilacoy. "It can't be anyone you knew," said Matron.

"My son, Tom," Greg insisted. "It is, was."

"I'll make enquiries," said Matron, feeling in her heart that there was little hope of this being "Jim's" son. She resolved to write to the Mayor of the town with the picture and ask if he had any ideas who it might be. At least it would be an avenue closed.

Greg could not settle after seeing the picture. He would not do his duties but walked up and down, looking into the distance.

*　　*　　*

Chapter 22

Back at the homestead Tom was frantically busy bagging potatoes. Then the cattle managed to break through a gate that really should have been repaired way back and he had to round them up and herd them into a safer paddock. He was run off his feet.

After smoko one day, he saw a rider trotting down the drive. It looked like a teen-age boy, with a good seat. Obviously an accomplished rider. As the boy dismounted, Tom came forward and shook his hand. It was a small hand but felt as if he had done manual work.

"Sian.," he said by way of introduction. "You'll be Tom? The magistrate sent me. Said you'd find me work. Nice place you've got here."

"Sian? What sort of name is that?" he thought to himself.

"Hi, Sian. Welcome. Bring your gear inside." Tom led the way. Sian undid his swag from the horse's saddle and followed him in.

"Say, you've got electricity, great," exclaimed Sian with approval.

"Yeah, my last helper set that up," he said, thinking that Kit had had his uses. "This is your room. £5 pound a week and board. Okay with you? You'll earn it," he added hastily.

"Too right. Sounds good to me," said Sian, looking at Tom in a friendly fashion.

"Geez, I hope he's not queer," thought Tom. "It'll be a short partnership."

"We'll share chores," he said. "See how you shake down."

They sat down on the verandah after a meal, thrown together by Tom. He was glad when Sian did the washing up without being asked, and didn't break any plates.

"Where've you worked before? Been on a cattle station?" asked Tom.

"Just my dad's. He sent me away to get wider experience," said Sian. He had a high voice for a fellow. Tom wondered how strong he'd be?

"How old are you?" said Tom.

"Seventeen, but getting older," laughed Sian, flushing. "I'll be eighteen next week."

"That explains it. He's a late developer," thought Tom. "Just as well you found me. There's some who'd take advantage of you," he continued.

"I think I can trust you," said Sian. "You look civilized."

"Am I?" he asked himself, "after what I've been through? I hope he's right."

They went to their rooms early and both crashed out almost as soon as they hit the mattresses.

Next day, Sian had their breakfast cooking before Tom was up. "Hey! This is the life," he thought. "He's got initiative and looks on the right track."

Tom threw off his clothes at the trough and had a good scrub. As he was drying himself, he noticed Sian eying him in an unusually speculative way. When he saw Tom had noticed him, he quickly entered the house.

"Oh no," thought Tom. "I thought it too good to be true. I'd better find an excuse for sacking him."

After breakfast, which Sian washed up in record time, Tom told him he could help him repair the gate that let the cattle through. They saddled their horses and set off with a saddle-bag containing, a bit and brace, spanner, nuts and bolts, hammer and a saw. The wood was too hard for nails. Till they had finished, Tom was quiet, wondering how he could get rid of Sian. It seemed a pity as he was expert with drilling straight holes and they had repaired the gate in record time.

The next test was drafting cattle for drenching for worms. They shed a hundred at a time into a holding paddock. Sian was first rate in the saddle and Kit's horse responded to him as if they had trained together for months. They worked the cattle from the paddock into the race, where Sian offered to use the pellet gun on the cattle, a potentially dangerous job for a beginner as one had to watch for sudden movements from the frightened beasts, which could break ones arm very easily. Tom pushed the cattle, one at a time into the crush where they were held by the neck ready for the tube to be inserted down their throats. He soon realized that Sian was a professional and became relaxed. Perhaps he could keep him on whatever. Just be on guard. The lad might well be harmless.

When they returned tired at the end of the day, Sian still got the meal under way, with no prompting. He seemed too perfect in every way. He also had a charming smile and seemed to anticipate Tom's needs in all directions. He was surprisingly modest when it was his turn to wash and Tom went into the house, to avoid embarrassing him.

As they relaxed over a beer on the verandah, Tom in the rocking chair, Sian said, "Well, what do you think? Have I passed the test?"

"Yeah, sure. You've obviously spent all your life on a cattle property. I guess you know as much as I do about raising beef cattle."

Sian smiled and shook Tom rigid with his next remark, "Then it doesn't concern you if I'm a girl?"

"What!" Tom jumped out of his chair. "So that's why . . ."

"Why I look at you the way I do, when I'm not mindful?"

Sian took off her cap and a nest of golden hair was revealed.

Tom looked at Sian with his mouth open. "Yeah, sort of, I mean . . ." He wasn't sure what he meant, especially after his recent experiences in the pub.

"Will you keep me on, now you know?" asked Sian nervously.

"Will I just! Yeah, if you want to stay." Tom hoped fervently she would. As he looked at her, he realized that she was actually quite a looker. Not much up front yet, but that would probably come pretty soon, and Hell, keep your mind on the job. She wasn't here for sex, but a worker. Would this complicate things? Suddenly Tom wanted to know her better. Uh huh. She wasn't legal for a few more days. But then?

Sian didn't need to be a mind reader to see Tom's mental tumult. It looked as if he liked her as much as she had liked him ever since she had ridden into his life. Even more so, since she had spied him at the trough. "Yeah, it could be fun. Lots of fun," she thought. "No Mum or Dad to interfere and what couldn't we get up to out here!"

"Will you stay?" asked Tom nervously, praying that she would.

"Oh yes," said Sian, blushing and shaking short dark hair from under her cap. "I think we'd better lock our doors for another week."

Both laughed, embarrassed.

Neither was in a hurry to retire that evening and when they did, Tom heard her lock her door. He left his unlocked, hopefully, but then told himself to not be a fool, and he locked it too. Without the temptation, he would sleep much better.

*　　*　　*

Chapter 23

In town Granger had time to consider his position. He had lost his partner in crime. In two weeks the auditors would reveal glaring gaps in the funds that should have been in Tom's bank account. Stupidly he had relied upon Kit to control the boy and had bought shares under his own name. The more he thought about it, the less he could sleep on it. Fraud was punishable by imprisonment, let alone huge fines, and forty thousand pounds worth of shares was going to need a lot of explaining. Perhaps it was time for a world cruise and to take everything he could grab? He worked late into the night scanning Tom and others' accounts to see what ready cash and shares certificates he could take with him. Then he checked his passport was up to date and searched for an international shipping company's phone number for the morning.

At the hospice, Matron Goodheart and her staff were in a flutter. They had been given a month's notice that the place would be closed and knocked down for development into a bar and gambling joint. She rang around but could find no alternative accommodation. In desperation she found a few beds for the most deserving cases, but Greg and a few others were to be out on the streets. She told them they had a month to find digs and employment. Since there was high unemployment already, starvation faced them.

Greg's mental state had simmered down from when he had seen youngster Tom's photo. He was approaching a normal state of mind, apart from memory loss. He could now remember happenings a few months after his "drowning". But there was still a long gap before that. In the meantime it was vital that he find employment. Search as he did, he could find no one who'd give him a job. There was a dole queue on Mondays, when Greg and other down-and-outs were given a couple of shillings, which would buy them enough tucker to stagger through the week, when added to the soup kitchen at mid-day. They all stared around them, dreaming of better days, with the hopelessness of those whose lives were out of control and no future prospects but an early grave. Some took refuge in drinking meths while one committed suicide. Greg had held onto the photo and kept it secure in his money belt. He nearly lost it, when sleeping under a tree one night, in the park, another vagrant tried searching his body for cash. Greg waited till he was properly awake and then drove the points of his fingers into the thief's throat. He stumbled off, empty handed, choking and was lucky to live. Greg felt anxiously for his photo and last shilling. They were still there. It was the photo that held him together; a link with the past, even if he could not remember where it had been taken or anything beyond.

Life staggered on with hand-outs and the occasional bonus when he helped at the petrol station, washing windscreens. There were some cruel comments about a man of his age doing this sort of labour but he smiled grimly and kept going.

On the property some weeks had passed by since Sian's arrival. Tom was happier than he could remember in his life. They worked hard together like a married couple in the same business, and nearly every night they made passionate love. Their self-reliant lifestyle with almost entirely home produced free food, discounting their labour, free electricity and horse transport meant no pressures they knew about. That is, until they decided to go to town for the next load of petrol, cattle medications etc . . .

They drove up to the bank and were surprised to find a new youthful manager, who introduced himself as Mr. Symmonds.

"Glad to meet you," he greeted them. "I'm just finding my feet here after the sudden departure of Mr. Granger."

Tom had a nasty turn as he felt something frightening in the pipeline. "He's left then?"

"Yes," continued Mr. Symmonds. "And since it's common knowledge, as you'll find out round the town, much of our money left with him."

"Is my money safe?" asked Tom, suddenly aware that once more the world was caving in around him.

"I'm afraid anything by way of cash, he took with him. Interpol are after him as he's thought to have gone abroad . . . Possibly Brazil."

"What about my proceeds from the last cattle sale?" Kit said. "They raised £10,000."

"All gone, I'm afraid. Your account, like many others is zero."

"The bank lost it so the bank should pay us back," said Tom, hotly, Sian nodding.

"In time, we'll be in a position to repay some of the rest," said Mr. Symmonds, looking at their statement. "I can't see any reference to ten thousand pounds. Perhaps Mr. Granger put it straight in his pocket. In the meantime, we can arrange a small overdraft to see you through for essentials."

Tom gulped. It was a couple of months before they could sell any more fat cattle. The young stock should fatten nicely by then, weather providing. But Tom and Sian needed to eat till then.

"We'd better just buy flour and sugar plus some coffee and tea. No beer," said Tom, as they left the bank. What else could go wrong? The weather? It hadn't rained for weeks.

Suddenly life was not quite so rosy. They drove back to the property in silence most of the way. "Not my fault, Love," said Tom.

"No," murmured Sian, still shocked. "But the problem's still there. And I think I'm going to have a baby."

In his turn, Tom was also shocked. "Well, we were rather asking for one," he smiled, hoping to reassure her.

"But we're so young," she said, tearfully. "They might take it away from us."

"Over their dead bodies," exploded Tom, thinking of the rifle he had hidden.

They quietened, each with their own thoughts.

That evening they chose not to make love. They went about their tasks, almost as if living on their own. Tom was frightened by their lack of cash and the thought that he could no longer trust banks. Sian was frightened by being so far from town. She'd have to live in town for the weeks before the baby was due and then what, when it was born? She had heard of aboriginal children being taken away from their natural parents. Could this happen in her case?

Before bed, they lay huddled together like two young children on the settee. Eventually Tom got up, gave her a quick hug and went to his bedroom, where he stripped and got into bed. He couldn't sleep for a long time. Their magical period had come to an end.

Sian rolled off the settee and made for the trough. A dip and a rough toweling made her feel better. At least Tom had accepted the idea of a baby and looked as if he would support her through thick and thin. She loved him and his youthful determination. At least she thought she did.

*   *   *

Chapter 24

A week passed and no rain came. Then a month, then another month. Still beautiful cloudless skies. Not a trace of moisture. The dams were getting low and the creek was only a trickle in places, between diminishing pools.

Tom decided to sell some cattle early before all the grass disappeared, even if they would not make good money. They rounded up two hundred of the best grown youngsters and to save money, did their own droving. After a week on the road, the stock living off the grass on the wide verge mostly, plus a few stock yards en route, where paddocks had been given over to passing stock, they rode into town. They drove the cattle into the yards and were glad that they would only have to wait a couple of days before the sale. Mr. Symmonds said he could loan them enough to pay for some hay for the cattle. It was at a premium price, with other farmers clamoring for it. They wandered round town with lecherous glances in Sian's direction and one or two in Tom's.

"Shall we arrange somewhere for me to stay when the baby's due?" asked Sian.

"Let's wait a little longer," said Tom, thinking that in the frightful event of the baby being born prematurely, it would be money down the drain.

They had enough money to stay at a cheap B & B and kept a careful eye on their cattle as rustling was known in these parts. Tom had the pistol hidden in his clothes in his rucksack. There was an atmosphere of a town in frontier America a hundred years ago and he trusted hardly anyone. On the morning of the auction they were watering their cattle and a large man in a smart Jakaru hat sauntered over to Tom and said, "G'Day, kiddo. I'm Frank Sawyer. These beasts yours? A bit young to sell."

"I need the money," said Tom uneasily. There was something he didn't trust about the man. He was overpowering.

"Tell you what, I'll give you £300 for the lot. Save you waiting about and it'd be cash in hand."

"You must be joking," said Tom. "Less than two pound a head!"

"They look as if you're short of tucker," said Frank. "I guess you're between a rock and a hard place."

Sian was watching nearby. She shook her head vigorously at Tom. He caught her out of the corner of his eye.

"Tell you what, I'll pay you $400 and that's my best offer. By the way I've bought the property next to you. Got it cheap as Jack Turnbull was about to walk off his property. He hasn't got the creek like you."

There was almost a threat like quality in Frank's tone.

"Sorry to see him go," said Tom. "He was a good neighbour. Give me £600 and they're yours. Save me the auctioneer's fee."

Frank nodded to a rough looking guy, unshaven and skinny but well-muscled. He strode over quickly. "Meet Joe. He works for me. Sorts out all my problems. Useful guy is Joe. Joe, this kiddo is Tom."

Joe nodded and squeezed Tom's hand hard, looking at him as if he could eat him for breakfast. "Tom Hartley," said Tom, trying not to wince.

"Oh, the boy off that nice piece of land bordering yours, Frank," said Joe. "Nice to meet you, kiddo."

"Tom wants £600 for those skinny little beasts. What you think, Joe?"

Joe took a long hard look and then said nothing for a moment, smiling at Tom in a nasty way.

"I reckon if the kid's going to stay on that land of his, he'd be wise to take your offer, Frank."

"Is that a threat?" said Tom, furious.

"No, just an observation," said Joe, meaning it was every bit of a threat. He looked very straight at Tom and laughed. "And we can include Tom."

"No thanks, Mr. Sawyer. I'll try my luck in the auction. Thanks for your offer."

Tom gave both of them a very hard stare.

"Be seeing you, kiddo," said Frank, smiling at Joe. They strolled away. Joe winked at Tom.

"God! I hate them," said Sian, striding up to Tom.

"They're evil," said Tom. "We'll sell our cattle in the next lot," he continued, looking at his bill of sales. They could hear the auctioneer giving tongue with the previous lot.

In minutes it was their turn. The auctioneer shouted, "Is Mr. Tom Hartley here?"

Tom leaped up onto the rails and shouted, "I'm here."

The auctioneer hesitated as he took in his client's youth. "Er, right. Gents we've got some nice young stock here. In need of fattening but in three months you'll double their value."

"Not a chance," said Frank Sawyer in a loud voice and glared round the buyers.

"Mind your manners, Sir," said the auctioneer, unabashed by Sawyer's aggression. "Now, what am I bid? Two hundred healthy cattle. They'll be a good buy at five pounds a head."

"One hundred pounds the lot," shouted a buyer.

"Two hundred and they're mine," said Sawyer, glaring round the buyers. Some took fright and left.

"Three hundred," shouted another buyer, looking totally at ease with Sawyer.

"Three hundred and twenty five," shouted Sawyer, joined by Joe, who also glared round the circle of buyers.

"Three fifty," said the other buyer. The other buyers had slunk away.

"Let him have them," whispered Joe to Sawyer. "Less money in the boy's pocket."

Sawyer nodded.

"Going once at three fifty," shouted the auctioneer. "Going twice. Last time. Going . . . Sold to Mr. O'Connor, of O'Connor Estates," shouted the auctioneer. Payment to Mr. Tom Hartley. Cash."

Tom and Sian strode over to Mr. O'Connor and he shook their hands, cheerfully, casting a hard glance at Sawyer and Joe. "I should keep a watch on them two, Tom." said O'Connor. "They look a mean pair of bastards."

"You bet and thank you, Sir," said Tom, as he pocketed the notes. "I'm glad they're going to you."

Mr. O"Connor patted Tom on the back and said, "Watch your back, son, 'bye."

Tom and Sian made straight for their ute, watched by Sawyer and Joe.

Sawyer murmured, "She's a pretty little thing. I'll have her. You can have the boy, Joe."

Joe licked his lips and nodded. "Tonight, before they spend the money?"

"A full moon. After they've gone to bed. Easy. Cherries off a tree."

*   *   *

Chapter 25

The journey home went more cheerfully, with money in their pocket and less cattle to eat the grass. As they drove up to the homestead, Sian went on into the house with the rucksack and Tom unlocked the barn to water and feed their horses. The mare was especially glad to see him. "I wonder whether she worries we might not come back," thought Tom, filling her hay-bag. He groped for the rifle and ammo box and locking the door, hurried towards the house. He had this funny feeling he was being watched. No, silly. He would have heard any vehicle and horses have a way of nickering to each other. He locked the door behind him and looked at Sian, blushing from the heat of the stove.

Sian cooked them a champion meal and after all the hassle of selling the cattle, they both felt ready for bed. "Okay for me tonight?" asked Tom, a sudden urge as he took off his shorts and saw Sian looking at him. She nodded sexily. "Just a minute," he said and left to re-enter shortly, carrying the rifle and ammo box.

"What!" said Sian. "You don't have to force me."

Tom laughed. "Just in case," he said softly and filled the rifle's magazine with ten bullets. He placed the rifle under the bed, easily reachable and the pistol under his pillow.

"Expecting company?" asked Sian.

"Always a good boy scout," he replied with a grin.

Soon after they were exploring each other and passionately occupied. So much so that they did not hear the front door's lock being picked. As they climaxed, the door to their bedroom opened and Sawyer and Joe stood there enjoying the spectacle.

"Just look at that," said Joe. "He'll be well spent and she'll be just right for you." They both advanced on their proposed victims, laughing. Tom just managed to slide off her and reach a hand under the pillow when both of them were astride the youngsters. He was turned over, which helped his hand find the trigger and swivel the pistol along his side towards Joe's chest.

"Git off me, you pig," he shouted.

"I'll enjoy this," said Joe, his last words. There was a muffled phut as the bullet passed through the pillow and into Joe's chest. He died instantaneously.

Sawyer paused in his attempted rape of Sian, frozen in paralysed astonishment.

Sian brought up her knee into his testicles and he rolled off her to lie yelping on the floor.

"Nice goal," said Tom, standing over Sawyer. "What part shall I shoot off first?"

"His balls," said Sian.

"No, no!" shrieked Sawyer. Tom stood, enjoying the bully's terror.

"No, we'll let him go and he can dream of what could happen to him any night. He kicked Sawyer, who yelped again.

"If you want to live, you get rid of your friend here and should he ever be found, you know we'll tell the police the whole story. Want to live?"

Tom rammed his pistol into Sawyer's mouth. He choked and nodded his head. "And should we ever meet again, you show me respect, understand?" Tom removed the weapon and Sawyer blurted, "Yes Sir."

Tom nodded in satisfaction. "Right, I'll help you get rid of this mongrel. Sian, the doors please."

Ten minutes later Sawyer was driving away in a cloud of dust into the night, while Tom having locked up, helped Sian remove the blood stains.

"Do you reckon we'll have any more trouble from Sawyer?" asked Sian, still shaking from her near miss of rape.

Tom held her in his arms. I'll be ready for him if we do," said Tom, more bravely than he felt. It was not every day he killed someone or was assaulted. What he had just avoided left him shaking like a leaf.

Next day, Tom was pulling out some hay from the loft in the barn when a feral cat sprang out and dashed past him for the door. There was a crash as a tin fell onto the floor. Tom picked it up and prised it open. To his astonishment it was full of £100 notes. He counted them out and it totalled £10,000. Kit's stolen horde! Tom thought for a moment and then decided to keep it as his secret, there for a rainy day. He put the money back in its tin and hid it in the rafters, more securely than before. It was a great weight off his mind. They could buy more cattle when the rain came, and could afford to buy vegetable seed and other items they had given up on.

*   *   *

Chapter 26

A month went by and nothing happened with Sawyer. "Learnt his lesson," thought Tom, while unbeknown to him, Sawyer was planning his downfall. No raw kid was going to divert him from his plans of taking over all the properties in the area. He already owned land on two sides of Tom's place. The time would come when Sawyer could apply the squeeze in several senses. He anticipated the moment with relish.

Sawyer waited another month and it had not rained. Grass was almost non-existent. He drove round to Tom's more distant neighbour, John Barrymore, a nice man with a young family, who was desperate to sell his place while it was worth anything. This was the final part of the jig-saw that surrounded Tom's property. Other farmers were walking off their land in droves. Some shot themselves. With the depression in full swing, the price of meat was at an all-time low. People were eating rabbits and kangaroos—anything that they could get their hands on. Banks repossessed properties, all with heavy mortgages with no consideration for the misery they were spreading.

Sawyer drove in slowly, taking in the skinny kids, the wife standing on the verandah looking hopelessly at the sky and John coming out of the barn, where he had been gathering the last of the hay before taking his handful of cattle to market. It was easy for Sawyer to drive a hard bargain, where he was handed over the title deeds for immediate evacuation and just

£1000 for a property worth fifty times that once the grass grew again. He handed John the money in cash and he gathered a few chattels into his beat-up ute, hugged his family as he urged them into the vehicle, and they all disappeared up the track in a cloud of dust.

Sawyer looked around him with delight. One day this place would be worth big money, but even better, he had that kid surrounded. No witnesses to whatever he might do. He got into his car and drove off to plan with his new hard overseer.

Time went by, with no move from Sawyer. Tom was relaxed. He had seen off the man. No more trouble. His mind was more set on Sian. Her belly was pretty large and perhaps it was time to book in to a home in town. He was glad of the money he had found and used some of it to pay in advance for a room close to the tiny hospital. At least it had a mid-wife, even if the nearest doctor was hours' drive away. Things would be clean and professional.

The day came when Tom and Sian agreed they should drive to town. He had half of the money he found in his pocket ready for the bank, which he now trusted under new management. When they arrived, he dropped Sian off at her room and visited the bank manager. Mr. Symmonds was pleased to see him. He thought Tom had come to seek a larger overdraft and already had 5% interest in his head, when Tom handed him £4,000 in cash.

"You can pay off my overdraft and interest," said Tom, and when that had all been paid, he arranged to buy some shares in the Bank of Australia, thinking that this was unlikely to fail. He explained to Mr. Symmonds that he had discovered a horde left by his dad. Only a white lie. It was his, after all.

While he was kicking his heels with nothing to do, Tom visited Kit's grave. It was already overgrown with weeds. "Appropriate," he thought. "At least he is well and truly under the turf. Funny how weeds will always grow. They've chosen the right patch!"

When Tom returned to Sian's room, he was alarmed to see her bed was empty. "Where's she gone?" he asked the nurse in a panic.

"She's being given a bath. It'll calm her down."

"Why's she in a state?" asked Tom, in need of calming himself.

"I'm so sorry. She's lost the baby. It was stillborn."

"Oh my God!" exclaimed Tom, sitting down heavily.

"And she shouldn't try for another," said the nurse. "The uterus was damaged and the midwife is seriously concerned that both might die another time."

Tom groaned. He suddenly thought back to their visitation by Joe and Sawyer. This might have brought on their child's death. Sawyer, he'd better never meet Tom again.

After her bath, he was told Sian did not want to see him again. Not yet, anyway. Tom felt he had been kicked in the teeth. He left a message for her that he would wait a couple of days and booked in at the hotel. Lying on his bed, staring at the ceiling, Tom wondered why he had been singled out for so much grief. He could have howled but lay there, dry eyed.

Later that evening he went to the bar and started on a drinking binge. His barmaid tutor joined him when he had finished his fourth pint and was getting bleary eyed, not used to so much alcohol.

"What's biting you, darling," she asked him with her arm round his waist, nestling up against him.

"You don't want to know." he replied, staring moodily into his empty glass.

"Come upstairs and we'll put it right," she said, squeezing his thigh.

"I'm hooked already," he droned. "Can't let her down."

"She won't know and I'll make you feel good, better than ever before."

Tom never thought about it. He just stumbled up the stairs obediently, not caring.

Kathleen—he learnt her name at last—undressed him, raising his desire on the way and in no time he was lying face upwards, rising up and down in the tide. She obviously had plenty of practice satisfying her customers but this time she enjoyed it every bit as much as Tom. The night lasted long and fruitfully, as Tom sobered up but could not wait for the next onslaught. Once more he awoke late and she had disappeared. He felt only a little shame since Sian had rejected him.

*   *   *

CHAPTER 27

In the months that followed Tom heard nothing from Sian. He felt a pang of regret but decided to get on with his life. He realized the difference between hot desire and true love. They had been two youngsters on a discovery mission only.

Most of the remaining cattle had to be sold. Hardly a blade of grass left in the remorseless drought.

Fortuitously the aboriginal family returned to Tom's property, Billy, his wife Bertha, Francie, a giggly girl of about twelve and Sammy a boy of fourteen. Tom made them welcome and gave them his empty barn to stay in. Billy was happy to work on and off and Tom asked him to help drive the remaining cattle to town. He decided to keep the bulls and a hundred young breeding stock, that he could feed with the branches of the willows that grew by the creek.

He left Bertha in charge, and they made for town on horseback, whips cracking under a relentless sun. As there was little feed en route, they kept the cattle going as fast as possible and made it in three days. The auction was for meat cattle only as no one needed breeders. His skinny beasts only made £1 a head, but it gave him £500, which would take care of his outgoings for some months, without touching his nest-egg.

They rode back to the property with some flour, tea and sugar in the saddle bags and were at the homestead in a couple of days. All was well and Bertha and her children were delighted to see them safely home.

News travels around country properties, via Bush telegraph, and Sawyer soon knew that Tom had sold most of his cattle and also that apart from a handful of "Blacks", he was on his own.

Sawyer licked his lips with the thought of getting his hands on that property and enslaving Tom. The boy would make a fine worker when tamed, he thought. He had heard of Kit's "accident" and wondered whether it really had been so? Well he'd teach him a lesson for sticking that pistol in his mouth and losing him his best stockman and partner he had had for years. The creek would be valuable and he liked the thought of living in Tom's smart home, ordering him around. He'd break him in a week.

The aboriginals moved on, as is their custom, leaving Tom a little lonely. He had enjoyed their cheerful company but they were nomadic by nature. He felt at an all-time low, longing for Sian and worrying whether she was all right. He had gone to bed one night wondering if he might not leave the property and join the army? He was eighteen and very fit. He could lie about his age but now it looked as if World War 2 was about to break out, they probably would not be too fussy.

Tom suddenly heard a rumble and thinking this was funny, as there had been no thunder about, he slipped on his shorts and went to the front door. By the light of a half-moon he could see a huge mob of cattle surging around his house like a sea. It had to be Sawyer at work. He must have cut the boundary fence and herded his own cattle into action. He heard whips cracking and shouts.

"Right, you want war, Sawyer. You've got it." He grabbed the rifle from under his bed and pocketed a box of ammunition. He made for the back door but there were cattle up against it. He rushed to the front door.

"Come out of there, kiddo. You're surrounded and finished. This is my place now, and everything on it, including you."

Tom opened the door a crack but a rifle shot splintered the wood of the architrave. Tom jerked his head back inside. He thought for a moment. He was truly bottled up but would not go down without a fight. He locked the door, made for the roof space ladder and pulled it down. He scrambled up it and pulled the ladder up after him, closing the hatch. In the darkness of the loft he waited and listened for developments. First he must learn where Sawyer and crew were situated. It would be silly to get his head blown off the moment he went outside.

Eager to get at the invader, he heard Sawyer's voice again: "Come out kiddo and you won't be hurt. You're no good to me dead."

Tom made for the rear of the building where the roof could not be seen from the other side and feeling his way across the rafters, clutching his precious rifle, he reached a place where he could stand upright. He eased up a roof air vent and squeezed his way out of it. He slithered up to the crest of the roof by the chimney, where he was in shadow from the moon, and searched for his tormentor. He saw three men still on their horses but had to shoot Sawyer first. He did not want to kill the others but just put them out of action. He could not see Sawyer but he must be down there somewhere. Then he heard him on the verandah, trying to force the door. No way could he reach him there so he had to draw him away. He drew a bead on one of the riders, aiming at his thigh. He fired and saw his target fall off his horse under the milling hoofs of the cattle. There was a strangled cry and then silence.

Tom immediately treated another rider to the same fate. The other vanished into the darkness.

"You shouldn't've done that, kiddo. Now I'm going to whip the meat off your bones. You'll only be good for dog tucker."

Sawyer jumped on his horse from the verandah and rode towards the shadows. Tom pumped two rapid shots after him and was delighted to hear him scream. The other horseman galloped off into the night. With all the shooting, the cattle panicked and made for the hills whence they came.

Tom could see Sawyer lying on the ground. He had been trodden into a pulp and would give Tom no more trouble. The other two men were badly battered but Tom rushed to give them first aid, checking first that their weapons were well away. He dragged them onto the verandah and bandaged their wounds with strips he tore from an old sheet. Frazer swore at him.

"You bastards would've killed me. I was only defending myself," said Tom.

"He was just going to make you his slave," said the other. "Not kill you."

"Yeah, and so that makes it okay, does it?" asked Tom, tightening the bandage so the man cried out. "Course, I could just put you under the cattle for another chance."

"No, we'll say nuffin'. Just git us to town," said Jones, groaning. "We need to git a doctor dig the bullet out of my leg."

"You're lucky. I could have killed you both," said Tom.

"Damn nearly did," said Frazer.

Tom helped them both onto the back of the ute, giving them a drink of water first and headed for town, with Sawyer's body and their weapons in the front. He drove fast over the bumpy track and delivered them to the district nurse, warning her they were dangerous, and then took their weapons to the police station plus Sawyer's battered corpse.

"Christ! Has the war reached Australia," said the sergeant when he saw the body and weapons. "You'd better come in and do some explaining, Tom."

Tom spent a couple of hours telling his side of the story.

"Well, if you were the murdering kind, Tom, which I know you're not, you would've finished those two low life as well, so I'm inclined to believe you. Plus three against one on your property! It tells us the whole picture. You admit you shot them in self-defence, so there's no need to check your rifle."

*　*　*

CHAPTER 28

With instruction to return in a week for the court hearing, Tom left the Police Station with a lighter spring in his step. He decided to try the army recruiting office before he left town.

There was no shortage of recruits as youngsters and older farmers left their farms in search of free food, a bed for the night and a little pay, plus a purpose in life, or death! After a long wait in the even longer queue, it was Tom's turn. The officer on the other side of the desk took one look at Tom and said, "A bit young, aren't you, laddie?"

"I'll be nineteen in August, Sir," lied Tom, out by six months.

"Hm. Well preserved," joked the man, liking what he saw. "You look just right for us. Pretty fit, eh?"

"A farmer, so have to be, Sir," replied Tom, relieved that his fib had been believed.

"Ever used a firearm before?"

Tom repressed a smile as he thought of yesterday. "I can shoot straight, Sir."

"I bet you can. All those rabbits," said the officer. "Yes, I think we can use you, laddie. Just write your address on this form and sign here."

"Can I join up in a week or two's time, Sir? I've a few things to sort out on the farm."

"Can't your folk do that?"

"No, Sir. Both are dead and I run it on my own."

"Crikey, a lad of ability. Well the war can wait for you. Yes, son, just let us know when you're free. Drive in here and offer your services. By the look of you, they'll greet you with open arms at the training camp at Townsville. Good luck. Oh, and I should get a haircut, son."

"Thank you, Sir." Tom thought he was walking on air as he left the office. He decided to look for someone to take care of what was left of the stock and the farm next.

He sat down on a bench outside the dole queue and looked out for a likely candidate. He did not have to wait long. A bronzed man of about thirty five, looking embarrassed at joining the queue, was added to their ranks. Tom jumped to his feet, liking the man's expression immediately.

"Can I buy you a meal?" asked Tom. "I might have something you'd like to hear. I'm Tom Hartley."

"Dick Deacon," said the man. "What do you want from me?" He looked at Tom in surprise at this youngster with so much confidence. A bit brash for his liking.

They were seated outside the pub, waiting for their meal. Dick had chosen the cheapest meal on the blackboard but Tom persuaded him, as he was buying, to join him with steaks.

"They're cheap enough," said Tom, and I'm not short." He ordered Dick a beer and was pleased when he wanted only a shandy. Not an "alcy".

Tom asked him for his experience and Dick stated that he was yet another who had walked off his farm, as the drought killed his prospects. Tom told him he wanted a caretaker manager, who would buy in more stock if the rains came, and generally look after the place, including the fences.

"What about the neighbours?" asked Dick.

"They'll be new," explained Tom and how they got to be. To his relief Dick had no hang-ups about Tom's battle. He was beginning to respect this "kid".

"What happens if you get killed in the war?" asked Dick.

"I'll sort it with the solicitor, that you keep running the place till the end of the war, unless I survive, in which case I'd like to keep you on, if you want to."

Dick smiled at his young employer and shook his hand. An hour later it was all in place with Dick receiving £3 a week, free access to the vegies and free meat, free board and lodging, of course and a healthy bonus, from any profits. If the worst came to the worst, there was money in the bank for his pay, whatever.

Tom had to go to court a week later. He felt apprehensive, but at least he was pleased with Dick's arrival. The man certainly knew his beef farming and showed his pleasure in his new job by working very hard.

Tom arrived in town in good time for the Court of Enquiry into Sawyer's death. They had sent out the police sergeant to check for signs of the cattle crush and he was not disappointed. Also the forced front door and the bullet lodged in the architrave were crucial evidence. Sawyer's two wounded men had been spirited away, so there was only Tom as a witness. He wished Sian was around still to give evidence of her near rape on the earlier occasion. But no one knew where she had disappeared to. Tom sadly realized he might never see her again.

After a very quick hearing and the magistrate impressed that Tom had volunteered for the army at his tender age, it was all over. Tom breathed a hearty sigh of relief as he left the court room.

News filtered through about the British army taking a hammering at Dunkirk but escaping with over 330,000 men, some being ferried across the channel in little fishing boats, pleasure craft and even two man canoes. A number of Aussies, who had no experience of war, thought it all exciting. Tom hoped he would come through unscathed but from what he had heard of the first World War, it seemed unlikely.

*   *   *

CHAPTER 29

Tom had no ties or responsibilities until a newspaper he was reading mentioned this strange man in a town fifty miles away, who was the age and build of his dad. The man was said to be living rough, having been pushed out of a closed down home for the mentally ill and vagrants. Could it be . . . ? He had to know. He ran to the post office and asked to use their phone. He got the number of the paper's editor from the small print at the end of the page and rang. Mr. Thomas, with a very Welsh voice, told him that the man in the blurry photograph had appeared after the flood two years ago, but had lost his memory and no one had managed to trace where he had arrived from.

Tom asked if someone could contact the man, who could be his dad, and keep him there for a couple of days. Mr. Thomas was very obliging, no doubt scenting a great story, and said he would be happy to put the man up in his own spare room.

Tom thanked him profusely and next rang the army recruiting office. He explained what had happened and asked if he might have a few weeks to sort things out. The sergeant he first spoke to was a bit huffy but Tom insisted he should speak to the friendly officer. He realized he had made no friend of the sergeant but still got through. The officer was sympathetic when Tom explained the history of the case, sounding quite tearful at times and he was granted two weeks to get organized.

Tom immediately rang Dick and told him the possibility. He wished him luck and offered to help any way he could. Tom almost forgot to re-fuel in his excitement and checked the oil and tires. He even bought an extra spare tube and tire levers. He bought two large containers of water and set off towards the distant town. It was getting dark when he arrived and he went straight to the pub for directions to Mr. Thomas's house. As he drew up, he braced himself in case it wasn't his dad and wondered what state he would be in?

Mr. Thomas had done his best. He paid for Greg to have a haircut and shave and he bought him some fresh clothes from a nearly new shop. He was outwardly presentable, but being discarded from the home had disorientated him and reduced his already fragile self-confidence. When Tom reached the front door, he steeled himself for anything and knocked. Mrs. Thomas answered it and stood studying Tom for a moment. "Who's this angelic looking youngster, Bill?"

"Why don't you ask him yourself?" called Bill Thomas. "I doubt he'll like being called that."

He arrived in the doorway and studied Tom. "I see what you mean. Come in, young man. You'll be Tom? I didn't realize on the phone how young you are. Come in, come in. You must be tired after your journey."

Tom felt exhausted from his drive but also the trauma of perhaps meeting his dad again. He followed them in and saw it really was his dad, older and a little haggard, standing waiting for he knew not what. Tom blinked away tears and nervously said, "Dad, Dad is it really you? Remember me, Tom, your son?"

He stopped a yard away, unsure of his welcome.

"Tom, Tom! Of course I remember. It's all coming back. How could I have forgotten?"

"It wasn't my fault," said Tom, struggling to breathe as his dad hugged him tightly. "The water dragged you away under a beam. I thought you must have drowned, especially when I heard nothing for years."

"Of course it wasn't your fault, son, my beloved son. Oh my God it's good to see you. How are you? Silly question. You're blooming. Someone please get the boy a hanky."

Mrs. Thomas obliged but needed one herself. Bill turned away and looked studiously into the fire.

"Oh thank you, Mr. Thomas. I can't thank you enough," said Tom.

"Don't worry son. You'll make the story of the year . . . You can sleep on the sofa tonight. In the morning I want you both looking nice and fresh for some pictures."

Tom slept like a log after telling his dad a little of his past adventures. He left out Sian for now. That would be too complicated and his emotions were stretched quite enough as it was. Sleeping on the sofa, he woke fresh and not really believing he had found his dad after all this time. Suddenly life took on a new meaning. There really was someone to live for.

They had breakfast with the Thomases and left for home after some staged photos and a grateful farewell. The journey home seemed much shorter as his dad told him what he could remember of his ordeal. Then Tom sprung the bombshell, hoping his dad was strong enough to take it. "Dad, I've joined the army. I've got just twelve more days at home and to settle you. Then I go to Townsville for training."

There was a terrible silence as his dad took it in. "So I find my son, only to lose him again! How cruel is fate . . . . Well, son I'm proud of you. Just make sure you come home safe and sound."

Tom breathed a sigh of relief. It could have been much more traumatic. He proceeded to tell his dad how Dick would run the farm and Dad could help as he felt fit, and to take it easy. "I want you in one piece when I come home," said Tom, fondly.

They drew up at the homestead to find Dick, already warned by phone, cooking a fine meal for them. When they were introduced, Tom was pleased to find Dick had cleaned the spare room for his dad and the bed sheet was turned down invitingly. Tom would spend his last few nights there in a hammock on the verandah. When Dad queried whether he would be all right like that, Tom laughed. "It'll be much tougher where I'm going."

Next day Tom showed his dad round the property, with its few livestock. At least the horses were in good condition and there was the beginning of a bore hole for water that Dick had organized. The borer's petrol engine growled all day till suddenly there was a gush as the Great Artesian Basin flowed forth. Dick had the good sense to drill on the slope above one of the dams so it ran down the hill into the dam. If that overflowed, there'd be some lush grass within a week or two.

"A good man, you've found there," said Dad.

"Yes, I've had my share of bad luck. He's a great find."

No way could Tom relate all that he had suffered under Kit's domination. He was careful to always keep his back covered, with its tell-tale scars.

Tom showed Greg where the hidden cash was, in case of an emergency. He also explained what was in the bank and how they were owed what Granger had stolen.

Before he left for the army, Tom had a couple of days to spare and he decided to try and discover any trace that Granger might have left behind him. If ever the war were to end, it might be too late if the thief had spent his ill-gotten gains. He tried Mr. Symmonds, the new manager first but he said he hadn't a clue where Granger had gone. If he had, he would have alerted the police.

Then Tom tried the local real estate agent, a not very bright young man, who had the task of selling Granger's house at a time when property was at an all-time low. There had been instructions left to send the proceeds to Granger's mother, since he lived alone. So Tom asked for and received her address, in a nursing home on the edge of town. He took with him a bunch of flowers and the receptionist showed Tom to her room, with an appreciative smile for this charming young man.

Tom knocked on her door, hoping that he might find a clue here, as there was no other trace to follow. "Come!" was her reply. So Tom entered to find a very old lady, who loved flowers.

She was only too ready to talk all about her beloved son, except she said he had vanished into thin air. While thoughtfully arranging the flowers in a vase provided for some withered cousins, Tom's eyes were flitting around the room for likely places for correspondence. He did not quite believe her professed ignorance of Granger's whereabouts. There was an element of cover-up in her expression. There was a drawer in the table on which the flowers stood, and he contrived to drop some on the floor, with a quick opportunity of opening the drawer a little. There was a bundle of letters, still in their envelopes and he glanced down to a post mark, "Hawkes Bay". That was all. He had to close the drawer in a flash, before she became suspicious.

"Oh they're lovely. Thank you so much. How well did you know my son? He's a bit old for you. Mind you he did like younger company."

"I'm glad you like the flowers, Mrs. Granger. Your son? Well, he kindly gave me advice on an investment. I just thought I would repay his kindness."

Tom grinned to himself: "Hey, that was quick thinking."

He bade her goodbye and left. In town he thought about Hawkes Bay, over a cup of coffee. The only one he knew was in New Zealand, and although close, he hadn't the time to go "swanning" over there before his due arrival in the army. So Granger would have to wait till he finished with the war, or it finished him.

*   *   *

Chapter 30

Granger had been canny in his choice of refuge. He reckoned that Interpol would expect him to choose Latin America as a place notorious for harbouring criminals with no extradition treaties. Granger had decided on New Zealand as the last place they would look, so close to home, and was correct. He would buy a sheep station with part of his ill-gotten gains, put in a manager and live in comfort in Auckland, which would be big enough to hide in. He bought a small but comfortable house in town and a remote property in Hawkes Bay.

He found a property of over a thousand acres near the Ruahine Mountain Range. It was approached by a dirt road and only had one neighbour, ideal for him to spend time there relaxing and checking on his manager. He advertised for a single man as women tend to gossip. He wanted an isolate, content to receive a fair wage and ask no questions; one who would work hard and run the place efficiently, perhaps employing a boy and having his sheep shorn annually by a shearing gang, as normal. Nothing was to connect him with Granger as owner and no one else would be visiting. Granger found his ideal man, one Roy Cobbold, a forty year old victim of a fire whose disfigured face made him seek anonymity. He would go in for his provisions and farm equipment to a tiny settlement, Waipukurau, late in the afternoon just before the shops closed. The store keeper quite understood Roy's reluctance to be seen much in public.

Roy was told to keep two dobermanns, whose fierce barking kept away itinerant life insurance policy sellers and the like. When Granger visited, he always brought a peace offering for the dogs by way of large meaty ox bones and they welcomed him. Mail was negligible and was left in the box at the end of the half mile drive. Roy lived like a hermit. He had a couple of sheep dogs that obeyed his commands lovingly and he rejected the idea of having a boy working for him. "They're only trouble, Mr. Granger," he said. "Best do it on my own."

Granger was well off enough to pay for female company in his town house and to go fishing off the Coromandel peninsula, when bored with their company. He was too old to be called up for the army so life seemed pretty good. He wondered how his benefactor Tom was faring from time to time. It had been like taking candy off a baby, running away with his and others' nest-eggs and life savings. There were many who would have given much to find him. Tom was one but that would have to wait. Just in case, he prepared a little hospitality, a "warm welcome".

So Tom's money was well invested way beyond his reach and unlikely to be repossessed except in some amazing coincidence.

The days flashed by, with Dick and Tom repairing the fences Sawyer had cut; only a couple of hours' work. And then they drilled another bore hole near the house and laid on water inside with a sink and a shower. Dad regarded the improvements with satisfaction. "Welcome to the Ritz," he joked as water sprayed out of the shower.

The young cattle had to be branded and drenched for worms, but with only fifty, they were done in a morning.

*   *   *

Chapter 31

The last morning Greg insisted on driving Tom in to the army office and kept a brave face as his son waved farewell. Tom signed on and was immediately in the sergeant's control, the one he had met before. The man was a power freak. He enjoyed shrieking at the top of his voice into the recruits' ears. "Git you 'air cut, you 'orrible little man," irrespective of the fact that the man he was addressing might be towering over him.

They were shown to their Nissen hut billet, a curved corrugated iron structure that roasted in summer and froze in winter. The sergeant showed them how to lay out their kit on their iron frame beds with bumpy mattresses. It was all done with military precision.

"And if one of you 'orrible lot let the side down by doing it incorrect, you'll all have to do it again. Understand?" He shouted this as if they were all deaf and a hundred paces away.

They had to be in bed by nine and up at six, shaved and dressed with bed set out perfectly by six thirty. Then they trooped into the mess tent and queued for their breakfast. There was porridge, except it was burnt and lumpy. Also eggs, half fried so slimy and bacon cooked but cold in congealed fat. There was plenty of burnt toast and Tom settled for that. "What a waste," he thought, like countless others. "It was just as easy to prepare the meal properly as to ruin it. Did the cooks have a malicious desire to starve them?"

They were allowed twenty minutes to eat and twenty minutes on the door-less loos to do their business. Then they were herded out to the drill square, where they watched trained soldiers march by, their arms straight as they swung them, and their boots and brass shining.

"Squad, shun!" roared a corporal and the squad crashed their heels into the tarmac in unison to a halt. A perfect recipe for varicose veins. "Dress by the right in threes!" The squad shuffled from their perfect formation to another perfect formation pivoting on their right marker, a soldier standing like a rock.

"Right, me lads," shouted the sergeant. "That's what you'll be like in a week. Anyone not up to it will be in the guard house for a week and join the next intake. Any questions?"

"Sir," called one brave but foolish youngster.

"Not 'Sir'. I'm not a ruddy officer," roared the sergeant at his ill-advised target, as if insulted. "It's Serg. Got it? Serg."

"Yes Serg." quavered the shaken lad.

"Well, what do you want, boy?"

"What do we do in the guardhouse?"

"You can find out if you open your mouth again, you miserable excuse for the human race. You do everything at double time till you drop, painting and polishing, all day for twelve hours non-stop, except one toilet break. And if anyone doesn't like it here, no going home to Mummy. It'll be the guardhouse for you too."

He then screamed at them to dress to the right marker, choosing Tom for that honoured position. "Christ," thought Tom. "I know where I go if I make a mistake. Was my first one joining up?"

After two hours of drill in the baking sun, during which three youngsters fainted and had to be carried into the guardhouse, they were already turning to the right in threes and so on like robots. Two unfortunates turned the wrong way and had to run in their heavy boots around the drill square, some thousand yards three times, with their rifles held above their heads. They were almost immediately soaked with perspiration.

As they were standing, waiting hopefully for dismissal, a fly landed on a soldier's nose. He wriggled it and immediately was noticed by the sergeant. "Stand still, you ignorant piece of camel dung. If that fly chooses to shit on you or investigate your left nostril, let him. You move and a sniper sees you and you're dead, just like that."

"Makes sense," thought Tom. "Perhaps there's a reason behind this torture after all."

That afternoon they were taught how to strip a bren gun, a light machine gun. It had to be stripped down to all its working parts and then re-assembled in one minute. "Gun jams," said the sergeant cheerfully, "and a horde of blood thirsty Gerries come storming at you, you're dead, unless you can do this without thinking. And don't forget, the barrel'll be red hot. Use your belt or anything to wrap round it. Change just the barrel in ten seconds. They wear out in ten thousand rounds."

"I wonder who counts," thought Tom, smiling to himself. Some of the things they were told were pretty basic—thus "Basic Training."

Perhaps it was his need for quick reactions in the saddle or his self-reliance managing the property, but Tom was the fastest there in every operation. The sergeant was too wise to praise his efficient trainee but there were some dirty looks as the others found it impossible to defeat Tom.

That evening a couple of his "mates" decided to take Tom down a peg or two. They marched up to him. Skobie said, "Stand up, Sergeant's pet. Let's see how good you are at being a real man, pretty boy."

"I couldn't compete with you," said Tom, not wanting a fight and the trouble it might cause.

"You're yellow. Yellow belly. Let's see if he's yellow all over," said Skobie, dragging Tom towards the shower.

Tom tried shaking them off, to no avail. There was no alternative if he were not to be stripped naked and humiliated.

No one noticed the far door open and the sergeant enter. He closed it quietly and made no move to interfere. Tom had both arms held tight. He slumped to the floor and in the same movement, stamped on Scobie's shin, breaking a bone. He shrieked and let go of Tom's arm. Kevin tried to hold Tom's right arm in a lock. Tom swung his flexed hand across Kevin's windpipe, and he sank gasping to the floor. "Thanks, Kit," thought Tom. "At least you taught me something useful."

"Anyone else want to join in?" asked Tom.

The sergeant strode down the aisle between the beds. "Enough, soldier. I want someone left alive for tomorrow."

"Serg," said Tom, relieved he had made his point. From then on he was on his own. People kept their distance, treating him like a dog with rabies. Tom did not mind. He was used to ploughing a lone furrow. When they were taken to the range, all lying on their bellies facing a line of targets, rifles beside them, Tom was told to fire first. He quickly sighted the target, having already estimated the cross wind and set his sights for distance too, and fired. He squeezed the trigger, rather than jerking it, and hit six bulls' eyes in a row.

"Jesus," said the sergeant under his breath. "Where did this kid come from? Give me a hundred of him and I'll take on the German army." He said nothing aloud but, "Next".

Kevin, with repaired windpipe, loosed off six rounds and the target marker showed them spread all over, one missing completely.

"Rifles down," commanded the sergeant. "No disgrace for this lad," he gestured to Kevin, who had the grace to look grateful. "He's never fired a rifle in his life, have you lad?"

"No Serg," said Kevin.

"On the other hand this fellow's been around a bit." He nudged Tom with his foot. "By the time I've finished with you, you'll all shoot like him. And you'll learn to depend on each other, no one letting the side down. Understand? Mate-ship."

"Yes Serg!" they all yelled.

After the practice back in the Nissen hut, Tom noticed a line of recruits approaching him, one after another. "Oh God! This is the end," he thought and got to his feet, resolved to go down fighting. The first was Kevin. "Does he never learn?"

Kevin simply put out his hand and shook Tom's before walking off without a word. The whole squad of twenty did the same. Tom realized he had been accepted and felt quite emotional. He lay down and went to sleep.

*　　*　　*

Chapter 32

Next day they had to change out of battle-dress into P.E. kit in one and a half minutes. Tom was panicking as he realized he had left the padlock key inside his locker. A skinny little fellow he had never heard say a word, saw his trouble. "Hat badge?" he asked Tom. He quickly undid it from his beret and handed it to the lad. He bent down and unpicked the lock with the pin faster than Tom could have turned a key.

As Tom rushed his kit on, he said, "Thanks mate."

"Any time," said the lad, Ewan. "I was inside for burglary."

Tom nodded. Everything was explained, including "Mate-ship" which was spreading.

Training went on at a steady pace, drill varied by learning new methods of killing, unarmed combat and grenade throwing. This was done one at a time. They were shown how the grenade was safe until the pin was removed and the lever it held in place was released. Then you had a couple of seconds before it blew up, so you released the pin only as you threw it.

One recruit froze as he released the pin. The Sergeant grabbed it from the lad and threw it, pulling him down behind the safety mound of earth in one motion. It exploded too close for comfort. When the lad had stopped shaking, the Sergeant made him take another grenade and throw it properly. Everyone breathed a hearty sigh of relief when that happened.

The Sten gun, a nasty little weapon made for two shillings and six pence, was liable to jam. It was not meant to be aimed but used in close combat, spraying the enemy with bullets. At the range, the sergeant warned them telling of his predecessor, who had a recruit with a jammed Sten gun, turn round to show his instructor, when it unjammed of its own accord and killed the sergeant.

"If anyone thinks of doing that with me, I'll kill him first," he said and probably meant it.

They ran at stuffed dummies of the enemy and plunged their bayonets into them, yelling at the same time to create fear and disorientation.

"Why is the bayonet so much shorter than the previous ones?" asked the sergeant. They were too wise to reply, wary of a trick. "It only takes three inches of cold steel to kill with. The First World War ones used to stick in the body and men were killed while they tried to extract it. Three inches. Remember that!"

"I'm glad he's on our side," thought Tom, hiding a grin.

After six weeks' basic training, some of them were picked out and sent for an interview to see whether they might make officers. Tom was not surprised when his name was read out. It was the last one. He wondered whether that was by chance, or to make him sweat a little. They were taken to another camp in the back of a lorry. They had to sit and wait for the interview, Tom last as usual. When his name was finally called, as he sat by himself on a long bench, he felt nervous but decided to give it his best shot. He entered a room and saluted the three officers facing him. He recognized a Captain as a face he had seen watching them drill at training camp. He relaxed a little. The other two were a colonel and a brigadier, the most junior of the General's.

"Hartley, you have two minutes to prepare a five minute talk on anything you like, from now."

"Jeez! What the Hell can I talk about that they don't know already?" Inspiration came just as his time drew to a close. The flood.

"Right Hartley, tell us what you're going to enlighten us with."

Tom snapped to his feet, trying to control his trembling knees. He launched into the cause of the flood, a little of its flow and then its results. He was relieved to see they were listening intently. When the timer pinged, they ignored it and let him continue. Eventually the brigadier said, "fascinating and how old were you then?" Tom saw the trap, hesitated and then gave his age correctly as seventeen at the time. He was not going to lie to these officers.

"So you fended for yourself all that time, having lost your parents? Amazing." No way would he admit to Kit.

Tom felt it was going his way. He stood very still and awaited events. The officers went into a huddle and he could not hear what they were saying.

"How you got past the recruiting officer, we'll ask no questions but so far, so good. You now have to go out and prove you can lead others. Well done, young man," said the brigadier," a twinkle in his eye. Tom felt he was walking on water but there was still the next hurdle, whatever might be asked of him. He saluted smartly and exited the door, shutting it quietly behind him.

A corporal was waiting outside to direct Tom to his next hurdle. He marched to a number of scattered trees where his comrades were engaged in some sort of initiative test. He waited his turn. "You have to get these men across that minefield using these drums and ropes," said a sergeant. "You have five minutes to think of how and tell your men what they have to do."

Tom looked at the signs depicting mines and wondered which branches he could string the ropes from. "We obviously have our weapons?" queried Tom. He noticed the captain from the interview and his training camp was watching and listening attentively. It nearly caused him to lose his thread.

"Yes, of course," said the sergeant, thinking this lad had lost his way already.

"That includes the rocket launcher," said Tom.

"Yes, but . . ."

"No buts, Sergeant. No time. I take the rocket launcher like this." Tom knelt down and aimed his imaginary weapon low across the minefield, "and fire, blasting a path through the mines. Men, follow me," and Tom ran straight across the, he hoped, exploded minefield, followed by his obedient comrades.

As they left the place of safety, the sergeant looked at the officer, out of the hearing of the potential officers, as they were to be called, questioning. "I've never had that solution before, Sir. Is it okay?"

"Very okay for me," said the officer. "Initiative and originality. Could go far, that boy."

The sergeant blew a whistle and made the "come to me sign." The P.O's ran to him. The officer strode off, deep in thought.

"The following will go over and stand there," said the sergeant, pointing to a tree. He read out a list of names, including Tom, last again. "The rest remain here. You will be returned to your units. Maybe you will be given another chance. Better luck next time, Gentlemen."

Tom and eight others were congratulated by the officer, as having passed that test. "The next hurdle at which you can fall, will be to see if you can pass a two month officer training course."

*　　*　　*

Chapter 33

Back on the property Dad and Dick were getting on fine. Dad was happy to let the manager manage. When it came to finance, he insisted he was consulted. It was his place after all. They had enough in the bank to get by and the promise of rain raised their spirits. After his last experience of floods, Dad said he would like a deep trench dug above the veggie patch, the earth deposited below, forming a levee, diverting any water diagonally past the buildings. He paid a council worker with a tractor and blade to do the work and they slept more easily the next night. They brought the few cattle and horses onto the high ground, which had proven safe last time.

Dad wondered how Tom was getting on. He knew the boy was as tough as the next guy, but one never knew if the training was dangerous.

Greg was right. They had to cover an obstacle course, which entailed climbing a high wall, a scrambling net, ropes, and leopard crawling under barbed wire, while machine guns were fired overhead. One P.O. stuck his head higher than he should have and was cut down. Tom flattened himself like a lion after a gazelle and was safe enough. When it came to unarmed combat, he excelled himself and was warned to pull his punches as two adversaries flew through the air with stomach kicks and leg throws, to land heavily. It was rumoured that they were allowed

2.5% casualties during training. Tom wondered what happened to the 0.5%, no legs?

They had to fire at miniature targets with .22 cannon on an indoor range, giving orders for High Explosives for anti-tank guns, Armour Piercing for tanks and Smoke to give cover. Tom showed a good sense of land use as he hid his model tanks in dried river beds and positioned them for enfilade fire, so his tank would hit the less armoured side of the opposition as it drove by. They completed their course at a tank range. They had to aim at beaten up old tanks. Tom's second shot sent the target's turret glowing red hot, high into the sky, to his joy.

On the last day Tom was told to report on his own to the Adjutant's office. He wondered if he had done something wrong. He was kept waiting for half an hour, which did nothing for his nerves. At last the door opened and a corporal ordered him inside. Tom came to a smart halt and saluted crisply. The corporal exited, shutting the door. To Tom's surprise the captain was accompanied by the brigadier, who had interviewed him earlier.

"At ease," commanded the captain. He looked at the brigadier, who nodded.

"We'd like to congratulate you Tom Hartley for coming top of your course, which you passed with flying colours."

Tom controlled his smile of relief.

The brigadier smiled. "But there's a cost for that honour."

Tom wondered what the Hell was coming next.

"We could just send you to join a cavalry regiment, where you'd be in charge of fifteen men and horses or maybe tanks. But we feel that might be a waste of your talents. You have initiative with individual spontaneous thinking, which might be more usefully employed in the Intelligence corps. How does that grab you?"

"Thank you Sir. Please could you tell me something about my likely duties?"

"You'd have a course in Japanese for a start. You'd be softened up in mock enemy interviews—not pleasant but not life threatening. You'd study many maps showing the likely war zone you would be operating in, possibly solo, behind enemy lines. I feel you'd have more chances of surviving than most, from what I've seen and heard. You'd learn interview of prisoner techniques and a modicum of military law. You'd learn to live in a hole in the ground or up a tree for three days at a time and not be seen. Your fighting skills will be kept up to scratch. There's a hidden advantage. Your training would take longer and so you'd be legal age when starting live Action." The brigadier paused to give Tom a moment to weigh it all up.

He was about to give his answer when the brigadier delivered his punch line.

All the time the brigadier was talking, the Captain watched Tom's reactions like a hawk. They didn't want a recruit, who was in on a wave of enthusiasm, only to buckle at the first tough demand on his body or mind.

"Of course, if caught, you might well be shot as a spy, so you'd always need to wear your uniform. So what do you say, Tom?" The use of just his Christian name made Tom feel he was about to join an exclusive club, not far from the truth.

Tom was mentally jolted at the thought of being shot as a spy, but then, he'd just as likely be shot in action with the enemy.

"I'd be honoured, Sir."

The brigadier looked genuinely pleased. He nodded to the Captain, who simply inclined his chin.

"Welcome aboard. You won't join your comrades after this. We "vanish" you. In the back of a truck tonight to start your real training. And you won't be able to tell your dad what you're up to, or anyone else. Is there anyone else?" He slipped that in so casually.

"No, Sir, no one." Tom felt apprehensive.

The brigadier had three sons of his own, all older than Tom. He had come out of retirement to conduct interviews like this, among other things. He felt for the boy and hoped he'd survive. A nice kid and with what potential.

*   *   *

Chapter 34

Tom had a rough time in his training for Intelligence. The aim was to see how much punishment he could take, if captured before he cracked. He held out for two days, with no sleep, being forced to drink masses of water and then have a soldier bounce on his extended stomach, and other indignities best not mentioned.

After that, he had to survive in the Bush with little to eat or drink for three days on his own, armed with a bayonet and little else. He hit a rabbit out for its evening stroll with the bayonet on his first night. He skinned and gutted it and cooked it, having started a fire with a soft and hard piece of wood, which he sharpened with his bayonet. He chose a spot between two massive rocks to site the fire and hide its flickers. He kept half the bunny for the next day. He had to find his way with a map, and the sun and his watch as his compass over fifty miles of rocks, creepers and snake ridden Bush. His target was a tiny town and when he eventually reached it, with three days of fine beard, mud spattered face and filthy camouflage, children in the streets screamed in terror, as he reached the Crooked Back Arms. The sergeant waiting for him, muttered, "You're three hours early. Should have waited for nightfall and avoided frightening the natives."

"Sorry," said Tom. The sergeant grinned: "Only fooling. Well done, laddie. We had guys stalking you all the way. Too precious to lose."

"Jeez. I never saw them," said Tom, feeling this was creepy.

"You weren't meant to, and by the time we've finished with you, you'll be as good as them."

Other trainees were at the camp but their tasks were different, judging by the way they were kept separate and the others spent much more time on unarmed combat and on the range. Tom joined the 2nd/14th Light Horse for a couple of weeks, just to get accustomed to being a "real" soldier. He enjoyed the easier training and was careful not to stand out from the crowd. He actually got through his time there without seriously hurting anyone.

Tom was allowed down town at night, with instructions to keep out of trouble. One night he was aiming for the cinema, a little flea-pit in the centre of town when suddenly a trio of youths surrounded him.

"Hi guys. What goes?"

"This, soldier boy," said one of the lads, aiming a kick at Tom's balls. Quick as a flash he caught and turned the attacker's foot, wrenching his ankle. Dropping that, Tom faced the other, conscious he had one behind him. The latter got Tom round the neck. Tom swivelled to one side and smashed back his elbow in the attacker's ribs, breaking some. He screamed and fell. The lad in front of Tom blurted, "Christ! He's a maniac," turned and ran.

Tom said, "Take on someone your own size in future. Better not be a squaddie." He walked off with no pity for the sorely wounded he left on the pavement. Hopefully they had learnt their lesson. He enjoyed the film.

On another town visit he met a girl in a dance hall. The men were all sitting on the right and the women on the left. There was a four piece band with piano, drums, trumpet and tenor sax. They sounded smooth. Tom wished he could play something but consoled himself with the thought that then he would not be free to dance. A pretty fair girl was eying Tom, who did not need any more of an invitation. When the music started again, Tom walked smartly across the floor before anyone else could ask the girl for a dance and soon they were stumbling around the floor, not much worse than the other couples. "What's your name?" he asked her.

"Sonya. What's yours?"

"Tom," he replied, thinking she looked inviting, with her sleek blonde hair and deep blue eyes.

"What regiment are you in?" she asked, as Tom had his beret folded and stuffed under his shoulder straps."

"Oh, I'm just a trainee," he replied. "Just a cadet," he lied. He had been told of the dangers of possible enemy spies and to give away nothing.

"And so just a learner . . . Are you a quick learner?" she asked, sexily. "You look too young to be in the army."

"And what do you do?" he asked, avoiding the inquisition.

"I worked for a travel agency before the war," she said. "Now I'm not sure what to do. Jobs are hard to find. Perhaps you could find me a job with the army? A secretary, or something?" She nuzzled his cheek.

"I think I can see which way this is going," Tom thought. "Well a one night stand. Why waste it!"

"Like a cup of coffee at my place?" she asked.

"That sounds inviting," he replied, thinking, "Great! She'll not be disappointed, in one way at least."

They slowly drifted towards the exit and as people were taking their seats, they were out of the door.

As they walked down the street towards Sonya's flat, she felt around his chest, playing with his nipples.

"Wow! The queen of the fast workers," thought Tom and by the time they were inside her rooms, he was fully aroused.

Sonya pointed him to the bed and said, "I'll have the coffee ready in a jiffy. Why don't you prepare for action, while you're waiting?"

Tom took off his shoes, socks and shirt and waited for the coffee. He guiltily thought of Sian but that was silly. She had ditched him. She probably still thought of him as being obliquely responsible for the loss of their baby. Yes "theirs"—not just hers.

As she returned, Sonya looked at him with appreciation. She handed him a cup and they both drank, almost back in one. Then, hands free Sonya went to work. She quickly had him where she wanted and then slipped in a question: "Where're you off to, soldier boy, when you're trained?"

Tom nearly went off the boil, except she was an expert.

"I don't know. We haven't been told yet." The lie passed smoothly from his lips.

Just at the peak of desire, Sonya asked, "Are there many of you in the camp? . . . I'd like to know for when you go away . . . more to break in."

"Jeez! She's breaking me in. Where did she learn such tricks?"

"They come and go. I've no idea," said Tom and although she kept him there all night, when he left in the early hours as the sun was coming up over the horizon, she learnt nothing except that Tom had real talent.

When he returned to camp, Tom asked to see the Captain who had interviewed him.

"What's up, Tom?" he asked. "Not getting second thoughts?"

"No Sir, but I thought you'd need to be warned, I think there's a dangerous woman in town."

"I've always wanted one of those," joked the Captain. "Unfortunately my wife might object."

Without too much detail, Tom gave the Captain her address and the questions she had asked. The Captain was delighted with the information. "Well done, son. You've shown the right touch. We'll pay her a visit. It may be a permanent one. And good luck. You leave tomorrow. I suggest you spend tonight in your own bed. Where you're going, you'll need all your energy." He smiled knowingly. Tom slept very soundly that night and a certain door was unlocked late the same night and Sonya hustled away.

*　　*　　*

Chapter 35

In December 1941, the Japanese attacked Pearl Harbour with no warning that they were entering the War. The destruction of American ships and men was terrible. It had one beneficial effect in dousing the anti-war faction in America, which included a large number of German and Irish expatriates. Troop training in Australia increased frenetically and Tom was summoned to the brigade office in Townsville. He wondered where he would be sent and was glad the waiting was over. He had been promoted to Lieutenant from 2nd Lieutenant and made a dashing figure in his uniform, which would be changed before long. Aged 18, he was the youngest Lieutenant in Intelligence but known already for having a wise head on young shoulders.

Tom was welcomed by a Major and a Captain and offered a chair. They had a map rolled out on the desk. "Good Day Hartley", said the Major. "We've found a job for you. The British fear a Japanese invasion of Malaya and Singapore, and we want you in under cover, solo to observe and report back to us any enemy movements. So you'll be on your own with a radio. It's essential you keep well hidden. They are said to take no prisoners and you're no use to us dead!"

"Yes, Sir," said Tom, shaken with the enormity of the task and its almost suicidal connotations.

"You will be dropped off on a beach in south east Malaya near Kota Tinggi. The British, Australian and Indian troops will be north of you. You'll need to infiltrate their positions and those of the enemy without being seen. Thick jungle, much of it. Japs up trees. Think you can do it?"

"I'll have a try, Sir," said Tom, bravely.

"And if you're near capture, hide the radio in the jungle. Then, hopefully you'll be taken as just another Allied soldier. We've decided to upgrade you to Captain, which might save your skin if captured. Anyone lower is expendable in hostiles' eyes."

Tom was shaken but pleased. If he survived, his pay would be worth saving. Playing such a vital role in the war gave him satisfaction beyond belief.

It was a moonless night as a fishing boat puttered into the Malaysian shore. Distant booms of heavy guns could be heard. "Ready, Tom?" asked the skipper.

Tom clutched his shoulder in reply as the vessel grounded on shingle. He dropped noiselessly into the gently heaving surf, water up to his knees, his radio strapped to his camouflaged shoulders, over a haversack with various packets of "iron" rations. At least he could go a few days without living off the jungle. He had been dropped at low tide so his footsteps would be rapidly washed away by the sea. He took a quick look along the beach but there was no sign he had been observed, so he strode across the sand and into the jungle.

It was hard seeing where he was going but at least no one could pick him. He heard the vessel making for the open sea. He suddenly felt very alone. Just nineteen and a rank already of acting Captain, he was expendable, or so it seemed.

The jungle night-time insects clicked around him as he parted the foliage in front of him. He must hide up until it was light enough to get his bearings. The sounds of firing seemed closer, a bad sign as the Allies were being pushed back, in spite of there being a hundred thousand of them but poorly trained in jungle warfare, many suffering from dysentery or malaria. When you suffered from those, you were in no way fit for fighting a relentless enemy.

As dawn seeped through the jungle, Tom checked his position, which seemed pretty well hidden, and then his radio. He turned it low as its crackling could be heard a hundred yards away. He soon made touch with base, wherever that might be.

"Hello Able Baker, Charlie 421 here. Fighting drawing closer. We're retreating. Definite. No contact yet . . . . Roger. Out." Communication had to be kept short for fear of enemy interception. It was good to feel he was not entirely alone . . . Well, forgotten.

Tom chewed on a piece of jerky, dried meat and took a sparing drink from his water bottle. If he could find that stream he had seen on the map and could replenish, it would be useful. An hour went by, heavy guns getting closer.

He thought of travelling towards the fighting, but then realized that at the rate it was advancing, he might get over-run too far and be in serious trouble. He gave a quick sit-rep (situation report) back to base. It gave him a spark of confidence hearing a friendly voice again.

Then he struggled through the creepers towards a more open area, stopping short of a track, wide enough for a man to pass and recently hacked out of the jungle. He hid up a few yards back, under cover and waited for what might eventuate. He didn't have to wait long. Heavy machine gun fire and the odd tank shell came from the Japanese, too close for comfort.

Scores of Aussie soldiers retreated down the pathway in front of him, some carrying wounded comrades, all oblivious of the observer, which gave him hope that the Japanese would not notice him either. There was a lull in the passers-by and Tom took advantage to give another sit-rep. "Many Australians retreating, many wounded. Can hear tanks. Must be Japs . . . . Roger (Meaning "understood") Over and out." He packed away the radio and was just in time as the advance party of Japs rode by on bicycles, some firing into the jungle not far from his position. "No wonder they advance so fast," Tom thought.

His position was nearly compromised as a tank smashed its way past him on the other side of the track. It seemed like a monster from outer space with its gun probing the jungle and its engine roaring. It was lucky it had not headed right for him. He could never have avoided it in this tangle of creepers. Oh for a grenade to pop into its turret! But he was not there to fight, he had to remind himself.

The next sequence flashed by Tom as a stream of Jap soldiers passed by his position, again, mostly on bicycles. If only he could capture or kill an officer, he might discover which branch of the Imperial army was invading and what their numbers might be.

Back in Australia Greg and Dick listened to the news of the Japanese invasion of Malaya and hoped Tom was still safe in his home country. They would have had a fit if they knew he was surrounded by the ruthless enemy.

As dawn broke Tom heard the relentless bombing by Japanese planes of retreating Allied forces. They seemed to have complete control of the air. His chief concern was to go south towards Singapore where the final stand would be made in all probability. He sent a last message: "All appears lost. No Allied resistance here. Out."

* * *

Chapter 36

Getting through the jungle would have been hard enough when there was no war. Now it seemed impossible. Tom knew he was doing no good where he was, so he hid the radio under creepers, destroying it first. He had to get some sleep so he curled up under a thick Medusa head of creepers. He fell asleep immediately, exhausted.

Midnight had arrived, if his watch was correct when Tom awoke. Its luminous hands avoided a give-away torch. Wondering what had awoken him, as battle sounds were distant, he felt a knife at his throat. Judging by the rustles all around him, he was surrounded by the enemy. He was dragged to his feet and into a clearing, where they stripped him and searched his clothes. A Japanese lieutenant faced him in a tent lit by a hurricane lamp.

"Who are you and why are you on your own?" he asked in remarkably good English. He gestured to Tom to put on his clothes. "What is a boy like you doing with the army?"

"We are short of men. I was forced to join up," said Tom, playing on his tender years and appearance. "They beat me when I didn't want to fight you."

"So, the scars," said the lieutenant, taken in. "You bow to me when you speak. Manners, boy! . . . And why on your own?"

"I was trying to get away from the fighting," said Tom, bowing meekly.

"Ah, a coward! We execute cowards," said his enemy. "What do you know of the Allied forces? Where's your unit now?"

"I only know my infantry unit has retreated, probably to Singapore. I don't know for sure."

"How many are left alive in your unit?"

"Half of them are dead," said Tom, not forgetting to bow.

"And that would leave how many?"

Tom thought quickly. Make it many more and that might slow their advance. "Only about a thousand."

"Don't try to trick me," said the furious Lieutenant. I know your regiment sizes are no more than eight hundred men." He slashed Tom across his face with his whip.

Tom overdid the pain and lay shaking and cringing on the ground.

"How many?" said the Lieutenant, whipping Tom across his legs.

Tom began to cry. "About two hundred, Sir." He forgot to bow, difficult in his position and so received another slash.

"Take this pathetic creature away and tie him up. We'll give him a chance to tell us all he knows tomorrow and then behead him."

Soldiers dragged Tom away, feet first, and tied him up, his wrists and his ankles. One laughed at him. He mimicked the lieutenant, "Boy! Head-less boy!" He laughed again and walked away.

Tom realized that they thought they had found a soft victim and his wrists were not bound that tight. As they tied him up, he had held his wrists rigid and slightly apart on the side away from the soldiers. So now the bonds felt comfortably loose. He looked around him but no soldiers were near. They thought the battle was nearly over, quite correctly and were relaxing with some sake, a Japanese rice wine. Tom used his teeth on the knot and gradually it loosened. He next freed his ankles.

A sentry approached him, so he lay curled up like a baby and snored softly. The sentry laughed, no doubt anticipating the beheading and sauntered away. Tom waited at least an hour till the camp was silent. Then he listened for a while, working out where the sentries were placed. "Do I just slink away in the dark, like a coward, letting these monsters decapitate many of our troops?" he asked himself. "No, seize the opportunity to become a fighting soldier." He would dearly love to take down the lieutenant if it were the last thing he did. Perhaps it would be.

Tom waited till the nearest sentry was sitting, listening for any enemy signs. Then he hid the rope and eased himself towards the sitting man's back. Once or twice the sentry looked behind him, but there were so many night sounds of rustling little creatures, he relaxed and gazed fixedly in front of him, a fatal mistake. Tom placed his arm across the front of the sentry's neck and the other behind it, in one quick motion. Then choking off his air supply, he strangled him.

Tom looked around to see if he had been noticed but all was quiet. He removed the sentry's bayonet and laid him down in the creepers. Then, moving so slowly, he crept towards the lieutenant's tent. Another sentry was stationed some hundred yards away, but yawning and hardly alert. Tom undid the bow knots that held the tent flap shut and peeped inside. As the only officer with the unit, the man slept on his own. He was breathing heavily, perhaps dreaming of tomorrow's execution. In his dreams, he imagined taking a photograph of Tom's head and posting it to an Australian newspaper. It would not help their morale.

Tom crawled in and placed his hand on the lieutenant's mouth to stifle any cry, and in the same movement, stabbed the bayonet well into his heart. There were death tremors but nothing else. Tom sat his would-be beheader in a life-like position, so he would not be discovered too soon. It was time to leave before his trail of destruction was discovered and a hue and cry started. Tom crawled out of the area by way of his dead sentry. There was a young soldier lying almost across his path, inviting death, but Tom eased round him, suddenly sickened by what he had done. Somehow a bullet put death at a distance and he could cope with that.

As dawn was breaking, and military activity re-started with a vengeance, Tom decided that to venture south, he must become a Jap. He waited till there was a lull in passing cycles. Then stripping off his outer garments, but hiding his hat inside his shirt, he waited by the track. Eventually another burst of Japanese infantry cycled by. The last soldier was unlucky. Tom leapt on him, stabbing him dead with his bayonet, and flipped on the Jap's hat, stuffing his own inside his tunic. To all who might see him, he was one of the invading force as he pedaled along with the enemy's rifle, hat and bike.

Keeping the rest of the party just in sight, he waited till they slowed for a rest or whatever and swerved into the jungle, where he lifted the invaluable bike under cover and hid. One more dangerous gambit and he was in sight of the sea and the causeway to Singapore. Just as Tom hid again, there was a terrific explosion and the causeway blew up, halting the Japanese advance for a while. It was accompanied by a wave of Allies' bullets, Japanese falling in all directions.

Now there was the problem of crossing the narrow strip of sea to Singapore Island. Tom would have to wait till dusk. He'd have to avoid being shot by his own side, too. He threw away the Jap hat. It had served him well. He noticed an old sampan tied up on the shore. That could be useful. He looked at the Japanese forces taking cover from the occasional burst of machine gun fire from the other side. There seemed thousands of the enemy, their numbers increasing all the time. He wished he still had the radio to report it but the information would be superfluous by now. The Allies would be only too aware of the deadly force about to invade. They could not get fresh supplies of ammunition nor reinforcements at this late stage. The last news he received on his radio was that the British battleship, Repulse had been sunk in addition to destroyers and other ships, the result of having no air support. Relentless attacks by Japanese dive bombers gave them no chance of survival.

From his position, well back in the jungle, he could smell the enemy soldiers and hoped they could not smell him. At least they would never suspect having an enemy agent so close. He snuggled down and hid his face, rubbing mud across it. The secret of not being seen was to keep still. With insects crawling across his face, this was not easy. Tom eased a bit of jerky from his back pocket into his mouth and chewed. It tasted like kangaroo that had been dead a long time. The hours dragged but eventually it was getting dark.

As complete darkness fell on a moonless night, Tom eased himself on his belly towards the sampan. After what seemed hours, he reached the vessel and crouched on its seaward side. He cut the anchor rope and levered the boat into the sea, swimming round to the Jap side. There was no sign that he had been spotted. He gradually pushed the boat ahead of him, still swimming behind it and drifted into the ocean. Oh, Captain, if you could see me now, he grinned, taking his mind off the possibility that he might be sliced into little pieces at any moment by a "friendly" machine gun. He hoped there were no crocodiles around.

The boat made such slow progress that anyone spotting it in the pitch black night would imagine that it had drifted away from its moorings, Tom hoped. He kept kicking with his legs below the water line, holding onto its low side. At least a couple of hours later he felt the vessel grounding on the other side. Now for the moment of truth. He donned his own hat, clearly an Allied officer's, from his back pack. He fitted it carefully and crept on his knees into the jungle. The relief of momentarily being free from the enemy was tangible. Tom breathed a sigh of relief and sank into the vegetation. He took off his sodden clothes and rang them out before replacing just his shorts and shirt, plus boots.

*   *   *

CHAPTER 37

A s dawn broke, the bullets began to fly from both sides and big guns opened up from the Japanese side. Tom leopard crawled further from the shore and relaxed only when well past an Allied troop position. He was dying for a drink, his water bottle being empty from hours back. He was wondering the best course to follow now. No radio so his purpose for being there was finished. He must get off the island somehow. Just as he was pondering his next move, the bullets started to fly. He flattened himself to the ground and prayed none would get him. Judging by big Japanese guns and heavy enemy machinegun fire, supplemented by dive-bombers, the invasion of Singapore was on. The Allied resistance seemed to be petering out and suddenly Australians started retreating past him, some clearly out of ammunition. Should he join them?

The urge to fight the enemy eased Tom's decision. He approached the Allied front line from behind and heard Australian voices. He gathered that they were a famous cavalry regiment, the 2nd/14th Light Horse to which he had been seconded while training. Entering a hastily scraped shallow trench he found himself beside some of his old buddies he'd shared a drink with before leaving for Intelligence, still as a Second Lieutenant.

"Strewth! It's Tom Hartley. Where'd the Hell've you blown in from, mate?" exclaimed a startled trooper, Pete Rathbone.

"A reinforcement of one," joked Tom.

"Hey guys! Look what the tide's washed up! Second Lieutenant Tom Hartley."

"Captain" corrected Tom with a smile, nearly his last as a bullet whistled past his head. He ducked behind the protective mound of earth.

"How many Japs did you kill to get that promotion? Jeez Captain kid Hartley, Sir?" laughed 'Shorty' Smith, a blacksmith before he joined the army.

"A few," grinned Tom, thinking: "one two, three, four, so far. Jeez, it's becoming a habit!"

The others looked at each other shaking their heads, unbelieving. This youngster wasn't a killer. He must have a friend in high places.

A tank fired from the other side deafening them for a few minutes, its shell exploding less than fifty yards to their right and showering them with clods of earth. Tom saw Shorty's mouth opening and shutting but couldn't hear a thing. By degrees his hearing cleared, to his relief.

An enemy attack was due, judging by the rain of tank fire all around them. They kept their heads down and prayed the next moment wouldn't be their last. Machine-gun fire was added to the deadly hail. Somewhere to their left, they heard a young soldier screaming for his mother as he lay dying in agony. Tom bit his lip and tried not to listen.

Suddenly a wave of Japanese was advancing on them, yelling like crazy and firing everything they had. Shorty's machine-gun fired incessantly, only pausing for a moment as he fed in a new ammo belt, assisted by Pete.

"Jeez, it's getting ho . . ." exclaimed Shorty, stopped short by a bullet through his brain. He slumped forward and Tom took his place, scything through the Japanese infantry, like corn being harvested.

"Bastards, bastards!" exclaimed Pete.

"Keep your mind on the job, killing the bastards," said Tom. "Another belt, quick!"

"It's our last," said Pete. "They're thinning out. Have a grenade." He passed Tom a bag of grenades.

Tom pulled the pin from one and threw it, glad to see the advancing wave have a hole blown in it as bodies flew in all directions. It had not exploded before Tom had the next in the air, then another and another. Suddenly there was a lull in the fighting. They could see the enemy retreating from their relentless onslaught.

A Jap soldier was screaming only twenty yards to their front. Pete rose to put him out of his misery and was rewarded by a shot through his chest. As he lay dying, Tom threw another grenade, silencing the screaming and pulled out a medical pad to press against Pete's chest, but it was too late. He died with a gurgle. "Oh God," thought Tom. "Two good mates—Their poor families will be grief stricken." He pulled off their dog-tags from round their necks for their families and pocketed them.

Tom suddenly realized he was on his own. The Aussies had retreated silently under cover of his grenades. He realized that to stay there was to invite instant death or capture and threw the machine gun barrel into the jungle, rendering it useless. Then he eased himself into the jungle, hoping to join the other Aussies.

Before long Tom reckoned being out of touch with his regiment, he had better hide in the thickest jungle he could find, awaiting developments. Perhaps he could make his way under cover of darkness into town and find a ship out, if there were any left. As he waited he watched a lizard cross his boots. Lucky little creature. It helped stabilize his nerves. Only mankind had to invent endless means of destruction. Tom wondered how his dad and Dick were getting on. Had it rained enough yet for them to buy more cattle? Well, it was their problem now. It seemed unlikely he would get out of Singapore alive, let alone survive the war that Japan were clearly winning.

*   *   *

PART 2
TRY AND STOP US

CHAPTER 1

I t is 1942. The Japanese are advancing through the Malayan jungle in huge numbers, while the British and Australian forces, thinly strung out and running short of ammunition, vainly try to stop them.

The cicadas are strangely silent in the Singapore jungle. An occasional bird sings its sorrowful song. A rifle shot sounds some distance away, to be followed by a cacophony of machine gun fire, shouted commands in a foreign tongue and screams of the wounded.

The whole nightmare rapidly rolls closer till retreating Australian troops sprint across the clearing and vanish into the jungle beyond.

A Japanese soldier rides his bike into view. Contrary to popular conceptions, he is neither short, nor wearing thick glasses. He wears trim tropical gear and is young and fit; full of life till a bullet explodes in his chest. He tumbles to the ground killed outright, his bike falling away from him.

Other Jap soldiers spread out into the clearing firing hopefully into the sea of green before them. Several of them fall dead or wounded. The storm of superior firepower silences the Australian resistance, betrayed by the futile clicks of their empty magazines.

An Aussie soldier flies back into the clearing, shredded by machine gun fire. Two more Aussies stagger into the green amphitheatre. One, a boy of eighteen, clutches his wounded leg, his face creased in pain. He looks so young and vulnerable. Good looking, in the prime of life. Some proud mother's son. Six Jap soldiers run in to join them. They surround the wounded lads, their bayonets poking the Aussies. Their sergeant studies them for a moment. He pulls out his pistol, cold as ice.

Peter, the youngster is petrified. "No mate. Leave me. I'm okay. Give me a stick. I can walk."

The sergeant shoots Peter in the heart and then the other Aussie. The sergeant smiles as he watches their bodies twitch and then lie still. The Japs advance through the murder scene and disappear among waving fronds. All is silent apart from continued distant firing.

A bush moves revealing a tall, athletic Captain in Aussie uniform—Captain Tom Hartley, aged only nineteen. His strong face radiates hatred. He runs over to the two Aussies and checks them for life. Dead! He freezes by the youngster. "Peter Brian. Sweet kid. From the next property to ours. Bastards! "Tom wipes away a tear. He mutters to himself: "You'll pay for this—by God, you'll pay."

Tom crosses himself. He folds the boy's arms tenderly across his chest. There is the noise of someone crashing through the bushes. Tom fades under cover.

A Japanese colonel strides into the clearing. He peers around but fails to spot Tom. He makes to follow his soldiers. Tom erupts from the bushes and springs onto the colonel, driving his bayonet into his back. The man falls dead. Tom flares the colonel's body a flash of hatred enough to fry it.

"That's a start," whispers Tom. He rapidly searches the body and retrieves a notebook and map from the breast pocket. He studies them briefly and whistles as he reveals a plan showing arrows from Burma pointing towards India. There is also a list of codes. Tom puts them quickly into his pack and slides into the jungle, oblivious of a Jap reporter, whose camera is revealed through the creepers. The reporter is clearly pleased with himself as he too merges with the jungle.

*   *   *

Chapter 2

Two ragged, deadbeat Aussie soldiers in jungle uniform drink at a bar. An immaculate barman in white monkey jacket reigns in the otherwise empty saloon. He tries a water tap. It trickles and fades to nothing. He shakes his head.

The soldiers' weapons, a rifle and a bren gun—a light machine gun—lie on a table beside them. Their packs are dumped on the floor. There is an atmosphere of dissolution, helplessness and defeat.

Ash Speidermann, twenty four, tall with square features tosses back a whisky. He has smile lines, a relic of the past. REME on his cap badge announces he is an electrical engineer. He is tense and ready for the unexpected.

Charlie Brock, only twenty one but a lance corporal, one up from a private, needs a shave. He has sun bleached hair and a soft face. He was only promoted to fill a dead man's shoes. He has lost the will to fight, if he ever had it.

Occasional machine gun fire and mortar thuds sound too close. A heavier gun fires and then remains silent.

"Bloody Japs running all over us; units scattered. God knows where mine's got to," moans Charlie, hopelessly.

"We've got no chance, Charlie," says Ash in an Austrian/Australian accent. "How can we fight with no bleedin' ammo?" Ash empties his glass.

The barman fills it again without being asked. No request for payment. Sporadic rifle fire is very close. It could be in the next street. As if to underline their predicament, Charlie aims his bren gun out of the window and pulls the trigger. There is just an empty click. He shrugs and lays down his weapon on a table. He flashes a wry smile, snatches up his glass and drains it.

How quickly things can change. Captain Tom Hartley, our colonel killer, blasts into the bar. He sums up the situation with a shaft of disgust. Greg Topping, twenty eight, tall, thin and tough follows Tom close behind. They both sport the 2nd/14th Light Horse cap badges.

Tom strides to the bar and sweeps all glasses to the floor. He accuses: "Why the Hell're you in here? Japs out there!" He points through the window.

"Why not? Stay alive. Be fed and set free when it all ends, eh?" returns Charlie.

"That was my drink!" says Ash.

Tom ignores him. "Japs take no prisoners. Find a boat out or die." He scorns their attitude.

Ash picks up his rifle and pack. Charlie makes no move to follow.

A red faced British colonel aged about forty five, with riding boots polished immaculately, trim moustache, gleaming pistol holster and Sam Brown leather belt strides in.

Tom makes for the door, his rifle in one hand and his pack slung onto his back. He seems keen to be rid of the colonel and keeps his head turned away from him. He appears to be alert, looking out for Japanese. He hesitates as the colonel speaks.

"What are you chaps doing here? Get down to the square and fell in. At the least we can make a jolly smart show surrendering." The colonel stands beside the bar, full of his own importance.

"We're not very good at that," jeers Ash, giving a mock Nazi salute.

The colonel bristles with anger: "Get down there now. I'll put you three on a charge in the morning. What insolence! Jankers for you lot."

A tracer burst through the window shatters the bottles on the shelf behind the bar, right in line with where Tom had been standing.

"Bloody Hell!" yells Charlie, shaking like a leaf.

"Enjoy the Jap hospitality, Sir," sneers Greg, contemptuously to the colonel.

Tom vanishes out of the doorway. The others grab their weapons and packs and follow. Greg brushes past the colonel. Ash makes him stagger backwards. He says in an affected English tone: "Enjoy your jankers, wanker."

The colonel looks to explode in anger, fuming at their retreating backs. "Bloody Colonials. Never have any discipline.—Barman, a gin and tonic please. You'd better make it a double."

The barman says, "There's no tonic left, Sir."

The colonel, "With water, then. How much?"

A bullet smashes the gin bottle.

*   *   *

Chapter 3

By the docks Tom, Ash, Charlie and Greg shelter in the shadow of a large ship. There is bright moonlight. A machine gun chatters on and off in the distance. Resistance has not altogether faded. Flames flicker as a building blazes in the next block.

Screams sound from the hospital, indicating the Japs bayoneting patients and nurses. They are indiscriminate in their murders, killing cleaners and doctors and even the hospital cat . . . Anything that has life. They haven't the wit to realize the staff they are killing could be attending their own wounded in hours.

"Bloody Hell! Can't we do something," explodes Ash, clenching his fists.

"What difference would we make," says Tom calmly. "Live to fight another day."

"You're yellow, Yank," grinds Ash, his face burning with frustration.

"Absolutely," says Tom sarcastically. He stares Ash down, stonily, daring him to say anything else.

Ash is shaken. He hasn't met such a hard case before, and so young.

Tom radiates determination. "I must reach Australia fast. Find a boat, provisions, water jerry-cans."

The others have one feeling in common: "Are we expendable?"

"Australia? You're mad!" says Greg.

"Obey a Yank?" jeers Charlie. "Why not follow the colonel and give ourselves up?" He pauses, looking closer at Tom. "Crikey! He's only a kid. How the Hell did you become a Captain?"

Tom burns Charlie with contempt. "Firstly, I'm half Aussie, so don't "Yank" me, and secondly, you'll do as I bloody well tell you. I earned my promotion."

There is something about Tom that freezes Charlie's balls off.

"We're not going to spend years in a prison camp, being dictated to by that silly bugger," says Ash, nodding back towards the colonel. "Go and join him if you want, Charlie. You can clean his boots every morning and kiss his arse."

Gunfire and explosions come menacingly closer.

"Take Charlie, Greg. Find provisions and fishing gear. Ash come with me," orders Tom.

Ash nods. Tom whispers in Greg's ear, "Watch Charlie. We need him for rowing." Then, louder, "Meet us by the Customs shed in half an hour and don't get caught." He points to a grey building illuminated by gunfire.

Greg gives a casual salute, ending in two fingers as Tom and Ash trot off along the quay side. Greg guides Charlie towards dark buildings, his hand on his shoulder. Charlie goes on muttering, "Only a kid. Can't be more than twenty."

"Stow it, Charlie," says Greg. "He's got the training and we don't. Do what he says. It makes sense so far."

Along the quay side a few street lights still work. Tom leads, crouched, slinking between vessels of all sorts. He stops suddenly and points. Ash cannons into him. He bounces off Tom, surprised by his hard muscle. A rowing boat lies tied to a ring in the concrete floor. Tom gives a thumbs up. They creep towards it.

Tramping feet approach. Tom and Ash scuttle behind a couple of fuel barrels, their faces tense.

A squad of twenty Jap soldiers runs by. They fade into the distance. Tom's face twitches. Hidden nerves. He's had his share of torture. He gestures towards the boat.

Water sloshes around in it. It is clearly un-seaworthy.

"Find another, quick," whispers Tom.

Running boots drum on the quay above them. Tom and Ash take cover pressed against the quayside wall. Tom has his bayonet ready. He'll die rather than be taken prisoner. Shadows of running Jap soldiers almost reach their feet. Tom and Ash's faces tense. The boots fade into the distance. Tom gestures up the steps. He leads their sprint up them. They race along the quay. Tom stops and points down below them. A boat. They run down more steps, panting.

The boat is only twelve feet long but it is dry, with a small rudder, two oars and a tarpaulin. There is no engine or sail.

"Find some water containers. Meet us at the Customs shed in twenty minutes," says Tom.

Ash nods, murmuring, "Crazy!"

Tom hears, smiles grimly and nods to himself unseen by Ash.

They disappear up the steps to the quayside as more gunfire rattles around them, ever closer.

In another street Greg tries to force open the door to a grocer's shop with his bayonet. He is getting nowhere fast. Marching feet can be heard approaching.

Greg explodes, "Bloody hell."

"It's not worth it. Let's give ourselves up now," says Charlie.

"Shut it," grunts Greg. "If we suddenly appear, they'll shoot us." He hacks frantically at the door, splintering the wood around the lock. The door opens and he pushes Charlie inside ahead of him. The marching feet sound closer. Both men are tense as Greg closes the door and leans on it to keep it closed.

"You give yourself up to those guys and you'll lose your head for real."

"You sound as if you've had experience?" says Charlie.

"Believe it! Still got mine," says Greg, grinning.

The feet march by. Greg and Charlie search the shop in the dim glow of a street light. Charlie holds up an empty flour sack triumphantly. Greg pulls a tin opener out of a drawer. He disappears into a room behind while Charlie continues searching for tins and fills his sack.

There is the ping of a telephone being replaced from the other room. Charlie looks at Greg, curious as he emerges from the room holding two mugs and a funnel. He ignores Charlie and throws them into the sack. Charlie searches Greg's face. What's he been up to? Greg still ignores him. He leads the way out, carrying the sack. Charlie shuts the door behind him as they emerge into the street. Machine gun fire smashes the next door shop front.

"Shit!" mutters Charlie.

In another street Tom enters a phone box. He glances quickly round for the enemy and feeds coins into the box. He presses the button with the receiver to his ear. The coins fall but the phone is dead. Tom smashes down the phone in frustration.

Greg and Charlie arrive at the Customs shed alone.

"Reckon they've been caught?" asks Charlie.

"Hell. Hope not."

Charlie's face reveals disagreement. A nice comfortable prison camp for the rest of the war would suit him fine.

A mortar thumps further down the street. Charlie and Greg take shelter, disappearing behind large canvas bales. There's a pause as the gunfire subsides.

"What the Hell?" exclaims Charlie, emerging with Greg and two girls.

"Janice Harper," announces a slim, pretty twenty year old in educated English.

"Shona Sing," copies the other girl. She is a totally desirable Malay, about twenty five, with flowing black hair. She wears a colourful sarong.

"What are you doing here?" counters Janice.

"Finding a boat, we hope. Must get away," mutters Greg.

"Take us with you, please," pleads Shona. "We escaped from hospital. They execute us if they find us."

Machine gunfire sounds very close. A burst ricochets off the building opposite. They all duck. Both girls are petrified.

"It's not up to me," says Greg. It depends upon the size of the boat, if Tom finds one." He looks doubtful. "That kid a Captain?" he wonders. "Something's funny here."

As if on cue, Tom and Ash arrive out of the shadows, each carrying a full jerry can. Tom has a pack slung over his back. Hard ammunition magazines' outlines show through the canvas.

Tom is less than pleased with the girls' presence.

"What the Hell?"

"They need to get out too," says Greg, winking at the girls.

"They'll never fit! . . . Oh, come on girls. We may have to amputate," says Tom melting a little.

Ash chuckles as Tom waves them forwards. Sounds of fighting draw nearer from both ends of the street. Along the street a Jap officer urges his men forwards. Some fall, hit by sniper fire from the roofs. He runs in Tom and mates' direction. A bullet hits his knee and he lies face down, clutching it.

*　　*　　*

CHAPTER 4

Tom and group have reached the boat. He stows his can aboard, followed by Ash. Tom looks at the girls and then back at the boat doubtfully. He shakes his head.

"Please take us. They've been beheading women as well as men," pleads Janice.

"You haff a beautiful head," jokes Ash in his native Austrian accent.

Janice shudders.

"We can't leave them here," urges Greg.

"Get a bloody move on, whatever!" says Charlie, looking at the approaching battle.

"It's too small. You'll never fit," says Tom.

Machine gunfire shatters a nearby window. Tom waves them all into the boat. "Move yourselves. Quick!"

Buildings burn all over in the distance as the boat leaves the war behind. The moon gives little light between the clouds. The girls squeeze up into the bow, leaning against the jerry cans. Charlie looks at the girls with interest. Shona's slim legs peep through her slit skirt. Greg steers. Tom and Ash row, grunting tiredly. The water murmurs, lapping the passing vessel.

Some hours later Tom stops rowing. "Stuffed! Your turn, mates," his Aussie accent more pronounced. He carefully and stiffly rises to slide beside Greg, who takes his place. Even so, the boat rocks dangerously. Charlie reluctantly relieves Ash. The boat drifts to a standstill.

Tom looks hard at Greg as he takes up his oar. "How come we're in the same regiment and I don't know you, Greg?"

Greg appears cautious. "I only caught up with you lot last night. We were a platoon of reinforcements. The others were taken apart or captured in an ambush."

Tom nods, only partly convinced. His eyes are hard and uncompromising. He hides his reservations. "Shona, you can steer. Just keep us straight and if a big wave comes, steer right at it."

Shona nods and takes her place at the rudder.

Dawn breaks. The open sea rolls in every direction; not a ship in sight. Tom and Ash row slowly, mechanically for hours, exhausted. Janice wakes up and can't believe where she is. Shona waves sleepily from her position slouched over the tiller.

"Want a spell?" offers Janice.

"Thanks all the same," says Tom. "You'd send us in circles."

"I've done it before," says Janice. "I used to row with my brother. He was at Radley, a school famous for its rowing."

She smiles at Tom. He is unmoved, too tired to react. Recent experiences would have sapped anyone's energy.

"What about it, Shona?" asks Tom.

"Give it a go," she nods wearily.

"Good girl. I'll take the tiller."

Tom and Ash stop rowing. Ash grins wearily. Tom is stony faced. Ash curls up in the bottom of the boat, asleep just like that.

"Take it steady. Don't catch a crab," says Janice.

"No find them this far out to sea," replies Shona.

Janice giggles. Both girls reach for their oars. Shona makes a vigorous sweep with her oar, misses the water and lands on her back. Everyone laughs, save for Tom, impassive as ever. He is re-living his ex-neighbour's death and grinding his teeth in fury, his eyes blinking. The iron man has feelings. Janice notices and buries it.

Shona smiles. She leans back on her bench and rows carefully. Janice matches Shona's uncertain pace. Spray from the oars wets everyone. Shona gets the idea and both girls pull strongly, with less spray. Tom and Ash slide under the tarpaulin.

Charlie is at the tiller, keeping them on a straight course. They continue, making good progress for a while.

Greg wakes. He can't believe his eyes. He yawns and stretches.

"Mermaids next! . . . Why are you in such a Hellfire hurry to get back to Aus., Tom?"

Tom hesitates. "You'll know soon enough—I'm seconded to your mob from Intelligence." He closes his eyes.

Greg pulls out a fishing line. He throws the sparkling spinner off the stern. Almost immediately the line jerks. He pulls in a small fish. Greg grins and shows it to the girls. He smiles at Shona. Charlie, jealous, notices and scowls.

Shona is indifferent to Greg. There is something phony about him. She just can't place it. Greg unhooks the fish and threads a larger hook through it. He throws the newly baited hook into the sea. He pushes his way beside Charlie and pays out the line well behind the boat. Their body language is hostile, with Greg contemptuously amused.

Tom is already asleep, his body jerking in a nightmare. Shona nods towards Tom, who looks absurdly young, and Janice is perturbed. "What's he been through?"

"Dead man's shoes," observes Greg, who has his own story to tell.

Tom is back on his property being tortured, a slave of the manager, Kit. His dream is less traumatic with Kit's death and he relaxes.

A lone Jap fighter flies in a cloudless sky. Inside the cockpit the pilot scans the sea ahead. He suddenly sees a boat and yabbers excitedly into his microphone. He listens for a reply, searching the wavebands with a knob on the facia in front of him but hears none. He cocks his machine guns and dives towards the boat.

Greg points towards the plane in the distance as it swoops towards them, "Under the tarp, girls, quick!"

Greg nudges Tom with his foot. "Tom!"

The boat rocks dangerously as the girls squeeze under the tarpaulin. Tom and Ash wake up. Tom sees the plane. "Ship oars. Greg. My pack!"

Greg opens the pack feverishly. He extracts two bren-gun magazines, smiling thinly. He hides them under the tarpaulin.

Tom pulls out a rod and pretends to fish. Ash does likewise.

"Greg, wave as it gets closer. With a bit of luck he'll think we're fishermen," orders Tom. Greg waves enthusiastically.

The plane passes overhead. It returns lower, its Japanese markings clear. Greg waves again. Ash pulls in on his line and has to fight a large fish. Tom actually grins. "An immaculate sense of timing, mate." Tom helps land the fish with his bayonet.

The plane disappears into the distance. Ash in his best Australian: "So long, Mate." He gives two fingers to the distant plane. They all laugh from relief.

"What if he comes back?" asks Janice, worried.

"Let him try and stop us," replies Tom, patting the bren-gun.

*   *   *

Chapter 5

I n a tent the pilot of the intruding plane stands to attention in front of a desk. Wing Commander Isamu of the Japanese Imperial Air-force sits with his neat haircut and immaculate uniform. He is about forty years of age and in his prime. He furiously throws back a map, spread out on the desk before him. He yells: "You let them go? They could have been escaping from Singapore. There's a Captain Intelligence want stopped at all costs. He may be with them."

"Sir," the flustered pilot gulps.

"Get back there. Find them. If we have any surface craft nearby, radio them to capture the boat's crew. If not, sink the boat. We need the Captain if possible. They can kill the rest."

The pilot salutes and backs out.

Back in the boat Janice worries: "Suppose the plane does come back?"

Tom grimly replies, "We'll fry the turkey. Change the subject."

Janice looks lost for ideas. "What do you do, Greg, when you're not playing soldiers?"

"I work on the family cattle property out of Warwick. Lost my wife in a car accident. I hope our boy's okay."

"Sorry," says Janice, with a "Can't win" look.

Greg nods and turns away.

"I worked for the Council, gardening. Made redundant. The army offered me a payroll. I took it," offers Charlie unasked.

Ash looks at Charlie. He knows a loser when he sees one. He winks at Tom, who ignores him.

They all tuck into a meal of tinned meat apart from Charlie and Greg, who row strongly.

Charlie accuses Ash, "How come you're on our side? You sound like a Kraut."

Tom freezes Charlie. Charlie wilts. Futile bickering is the last thing a party leader needs.

Ash responds, "No matter. You'd better know. Patriotism made my Austrian dad fight for Germany in the First World War. After that disaster, he sent us to Australia to start a new life. I'm an engineer for a small boat firm."

Charlie opens his mouth to say something, glances at Tom and says nothing.

"How about you, Tom?" asks Janice a little nervously.

"Got a property my wife used to help with. She lost a baby at birth and that was the end of our relationship. Women!"

"Wife!" he thought. "Well close to one."

Janice has the "hots" for Tom. A quick glance from Tom shows he might be interested. The expression fades as the man of steel kicks in. Kit's treatment, mental and physical has honed a fighter not to be matched against. The others, knowing nothing of his past, instinctively know this is a dog that bites, going for the jugular. Charlie is a bit slower in the uptake.

"A labourer," derides Charlie and then shrivels as Tom's return look blasts him.

"There's another island ahead," observes Tom. "Sumatra? Could be."

They follow his pointing finger.

"How far to . . . to Aus?" asks Charlie nervously.

"About three thousand miles."

"Jeez! We'll never row that far," moans Charlie.

"Won't have to, Charlie. Over half of it's land." Tom wonders how far he's doomed to lug this weakling.

The wind is increasing fast.

"Couldn't we rig a sail? The Tarp?" asks Janice.

"She's not just beautiful," says Greg, admiring her. Janice is more interested in Tom.

"Oars in," says Tom. "We'll use one as a mast." He raises an oar as Ash disengages it from the rowlock. Tom holds it upright in the centre of the boat.

Ash pulls out a roll of rope and ties one side of the mast to the rowlock. Charlie ties the other side. Ash ties his so fast the mast leans his way, as Charlie's rope comes undone. Charlie gives a dirty look. Ash looks at Charlie with a contemptuous grin.

*   *   *

Chapter 6

Back in the plane the pilot flies high over the sea searching for the boat, looking worried. Knowing his wing commander, failure may mean he'll be grounded.

The sea stretches forever. In the distance a destroyer appears. The plane climbs and flies off towards the warship. The pilot speaks into his microphone. "They have to be stopped at all costs." The discipline of radio silence curtails their communication.

The destroyer thrusts through the waves at full speed towards Tom's boat.

"If that plane was sent back after us it could be closing fast," says Tom.

"Prophet of doom," laughs Janet.

There is the distant hum of a plane's engine.

"Jeez. He is a bloody prophet," says Greg.

Tom looks irritated. "Greg, take the Bren. Girls keep down below the gunwale." Tom beckons Greg to the two Bren magazines.

Janice ducks down, followed by Shona. Greg checks the bullets are seated correctly and snaps a magazine into the machine gun. "How far ahead should we aim?"

"Swing with it. About a plane length should do it and then let it fly through your spread. We'll fire at him with rifles and try to break his concentration." Tom hides his apprehension.

What chance has their puny fire-power got against a fighter with cannon, a Mitsubishi Zero, by the looks of it.

Tom passes rifle magazines from his pack to Ash and Charlie, clicking one into his own. There is dried blood on it; Tom's last kill. They pick up the weapons and hold them ready.

"Janice, do you think you can hold the tiller steady with one hand up?" asks Tom.

"I'll try."

"Good girl."

The sound of the distant plane quickly closes.

"Himmel! There," says Ash, pointing as the destroyer breaks through the haze about five miles distant. Tom watches it, shading his eyes with his hand.

"One of ours?" queries Charlie.

"Unlikely," says Tom. "The Japs will have sunk everything of ours in these parts."

"How do you know that?" asks Greg, as if Tom is making it up.

"Believe me, I know," says Tom.

Charlie blanches, biting his lip. A sitting duck! Not what he had signed up for!

The plane flies from the destroyer's direction.

"A little prayer, everyone," says Tom.

Greg looks sardonic. Not a hope in Hades! Janice's lips murmur in prayer. The plane zooms closer. Silence reigns in the boat. The plane dives towards them.

Tom directs, "Wait, wait . . . Fire!"

Machine gun bullets spray the water just ahead. Greg opens up with the Bren-gun followed by their rifles.

"It's bound to get us before we reach land," says Charlie.

The plane swoops away and wheels for a second dive.

"Belt up and concentrate," snaps Tom.

Janice jolts up and pulls on the tiller with all her might. The boat swings away from certain death. Machine gun bullets hit the water where they should have been. Their bullets have missed the plane.

"Yahoo!" from everyone. Their euphoria evaporates as they prepare for the inevitable confrontation.

Janice swings the boat back on course.

"Good girl. Only half a mile now. If we're sunk, swim for it," says Tom. Janice flashes Tom a smile. Tom's face twitches. He turns away from the others, unnoticed except for Janice. "He has feelings!"

Greg loads his last magazine. The others follow the plane in with their weapons. Greg fires earlier this time aiming well in front. He holds his Bren steady so the plane has to fly through his bullets. The plane strikes the side of the boat with two bullets above the waterline. A third strikes Tom in the arm. He gasps, dropping his rifle into the bottom of the boat. He holds his wound tight unnoticed by the others, who are watching the plane intently. Greg's gun runs out of ammunition. The plane flies straight over land. They regard each other, wondering. The engine cuts and splutters.

"Got the bugger!" says Charlie.

The plane's engine starts again. Ash looks at Charlie as if he's an idiot. There is a loud bang and smoke billows up over the ridge. They cheer. Charlie pats Greg on the back.

Shona points at Tom. "Tom, he's been hit!"

Janice leaves the tiller and turns Tom's arm a little. The bullet exit path appears through his bloody sleeve. Ash pulls out a field dressing from his breast pocket. Janice snatches it and carefully rolls back Tom's sleeve. He winces. She finds a morphine syringe and gives his arm a shot. "Got any sulphonamide?"

Ash produces a tin from his medical kit. Janice sprinkles the powder on the dressing. She bandages Tom's arm. "Painful?"

Tom smiles gratefully. "I'll live. But it's bloody sore." He thinks to himself, "That's an under-statement but don't show them any sign of weakness. I've had worse."

Charlie points at the destroyer. It is closing in on them fast.

The island looms much closer. "It'll mince us." They all look tense.

"We'll land. Find cover," says Tom as they near a long sandy beach stretching fifty yards back from the water's edge to the tree line. "Take rifles, provisions and water. Drop the Bren over the side, Greg. No good without ammo."

Greg does so. "Sink the boat? They might think the plane sank us and we've drowned," says Charlie.

"Worth a try. Good one, Charlie," says Tom.

Charlie looks pleased. He's not accustomed to compliments.

A reef bars them from the shore as Ash commands the helm. A good three feet of surf explodes on the reef. The boat pitches and tosses ferociously. Tom slides against the side of the boat banging his wounded arm. He winces but remains stoic.

Ash takes the boat parallel with the reef for a while, heading towards the rocks. They roll worse as the waves hit them broadside. All look up tight apart from Ash. He suddenly turns the boat towards where the surf lessens. Water is flowing towards the beach in a strong current. He guides the boat through a narrow gap in the reef. There is an audible sigh of relief from everyone. All are silent while Ash steers towards the rocks. Tom watches the destroyer through slit eyes, gazing into the sun.

"What are you doing, you moron? We've got to get out before you sink her!" explodes Charlie.

"Stow it." At the last moment Ash steers the boat onto a patch of sand. They jump out onto rocks. Larger rocks hide them from the open sea. Ash and Charlie pile the provisions into the tarpaulin. They lift it and run across the rocks to the trees and jungle. They hide the tarpaulin under the bushes.

Tom takes his rifle. Greg carries the jerry cans. Janice struggles to carry Greg and Tom's packs. Shona brings up the rear with two rifles. Greg, Ash and Charlie return to the boat. They push it out shoulder high in water and wade round to one side.

"Heave," says Ash. They overturn the boat, which fills with water and sinks. They run up over the rocks. From the cover of the trees they halt to catch their breath. Without war, it would be an idyllic scene, crystal clear water and azure blue sea, golden sand and dark green jungle of many hues.

The destroyer churns forward less than a mile out, approaching fast. "I wonder it's not firing at us," says Tom, grimly, as they disappear into the jungle. He thinks to himself that the destroyer captain must be sure he has the escapers now.

Each face registers concern. Out of the fire, into the frying pan! They slap at flies. The jungle feels impenetrable.

"Take the lead, Greg. Ash, bring up the rear. Try to cover our tracks. Quick!" says Tom.

They pick up their rifles and packs as they disappear into the jungle. Greg nods. He starts off into the jungle using his bayonet to slash through creepers and thick, juicy leaves.

A little further on the jungle thickens. Tom takes the lead, slashing a path with a stick, his rifle slung over his back. He's looking for a likely killing field. They sweat and slap at the ever present flies. A snake slithers out of their path. Janice gives a little yelp. Smiling, Shona taps Janice's shoulder, "A green snake. Not poisonous."

"Now she tells me," laughs Janice still shaken as they continue on their way.

*　　*　　*

CHAPTER 7

Relentless rain drenches Tom's party. They pause for breath in a tiny clearing. Each slumps to the ground, looking at Tom expectantly.

"They'll probably only send a boatload. The pilot will have told them our strength before he attacked."

"Ambush?" suggests Ash.

Tom nods. "Go back and kill off their rear, Greg. We need the rifles." Tom taps his bayonet. Greg nods. "And no prisoners," continues Tom grimly. The other men nod. Janice is horrified.

"It's not tea with the bloody vicar," erupts Tom.

Ash stifles a smile. Tom's a man after his own heart. He's beginning to like and respect the young Captain. In spite of his wound, he still takes the lead and plans well.

"Let me go too," asks Shona. The others look amused. "I'm a street girl." Water cascades down her face as a leaf discards its contents. She ducks and laughs. Tom nods and hands her his bayonet. She kisses it. Greg leads her back down the path.

"Keep together so we don't shoot each other," says Tom. He signals to Janet to keep low. She nods thinking, "He didn't need to tell me. But what a man." It's a curious fact that when one's life is threatened, many of us are tempted to sex. Janice is no exception.

Tom, Ash and Charlie hide one side of the track, Janice slides under the undergrowth behind them, her face petrified, fading into the greenery. Perhaps she should have taken her chance in the hospital.

Back on the beach a motorboat pulls up close to the sandy shore. Twelve Japanese soldiers including an officer scramble out holding their weapons high. The officer gestures towards the trees. They spread out to search for footprints. As they near the rocks, they converge. They follow up the rocks to the trees. For a while they find nothing. One points to a mark on the ground shouting, "Ai." The other sailors converge on him. One slaps him on the back, laughing. They disappear into the trees, not anticipating much resistance.

"Girls," one laughs. "One for your and one for me."

Greg and Shona hide off the track. Both listen for the approaching enemy. Shona lifts her finger and points. Greg nods. Feet trample through the undergrowth. The Japs make as little noise as they can but their rustles can be heard distinctly. The sailors file by. They are strung out, several yards between each. They nervously peer through the jungle. The rain lessens to a light patter. Greg rises to pounce on the last man when another appears. Greg sinks back. He gives a thumbs up. Closely followed by Shona he springs on a Jap as soon as he has passed. He drives his bayonet into the man's spinal cord. He grunts and slumps to the ground, dead.

A movement behind them reveals a last Japanese, astonished and petrified. He swings up his rifle to point it at Greg, finger on the trigger. Greg freezes. Shona dives under the rifle and drives her bayonet up through sailor's chest. He grunts, drops his weapon and falls to the ground, dead. Greg gives Shona a grateful smile and they drag the bodies off the track. They pull the rifles into the jungle.

Off the clearing Tom sweating heavily struggles with his wounded arm propping up his rifle. He leans it against the V of two creepers. Charlie crosses himself. Ash and Charlie are on either side of Tom, their fingers on their triggers. Tom points, Ash to fire at the left, Charlie, the right. They nod.

The crunch of approaching Japanese through the undergrowth is audible. The officer and three others appear on the far side of the clearing. They scan the jungle. Tom nods and all three fire as one. The officer and two others fall. The other fires blindly into the jungle. A bullet hits a tree trunk in front of Janice. She winces. The three work their rifle bolts, Tom with difficulty. Charlie and Ash fire together. The fourth Japanese falls dead. The remaining Japanese can be heard running away.

Charlie points to his rifle and shakes his head. His ammo has run out. Tom snatches up the semi-automatic from a fallen Jap and thrusts it into Charlie's hands. Ash takes another weapon, throwing his rifle bolt into the jungle, rendering it useless to the enemy. Tom gestures down the path. Ash and Charlie follow the Japanese cautiously. Tom checks the Japanese are all dead. Some are as young as Peter. Tom flashes a sudden look of sorrow. His war front kicks in again as hard as a rock. He looks behind him.

Janice emerges from the jungle, shaken. Tom rests his hand on her arm. "You okay, Janice?" She nods doubtfully. "Good girl."

She smiles. Tom kisses her cheek quickly. Janice is pleased and surprised. He turns away, embarrassed by his lapse.

Greg and Shona wait in ambush off the track. They hear approaching running Japs. Two crash onto the ground before them, tripping over the vine Greg has stretched across the pathway. Another falls on top of them. Greg and Shona spring onto the Japs killing the man on top. The other two rise to their feet. There is a fierce struggle. Greg tries to knife his opponent. Shona struggles to break free from hers.

Greg falls on his back. The Jap dives on top of him. Greg kicks him in the groin as they fall. The Jap curls up in agony. Shona's opponent scratches her thigh with his bayonet. She gasps. Greg knifes his opponent dead. Shona uses both hands to try to keep the bayonet from entering her thigh. Greg springs on him, killing him with his bayonet, thrusting it into his backbone.

Shona is shaken as she picks up the bayonet. Greg helps her back into the jungle as more Japs approach. They stop short before the bodies. They gasp and then fire blindly into the jungle. They continue running down the path towards the sea. Ash and Charlie are close behind. Two rifle shots ring out and a few seconds later a scream.

Tom appears carrying his fresh weapon; Janice behind him. Under his breath, "A bloody abattoir!" as he takes in the pile of bodies: "For you, Peter." Janice looks at him, enquiring. He ignores her. He strides through the jungle, leaving her struggling behind.

Greg reappears from the jungle, with Shona, her thigh bandaged and limping slightly.

"Bad?" Tom asks her. She shakes her head.

Another shot rings out.

"By my reckoning that's the lot, says Greg.

Janice appears from the path. She sees the bodies and blanches. "Butchers!"

Tom looks wooden. "This is war. Kill or be killed. What do you think they were firing at us? Peppermints!"

"Aren't you going to bury them?" asks Janice.

"No. Leave them for the next boatload to think about. Take their weapons and ammo."

They follow his instructions, checking the bodies for any signs of life. The Japs were well known for "playing possum" and then shooting the enemy in the back.

Arriving near the beach, Tom and the rest survey a body on the sand. Another hangs limply from the side of the motorboat.

"Great. We'd better put some distance between us and the next patrol." Tom is concerned by Shona's limping using a forked branch as a crutch. "How's it going?"

Shona gives a thumbs up and smiles bravely. "I'll live."

He smiles. "Good girl."

They pull out the provisions and stuff them into their packs. Ash conceals the tarpaulin under the bushes.

Tom glances at Shona. "The best of the bunch" he thinks. Then aloud, "Well-honed in surviving the streets' rat run."

She nods and grins. "Preserved my virginity." She wipes clean Tom's bayonet and returns it to him.

Ash leading, they stride off into the jungle.

*   *   *

CHAPTER 8

Tom and group stagger through the jungle. They are beat, dirty and sweating. The vegetation thins.

"Can't we stop for a rest? I've had it," says Janice. A wild pig dashes across her path, scaring the living daylights out of her.

Ash leads, scanning ahead. "A village, there," he points below the ridge they have been struggling along.

"Keep going everyone," Tom tells them. "You're doing okay." His arm throbs and his energy is spent. "We'll stop there."

The welcome words energize them. They lengthen their strides. Half an hour later, is it safety awaiting them? A large clearing reveals huts on stilts around the edge. They are all one storey with thatched roofs and some with verandahs.

Tom signals to take care with one hand, waving and pointing. They spread out and search the huts covering each other. Ash takes one hut, Greg another. Charlie covers them with his Jap light machine gun. The girls wait in the jungle. Shona has a rifle at the ready. Tom is watchful but bleary eyed. He leans against a verandah support, not much use in a fight, should the enemy be lurking in ambush. The village appears deserted. The others return. They wave Tom and company towards the huts.

"A rest at last," says Charlie.

"Thank God," says Janice.

Tom staggers. Ash runs to his side and props him over one shoulder. A cute eleven year old boy, dressed only in a pair of tattered shorts, part hidden by shade screams and runs inside a hut. His mother, well rounded but attractive, in her early thirties, peers out. She wears a sarong and sandals. She stops on the verandah and takes in the scene. She descends the steps smiling and meets Tom and Ash. "Welcome," she points to herself. "Maria . . . . British?"

"Australian, mostly," says Ash. "Any Japanese?"

Maria shakes her head. She peers at Tom propped against Ash and looking way out. "Bring him inside." She sniffs. "The rest of you take a shower. It's round the back."

Janice offers wearily, "I'll help with Tom."

"He'll be okay," says Maria.

Janice elects to stay.

Ash looks doubtful. Can she be trusted? Maria helps Ash carry Tom up the steps. Janice frowns, worried about Tom as she staggers up the steps. He is oblivious of her. The others disappear round the back.

Tom is lifted by Ash and Maria into a hammock, delirious. Janice sits beside him on a stool. She bathes his forehead from a bucket.

"Kill the bastards. Kill!" mutters Tom. Janice pulls back alarmed. Tom is reliving the murder of Peter and his mate. He half rises from his hammock but Maria restrains him. He falls back, exhausted. Maria looks at Janice, questioning?

"He must've had a bad time before he found us," says Janice. "I don't know what happened and don't want to know."

"You go and take a shower, dear. I'll take good care of him," says Maria, a smile on her kind face. Janice, seeing Tom is in good hands, leaves for a shower. After Janice has left, Maria takes off Tom's ragged shirt and bathes his top half. She sees the scars on his back, Kit's handiwork, and shudders." You poor, poor boy," she murmurs. "These are old ones, not from the Japs. So young to be beaten like that. Who in Hell did that? May he roast in Purgatory!"

It is later in the evening. Janice looks around her. The room is poorly furnished with only a cane table and chairs, a crude wood stove and hammocks. A lit oil lamp hangs from a rafter. Ash slumps on a mat. The boy, Subul, a bundle of health watches from the other side of the room. Maria bathes Tom's face from a bowl of water. "This will have to come off," says Maria.

Tom, only part conscious, is alarmed: "My arm?"

Maria: "No silly, your shirt."

Ash heaves with laughter. Maria takes off Tom's shirt very gently while Ash watches out for enemy activity in the jungle. Then Maria removes Tom's bandage and inspects his wound critically. She is concerned.

"Could be better," says Tom, groaning.

"Lie there while I boil up medicine. I have to find some plants," says Maria.

"Will he be okay?" asks Ash.

"If he doesn't get a fever. You may have got here just in time."

"Thank you," says Ash, his face saying much more.

Maria smiles.

"Any sign of Japs yet?" asks Ash.

Maria crosses herself. "No, thank God. Some villagers are hiding in the jungle. The rest have gone east . . . . Subul, come and help me."

Subul emerges from the shadows. He exits with his mother.

Tom awakens and smiles at Ash, a friendly face.

"Can we trust her?" asks Ash.

"She speaks good English. I guess she's worked for them," says Tom, as if that is a guarantee. He shifts his position in the hammock and winces. He checks to see if they are alone. "Ash, can I leave you to carry on if anything happens to me?"

"Too right mate. But nothing's going to happen to you."

"Listen," Tom lowers his voice. "I'm carrying vital information for the Allies. It could save many lives and shorten the war if we get back to Australia in time."

"Yep."

"Don't trust Greg."

Ash looks puzzled. Greg wanders by outside, concealing his interest in their conversation.

"He's . . ." Tom expresses his feelings by waving his hands up and down.

Ash partly understands. "I'll watch your back, Tom." He wonders whether Tom is hallucinating.

Marie enters with a basket of plants. She dumps them on the table and begins cutting some into a wooden bowl. Then she adds water and boils them over the stove.

Outside, under the shower, a jerry can with its top cut off and its bottom punctured by nail holes, stands Shona. Greg fills it with another jerry can. Shona is partially hidden by a bamboo screen, about eighteen inches off the ground and rising neck high. Her bandage drops off her leg. The wound is healing well.

Charlie, close by, grins and tries to see more of Shona.

"Wonderful," murmurs Shona.

"Could be," mutters Charlie.

On the hut verandah that night Ash, Charlie and Greg recline on a mat on the floor, their backs to the wall. "What happens if Tom dies?" asks Charlie.

"One of us has to take command," says Greg, looking at the others cautiously.

"Who? Charlie? No way," says Ash.

"I'm the bloody Corporal," says Charlie.

"I'm not taking your orders," laughs Greg.

"Tom's delegated me," says Ash. "But it's not going to happen." They watch each other with mutual distrust. Ash stares them down.

Inside the hut, Tom lies on a mattress on the floor. There is a poultice bandaged to his arm. Maria watches him from a stool. "How are you feeling?"

"Okay, thanks to you. How come you speak such good English?"

"I worked in Jakarta for an import company dealing with Great Britain mostly, as a secretary."

"Subul's dad?"

"Lost at sea in a fishing accident." Maria brushes away a tear. "Do you really hope to reach Australia?"

Tom looks warily around to check they are alone. He lowers his voice. "All of us? Not a chance in Hell but we've got to try." He grins, determined.

*   *   *

Chapter 9

t is two days later. Tom sits on the verandah in a cane chair looking much fitter, his arm in a crude sling. Charlie and Greg eat out of wooden bowls.

Ash plays with Subul on all fours. He growls like a tiger. Subul pretends to be frightened. A bond has developed between them. Subul dashes past Ash to freedom, the doorway at least. "Okay, Subul. I've had enough. Too fast for me." Ash slumps down beside the others. Subul climbs into a hammock. Shona idly swings the hammock. Subul smiles at her. It's a long time since he has had such a large audience. She gets up and hugs him.

Maria joins them. She sits in the remaining chair. Tom looks at Subul fondly. He says softly to himself, "Oh Subul, don't grow up before this bloody war finishes."

"I could stay here and last out the war," says Charlie, lying back relaxed.

"You're a soldier. We kill Japs," says Ash, coldly.

"And stay alive," adds Charlie. He puts down his bowl.

Janice joins them. She leans against a verandah support. "Not a bad idea."

Maria looks at them as if they live in cuckoo land. "You can't stay here. They've landed round Jakarta and Padang. I heard it on my radio this morning. They'll be here as soon as they've crossed the island."

"You reckon?" says Tom. "Hardly worth their while."

"They're spreading everywhere," says Maria.

"Like a rash," says Ash.

They smile. Except for Maria. She knows she will die if caught helping them.

"Keep your weapons with you at all times and be ready to leave. In the meantime we might wait here a day or two while my arm heals and we get our strength back," says Tom.

Charlie is rebellious. "Says you."

Tom freezes Charlie with one of his deadly looks. "That's right."

"Suits me," says Ash. He stares at Charlie, expressionless. Charlie avoids his stare, uneasy. Ash sharpens his bayonet on a large stone.

"Me too," says Janice. Tom flashes Janice a grateful smile.

Later that evening, as dusk settles, and insects tick, Janice skims stones into the stream. She is wondering what the future holds? Will they ever get home?

Greg emerges from the blackness behind her. Janice starts. "You move so quietly."

"A pity to waste this moment," says Greg.

Charlie observes them from behind a bush, biding his time.

"Don't get any ideas."

"So you couldn't fancy me a little?"

Janice smiles. "Maybe. It's silly getting involved. We could all be dead by tomorrow."

"All the better to enjoy the present."

Janice says quickly, "Let's see what happens when we reach Australia."

"If!" Greg strolls off into the night. A slither of moonlight filters through the trees. Charlie sidles up, unsure of himself. He drops down beside her. Janice sounds nervous. "What're you doing up so late?"

Charlie responds, "How about a little you know what?"

Janice rises. She's met so many "Charlies" in her time in hospital.

"No thanks, Charlie. You've got nothing I want."

Charlie grins. "I've got one thing every girl wants."

"Nothing new," says Janice. "I'm a nurse. Goodnight." She takes off towards the huts at a brisk pace.

"Damn!" Charlie throws a pebble viciously into the stream. He spins round to follow Janice. Ash strides into the light. He is steamed up. "Leave her alone, Charlie."

Charlie wheels around. "Been spying on us, bloody peeping . . ." Ash throws a punch at him. Charlie sways out of the way. "Mind your own bloody business."

"Sex maniac!"

"Queer!"

Ash connects with a savage thus on Charlie's cheek. Charlie falls to the ground, Ash towering over him. Tom sweeps out of the bushes. "Enough! What the heck's going on? Get to the hut, both of you."

Ash gives Charlie a filthy look as he slopes off into the darkness. Charlie reciprocates and slowly gets to his feet.

"Time we were moving on," thinks Tom. "They can use their energy to get us to Australia."

* * *

Chapter 10

I n the hut everyone sleeps. Subul dashes in. He runs round snoring bodies, shaking everyone. They awaken. Greg sparks, "Damn you Subul!"

"Men come. Japs from the air."

They react frenetically and dress quickly. The men snatch up their weapons. Maria dashes in and rolls up the hammocks, to stuff them under a table. Tom leads them out. Ash checks the room, throws on his pack and exits carrying Tom's pack.

Japanese paratroopers are only about five hundred feet above them and descending fast. Tom and company emerge from the huts, weapons in hand plus ammo pouches. Janice has a haversack. All leave except for Maria, staying in her hut.

"Janice, Shona, Subul, under cover, quick!" shouts Tom, pointing to a thick jungle area. "Ash and Greg on the shade side. Pick them off in the air. Single shots. It's a turkey shoot. Make each one count." Ash and Greg disappear into the jungle. Tom and Charlie dash to the side adjacent to Ash and Greg. A stream of bullets follows them into the jungle from the nearest paratrooper. It ceases abruptly with a shot from Ash or Charlie. Tom fires single shots. Charlie, Greg and Ash copy. Machine-gun fire sprays the jungle from above but fails to find any targets. Each of their shots hits a paratrooper. They slump in their harnesses. Not one lands and rises.

Janice from behind Tom sounds shocked. "God! It's carnage!"

"Them or us," says Shona. "I like it this way."

Suddenly there are no more Japanese. An uneasy silence reigns. Subul dashes out to the nearest body. "Come back. They may not all be dead," shouts Tom. As if to stress his point, a shot rings out, narrowly missing Subul. He falls and lies prone.

Ash fires once and a body jerks and lies still.

Subul rises and runs carrying a light machine-gun. He dives into the jungle beside Tom. "You silly, brave boy!" Tom takes the machine-gun, lying flat.

There is the sound of a distant aircraft. Greg shouts, "Check the others?"

"No, lie still. There's another stick coming,"

A further twenty paratroopers descend, as Ash shouts, "Getting short of ammo." Tom stares up at the paratroopers less than a thousand feet above them. "Grab some. We'll cover you."

Ash sprints twenty yards into the clearing and the nearest bodies. A stream of bullets kicks up the earth as he reaches them. Tom opens up on the nearest paratroopers with his machine-gun. Six bodies slump. The bullets cease. Ash grabs two machine-guns and sprints for cover. A stream of bullets follows him. Tom fires short bursts and Charlie, single shots. Ten more paratroopers are only fifty feet or so above them. Tom's weapon runs out of ammunition. "Shit! No ammo."

Machine-gun fire rakes the huts, setting them alight.

Behind Tom, Janice feverishly searches through his pack. She pulls out two grenades. "These any good, Tom?" He takes a quick look behind him.

Three paratroopers land alive and spray the jungle with bullets at their unseen targets. "You beaut! Throw them over here but don't touch the pins." The grenades land beside Tom.

"Bloody Hell," exclaims Greg.

Tom pulls out a pin, rises to his knees and hurls the grenade at the paratroopers. The nearest points his gun at Tom. As he squeezes the trigger, the grenade explodes and his bullets soar skywards while he falls onto his back. His comrades are blown apart too.

More bodies land. One is still alive. He puts his hands up. Charlie shoots him dead.

"Murderer!" shouts Janice.

"You still think this is a game?" says Tom.

"He was surrendering," smoulders Janice.

"Till our backs are turned," retorts Tom.

As if to emphasize his point, a bullet rings out from the far side of the clearing. Greg returns fire, killing the soldier. He methodically searches the bodies for any sign of life. He shoots two and searches on for signs of life till he is satisfied they are safe.

They all leave the sanctuary of the jungle. Subul screams. He runs over to the body of his mother, killed by the last bullet. He lies down beside her, sobbing his heart out. Janice follows and puts her arm round Subul. He shakes her off. She waits a moment to let him grieve and tries again. He throws himself into her arms, burying his head in her breasts. She cuddles him, then rises to feet, shaking, out of control. Tom puts his arm round her. He cuddles them both and she responds with a grateful smile.

As they unclasp, Ash lifts up Subul, hugging him. Shona's street-wise culture surfaces. "Japs, we kill, kill, kill!"

They are all feeling emotional at their narrow brush with Death and Maria's departure.

Tom releases Janice, bristling. "This is only a start."

Ash tries to bring everyone back to earth: "Better be out of here fast."

"We'll cremate Maria first," says Tom in a tone no one dare face down.

They rapidly gather dry wood from inside the remains of the huts for Maria's cremation. Ash lays her body reverently on the pile. Janice and Subul join them. "No, you can't," he cries. He runs to the pyre and tries to touch Maria's body. Janice runs after him. She puts her arm round his shoulders.

"Come away my love. I'll look after you."

Subul buries his head in her dress. She leads him gently away, sobbing quietly.

"Someone say a prayer," says Janice.

They line up by the woodpile. Tom is visibly moved. "Goodbye, brave Maria; my saviour. May God protect your soul." Tom crosses himself to the surprise of the rest.

They all say, "Amen."

Charlie lights the pile with his lighter. The fire catches fast. They wait till it burns furiously, then back off.

Ash remains staring into the flames, wooden. Tom rocks unsteadily. "Come on Ash. Time to go."

Greg wanders over and joins them.

Charlie: "What about Subul?"

Subul is lost in his misery.

"We'll take him with us till we find his people," says Tom.

"He'll slow us down," says Greg, looking hard.

Ash radiates fury, "You want to leave him here to bloody starve?"

"Sit, everyone," says Tom. They form a half moon round him near the jungle's edge. Subul stares into space, oblivious of what anyone is saying, traumatized.

"I need to know you're all with me," says Tom, still standing. He pauses, gauging their reactions. "There're two choices: One, you can stay here, wait for more Japs and give yourselves up." He points to the many bodies. "I wish you luck."

"Torture, death," says Ash. Tom nods.

"Otherwise I can only promise you a fifty/fifty chance of getting back to Aus. It'll be tough surviving off the jungle and storms at sea." He pauses to let it sink in. "The Japs'll be after us like hornets after this, and we'll have to fight for survival. If you come with me, you take my orders whatever." He stops and stares at Charlie.

"I'll come, boss."

"And?" continues Tom.

Greg watches the others. Ash and the girls give thumbs up or nod. Greg raises his hand. Tom notices Greg's hesitation but says nothing. He's not happy with it. This one will need watching. "Let's go."

They stretch and rise to their feet to follow Tom, Janice and Subul first, then Ash and Shona, Charlie and Greg. Tom pauses. "Take as much water and food as you can carry with your ammo."

They pick up their weapons. With a last glance at the village's smoking ruins, machetes in hand, they follow Tom into the jungle.

Some hours later, now led by Ash, they hack their way through the undergrowth with their machetes, getting progressively slower. They stop for a rest. They drop where they are, wiping their sweating brows, shattered.

"How far do you reckon we've come?" asks Greg.

Tom consults his watch. "About five miles. We've been walking five hours. Good going."

"Gives us a start on the bastards," says Ash.

"How far have we got to leg it?" asks Janice.

"About five hundred and fifty miles, if we stick to the island. Then sail for Java."

There is a shocked silence as they take it in.

"A bit far for a city girl," says Shona, smiling to show she's not complaining.

"I can never make it. Have some sense. Wait and give ourselves up," says Janice.

"You will make it," says Tom. "They take no prisoners."

"How can you be sure?" asks Greg.

"Believe me, I know," says Tom grimly.

Janice cracks. She jumps to her feet, advancing on Tom. He rises. "I'm not a flaming trained soldier. Slave driver!"

She tries to slap him. He catches her wrist. She bursts into tears. Tom hugs her. She struggles, then gives in. "You're doing all right, girl."

Charlie's face shows jealousy. Greg is coldly amused. Subul looks worried. Tom releases her. He softens. She smiles. Ash watches Greg, taking in his attitude but masking his own suspicions.

Eventually they reach the beach. "Have a drink, everybody," says Tom. "Make it a small one. By my calculations we should be twenty to thirty miles from where we landed." They drink eagerly from their water bottles.

"How're you doing, Subul?" asks Ash.

Subul is as tired and hot as the rest. He gives a thumbs up and flashes a sad smile.

"What now?" asks Charlie.

Tom gestures along the beach. "We walk by night and rest up during the day. Then the going will be much faster and no one will see us."

"You hope," says Greg, unfriendly.

"That's right." Tom gives him a withering stare. Greg turns away.

That evening under a full moon they eat bananas around a small fire, concealed from the sea by a huge rock.

"We could have raised the boat and hugged the shore in it," moans Charlie.

Tom glances at his impatiently. "No, Charlie. We'd be sitting ducks if they sent another plane and these weapons haven't the Bren's punch."

Greg regards Charlie with contempt. "I don't fancy taking on a destroyer."

"Couldn't we spend the night here?" asks Janice. "Go for a swim. Have a bit of fun?" She eyes Tom provocatively. He pretends to ignore her.

"You're all doing well. Keep faith in yourselves." Tom glances at Subul gazing blankly into space. "Poor kid."

"He'll come right," says Janice. Tom nods doubtfully.

*   *   *

Chapter 11

A Japanese Wing Commander, lit by a hurricane lamp, drums his fingers on his desk. A Morse code operator takes a message on a note pad using the same desk. The message ends. "Well?"

"The destroyer captain says they sent a boat but its entire crew, a dozen men were wiped out in an ambush."

"Impossible! Ask them to confirm the message." The "Winco" does not tolerate fools gladly. How many were in this small boat the local spy had reported leaving? Could not be more than five or six. He lights up a cigarette and studies a map of the Indonesian islands. His clerk taps away at his Morse keyboard.

Tom's party have reached a beach as they move cautiously through the trees. They are tired, hot and hungry and slump to the ground. Ash swings Subul off his shoulders and stretches. They look at Tom expectantly. He ignores them and approaches the edge of the jungle to scan the beach. There is no sign of human presence, to his relief. They are certainly not in a fit state to take on any enemy. Relaxation is of the essence.

"We'll stop here till morning and recharge our batteries," says Tom on his return. "Watch out for boats and when you've found the energy, we could spear fish for dinner."

There is a universal sigh of relief. "Subul, you should be fresh. Scout around for some dry wood for a fire. We don't want any smoke."

Subul smiles at his responsibility and runs around the perimeter of the clearing, glad to feel important.

Greg pulls out his bayonet from his belt and cuts some bamboos. He hands them to the others, keeping one for himself, which he sharpens.

"What about one for us?" asks Janice.

Greg cuts one for her, Shona and Subul. Ash offers to sharpen the others. Subul aims his at an imaginary foe. Ash grins. "Going to kill Japs with that, Subul?"

Subul nods vigorously. Then his face falls as he re-lives Maria's death.

"I'm hungry and thirsty," says Charlie.

"I'll look for water," says Shona.

"Count me in," says Charlie, jumping to his feet.

Tom nods his agreement and Charlie collects their water bottles before disappearing into the jungle with Shona.

"Be back inside the hour," calls Tom.

They approach a rocky outcrop with clear pools and Greg and Tom try spearing fish, with Janice. They have no success. Subul stands on the edge of a pool, the sea lazily lapping his feet, watched by Ash.

"You remind me of my boy, about your age. Wonder if I'll ever see him again," says Ash, his face tautening with emotion.

Subul jerks his spear out of the water, a fifteen inch fish impaled on it. He grins delightedly showing it to Ash.

Distant aircraft approach rapidly. They all dash for the tree cover. Ash and Subul are still yards out in the open as the plane flies overhead. A burst of machine gunfire scatters the sand. Ash grabs Subul and staggers under cover of the trees.

"Verdammt!, they'll know we're here," says Ash.

"All they saw was a man and a boy," says Tom. "No way can they tie that up with all of us.

Meanwhile Charlie and Shona stumble through the jungle. They suddenly break out from the trees onto the edge of an idyllic pool complete with the shade of palm trees and a tinkling waterfall. They look at each other, smiling. Charlie strips to his underpants and dives in.

"Any alligators," calls Shona.

"Not yet. Come in. It's paradise," says Charlie.

Shona joins him in her pants. They splash each other and swim like porpoises, brushing against each other. Shona is the stronger swimmer. She keeps just out of his reach, flirting. He chases her. She laughs and dives out of sight. As she fails to re-surface, Charlie is worried. Suddenly she surfaces behind him and ducks him. He springs up assisted by a hidden rock. They swim closer till Charlie puts his hand up and Shona matches it—the first high five, pressing hers against his. They kiss, the war forgotten, and nibble each other. They swim to shallow water. Charlie slides down their pants. They join and make love, the water reflecting pure ecstasy.

Back in the clearing the group relaxes under tall palm trees. Tom takes off his bandage. His wound is healing well. He pulls a tiny map out of his pocket. It is headed with Japanese writing. He studies it intently, including the arrows indicating an impending advance into India.

A small fire burns. Three sticks joined at the top with a strip of vine, suspend a billycan. Fishtails peep out of the water. Ash watches them cooking.

"I wonder where those two have got to?" says Greg.

"We'll have to do something about those planes. They'll slow us up," says Tom, inwardly relishing the chance to take the war to the Japanese.

Ash glances at Grég, shaking his head as if Tom is mad. "Travel by night?"

"We'll never get to Aus. in time," says Tom, thinking it will be a long shot anyway.

Charlie and Shona climax in the pool. A fighter plane flies overhead, only its wing tip visible. They freeze. "Japs," mouths Shona, as if the pilot might hear her. They sink below the surface, bubbles marking the spot.

Sitting on a fallen branch, Greg pulls out a photo. It shows his brother and himself leaning against a fence smiling. There are sheep yards behind them. He shakes his head. Why had he left that satisfying if hard farm life to fight for his country and to end up on the run? Nuts! Even with his hidden agenda, he'd support Tom in a hit at the Japs.

Three fighter planes pass above the trees, heard but not seen. Greg pockets the photo. Ash seizes the billycan. Tom scatters the burning embers. They all dart further into the shelter of the trees. They lie under bushes. The fighters keep flying inland. Their engines change to a rougher pitch.

"An airfield," exclaims Tom. "This side of the mountains. Know what I'm thinking?"

"Give them a nice surprise?" asks Greg.

"Crazy!" explodes Janice.

"Don't do it," says Ash, the cold hard voice of reason.

"A debt to repay," says Tom as Charlie and Shona stride into the clearing with water bottles suspended from their shoulders by vine loops. Charlie gives a thumbs up. His hair is slicked back. Shona's shines.

"Took your time," says Tom. "Was it far?"

"About half a mile," replies Charlie. "We had a struggle getting through the vines. Beautiful water. You should try it."

Ash grins, understanding. Tom is thoughtful. Janice smiles.

Perhaps she might fetch the water next time, with Tom?

"We'll take a look," says Tom. "Lead on, Greg." Greg rises to his feet. "This'll test him," Tom thinks, smiling grimly.

*   *   *

Chapter 12

Greg leads off, hacking his way through thick jungle with his machete. They all drip with sweat. Cicadas blank out their noise with an orchestral cacophony of chirping.

Tom has his Japanese light machine gun at the ready. Ash lifts Subul over obstructing creepers. "Don't let the enemy destroy this dear child," he thinks.

Janice and Shona follow, carrying their fishing spears, followed closely by Charlie. He stops and listens, his automatic at the ready. A not so distant rev of an aircraft engine shows they are nearing their target.

Greg halts. He waves his hand pressing down, warning them to take cover. A six foot high fence bars their way. They crouch and listen.

Greg speaks in a low tone: "I'll go forward and recce."

Tom steps forward to join Greg. "No, stay here with the others. Be ready for action, everyone." He shakes his head sharply.

"You okay, Tom?" asks Janice, worried.

"I'm leading," he replies curtly.

"No good for any of us if you pass out, Tom," says Ash, looking equally apprehensive.

"Just a bit giddy. I'm bloody leading. Ash, come with me." Tom rises, shakes his head and strides forward towards the fence. The two disappear into the jungle.

"Have a drink," offers Greg and they glug from their water bottles.

"Can I kill a Jap?" asks Subul, seeking revenge for his mum.

"No, love. You stay with me," says Janice, hugging him. Subul wriggles free, furious.

A plane skims the jungle above them. They all tense. It lands close by.

Reaching the fence Tom and Ash creep forward on their knees. Tom points to the bottom of the fence. It is not dug in.

"They don't expect any trouble. No settlements around here. Watch out for my signal and then fetch the others. Meet me at the petrol drums."

"Take care," says Ash, lifting up the bottom of the fence, aiding Tom. It gives and Tom scrambles underneath. He disappears into the darkness of the airfield, on his stomach.

"Just don't get giddy out there" thinks Ash. "That'll wreck the plan. Lack of proper food."

He watches the airfield as lights flick on near the planes and has a sharp intake of breath. No sign of Tom—relief. There are no hangers, just a long line of planes ready for take-off, on an airstrip cut out of the jungle. Masses of petrol drums are piled at the near end. Two Nissen huts provide accommodation for the pilots and ground crew. There are two smaller huts further away, possibly a communication hut and cookhouse. The start of a control tower pokes out of the darkness beyond them.

Tom looks back at the fence, lying on his belly. Someone has lit a cigarette. Who the Hell? He swears. Ash doesn't smoke. Will the sentries see it? Their plans could go up in smoke literally. He observes two sentries at the far end of the planes. They stroll towards him, chatting. They seem oblivious of the tiny glow. Their weapons are slung on their back, totally relaxed. Tom counts the planes: forty. What a killing that would be!

Tom slithers towards the petrol drums, shielding him from the sentries. A petrol hose protrudes conveniently from one upright drum. He smiles, then it fades as two men exit a hut.

They lean against its upright end and light cigarettes. "Jeez! They must see me!" Tom hugs the ground and slides behind a runway light in deep shadow. He lies there for a while.

In the jungle, lit by a fading crescent moon, Janice queries Charlie: "What are we doing, while you guys are playing at heroes?"

"Stay here out of harm's way and be ready to move out quickly if things go pear shaped."

"I'd like to help," says Shona.

"Let me too, please," adds Subul.

"Not for kids," says Charlie.

Subul picks up his spear and jabs it viciously.

"Stick to fish," chuckles Charlie.

There is no sign of Greg.

On the airfield the men stroll towards Tom. He flattens himself in the light's shadow. One flicks a cigarette butt, it landing close to Tom. Surely they must see him. They turn and wander back towards the hut. Tom lets out his breath in a sigh of relief. They enter the hut.

Tom creeps across the close cut vegetation towards the huts as the sentries disappear behind the line of planes. He stops and looks towards the sentries. Then he runs to the deep shadow of the hut. He rounds the corner and lets out an involuntary whisper: "Yes!" There are crates of empty beer bottles. He lifts two crates of twenty four, and peers round the hut corner. The guards are walking towards him. "Shit!" He crouches in the shadow.

They turn and stroll towards the far planes. Tom runs with the crates towards the nearest petrol drums. He lowers the crates and fills the bottles, one at a time. His hands tremble and he spills some petrol.

"Control!"

Back in the jungle Charlie, Janice, Shona and Subul sit, waiting. They hear a faint whistle.

"Let's go," Charlie looks at Shona. He picks up his weapon and they creep along the path left by the others.

On the airfield Tom hides the filled bottles among the petrol drums. He pulls out an old handkerchief and waves it in the direction of the fence, while watching the guards, whose backs are towards him. He checks the huts and waves his handkerchief in the light.

Ash see the signal and backs into Greg. "What the Hell!"

Greg crouches over Tom's pack, searching its contents. He pretends to be hiding it.

Ash dives under the fence, held up by Charlie. Greg, Shona and Charlie follow, while Ash holds it up. All through, Ash beckons them to follow him and they sprint unseen to the petrol drums. They reach Tom without incident.

"Greg and Ash, roll the drums quietly as close as you can to the huts. Charlie give covering fire if needed."

Charlie nods. "Willco."

"Shona, work with me."

"Light them?" she asks.

"Hell no. Not yet. Don't want to fry." Tom freezes. He has a sudden vision of a Bush Fire roaring towards him. Mind wins over matter. He leads off with the bottle crates, checking the position of the sentries, still the other side of the planes.

Ash and Greg quietly roll their drums towards the huts. Charlie covers them with his LMG. He aims his weapon at the nearest doorway, lying on his belly. With the runway lights on, he would be invisible to anyone exiting the hut. The drums reach hard mud and rumble.

Tom holds out two bottles to Shona and they approach the planes. He carefully places one under each plane, Shona copying.

Inside the hut a pilot opens his eyes, alerted by the approaching rumble. His eyes widen as he realizes something is not right. He stretches and rises to rest on his elbows. The rumble is very close. He shakes his head till fully awake and swings out of his hammock. He runs to the window, tripping over clothes on the floor.

Beyond the perimeter fence Janice watches Tom and Shona, and lets out her breath. The tension is unbearable. Just suppose they are seen? She watches the sentries the other side of the planes almost opposite Tom and Shona now, but they have seen them and hide under a plane wing.

"You'll have your revenge tonight, Subul." There is no reply. She turns and finds no boy. "Subul, Subul!" He has gone. "Oh God! He'll be caught and then . . ."

The pilot peers through a window and sees the drums rolling ever closer. "Ai, the planes! Someone . . ." he shouts.

"It's the sentries, fool! Go back to bed," calls a sleepy voice.

The pilot throws on some clothes and appears at the door, pistol in hand. He shouts, "Quick! The planes!"

Other pilots rush to get dressed. Two seize their weapons and dash for the door, clad only in underpants.

The pilot steps outside, aiming at Greg, who has just left his drum. Ash gasps as he sees Greg's danger. There is a swish and a thud as a spear sticks out of the pilot's back. He folds onto the ground. Subul yanks his spear from the body and vanishes into the shadows.

Doors open in both huts and men pour out, blinking, pistols at the ready. A siren sounds. More lights flash on. Greg and Ash are spot-lit as they dash for the shadows. Charlie waits till they are clear of the drums, taking pot-shots at the pilots as they are framed in the doorways. Then he shoots at the petrol drums, which explode catching most pilots alight . . . a scene from Hell.

Burning pilots roll on the ground in vain attempts to extinguish the flames. Bullets fly in all directions. Charlie has a turkey shoot.

"Run, the fence," yells Tom to Shona. "Shit! We'll never make it," she explodes. She needs no encouragement.

Tom runs from plane to plane leaving a trickle of petrol as a fuse. He reaches the end nearest to the fence and lights the trail, with a shot into the stacked petrol drums. They explode and the planes catch fire and burn furiously one after another in chain reaction. A raging inferno.

Tom reaches Charlie and both pour heavy fire into the staggering pilots and ground crew. Tom's face twitches as the fire rages. The odd bullet flies in their direction but soon they cease.

At the perimeter Ash, Greg and Shona squeeze under the fence, held up by Janice. "Where's Subul?" she queries, in dismay. He emerges out of the jungle with a smile, holding his spear. "Here. Just been taking care of my business."

Janice clasps him. "Thank God!"

A little hut beyond the two Nissen huts has its lights on. Officers dash out firing their weapons. Their bodies tumble down the steps as Tom and Charlie rain bullets in their direction.

Tom rushes the hut, stumbles and collapses. Charlie sprints after him. He halts by Tom. "I'm okay. Check the hut."

Charlie dashes forward.

Tom shouts, "Charlie . . ."

He is too late. Charlie vanishes inside.

Inside the hut a last officer tries to get through on the radio: "Hello, hello! . . . Shenko airfield. We've been attacked. A large force. Commandos. What!"

The door opens. Charlie enters, weapon in hand. The officer freezes in horror. He tries to draw his pistol. Charlie shoots him once in the head. He fires into the radio, checks for anyone else and exits. As he runs down the steps from the hut, two Japanese confront him. Charlie shoots one dead. A shot rings out. Charlie freezes. Has he been shot? The other soldier drops dead. Tom lets his rifle fall.

"Thanks Tom. Saved my bacon! . . . You okay?"

"Yeah. A radio in that hut?"

"Was. Not now."

"Bugger! I needed that. Never mind. The radio op. may have called in reinforcements. We're out of here."

Tom forces himself to his feet, shivering and frozen by the flames. Dante's Inferno! Planes explode, the bullets from their cannons fire in all directions. Charlie jumps to one side as a line of tracer bullets scythe towards him. He shouts, "Tom!"

"Sheet! Yeah. I'm away." Charlie sprints, closely followed by Tom, to the fence.

Janice and Ash pull up the fence and they scramble into the jungle.

"Jeez, that was a hit and a half," exclaims Ash, enjoying the blazing scene.

"They'll not be strafing us for a while," says Tom, with a wry smile. "All here? . . . Right, let's go."

*   *   *

Chapter 13

om's group heads for the sea, making slow progress due to the heat and exhaustion. His fire phobia has eased off but he has little left to give, energy-wise. He is buoyed up with the thought of what they have just achieved. The Japanese High Command will be seething but he has drawn their teeth.

"Can't we stop for a rest, Boss?" asks Charlie.

"Soon Charlie. Just think what we did today. The Japs'll be hopping mad."

Janice looks at Subul, wondering why he is so cheerful. He can't stop grinning to himself, wiping it off his face, every time someone looks in his direction.

Ash looks at Greg thinking back to the haversack incident. What the Hell had he been doing going through Tom's pack? An innocent motive was hard to consider. Greg plods on, deadpan.

"Each one of them deserves a medal for today's exploits." thought Tom.

Shona was also smiling, re-living the exploding planes and her part in it. Better than festival day fireworks by a long way. She was less cheerful as she thought back to her house in flames as the enemy torched whole streets, to drive out the Allies.

In a distant tent on a Japanese airfield a Wing Commander snores the night away. Outside the duty clerk is hopping from one leg to another. He talks to himself, as the only person awake apart from the sentries on the main gate.

"He hates being woken. He hates bad news. He hates indecision but he insists on being told important events before they happen. Oh well, we only die once."

He enters the tent and pauses before the corpulent form.

"Sir . . . Sir . . . Sir" increasingly louder.

The Wing Commander opens one eye. He does not care for what he sees. He shuts it. He opens both.

"What the Hell are you doing in my tent?" he explodes.

"Sir, I thought you should know we've . . ."

"Get out of here! Can't you see I'm trying to sleep!"

The clerk persists with his message and backs out of the "volcano", hands over his ears.

The message delivered, he runs to his office.

"Can't believe it! A whole airfield! . . . Everyone dead! . . . Not possible . . . . My precious planes!"

The Winco yells to a sentry, frozen to the spot: "My plane! Quick. Rouse the lazy ground-crew."

A crewman, clad only in underpants, runs to the nearest plane and opens the cockpit. He stands to attention beside the plane. The Winco jumps in and starts the engine. "Tell my squadron leader to have them ready for take-off on my return."

"Sir!" replies the crewman. He closes the canopy.

The engine splutters and roars into life. The crewman removes the wheel chocks. The plane lurches forward and takes off. The crewman runs to his billet.

In his cockpit the Winco growls, "I'll bloody well see for myself." He seethes with rage.

Some hours later a solitary plane zooms over the jungle airfield and circles, while the Winco takes in the scene of smoking devastation for himself. There is no sign of life. Just bodies and wreckage. His expression changes from horror to anger as he soars away, his fuel gauge on just below half full.

In the jungle Tom and company stagger through trees, thinning as they reach the coast. They slap at mosquitoes and midges. They raise weary faces to Tom as he pauses in a clearing.

"We'll stop here." There is relief all round as they slump to the ground. Charlie heats a leech off Shona's thigh with his lighter.

"Thanks."

"It shows good taste." He grins. They too lurch to the ground.

Ash swings Subul off his shoulders, the only fresh member of the group, and slumps.

They gulp from their water bottles, savouring the last drops.

"How many do you reckon we killed on the airfield, Tom?" asks Ash.

"Pilots—forty plus and ground crew, at least twenty, plus signals and cooks." They all look stunned apart from Tom and Shona. She smiles.

"You a farmer, Tom! How many cattle did you kill off?" asks Ash, grinning.

"When I got hungry," Tom forces a laugh, thinking to himself that Kit nearly killed him.

"Have you always been such a ready killer?" asks Janice.

"Only since Singapore. It's the Japs or us. Remember the hospital?"

"Has Fear no meaning for you?" pursues Janice.

"I'm trying to give it up," grins Tom. He scrutinizes Greg and Ash. "Were you on your own all the time by the fence, Ash?"

"Yes, Boss. Till Greg joined me. Why?"

"Just wondered." Tom looks hard at Greg, who studies the jungle, pretending not to recognize the meaning of Tom's question.

"A pity you weren't in charge at Singapore, Tom," says Ash.

"He'd 'ave killed the lot of us," mutters Charlie, unheard by Tom. Greg nods and Ash looks at Charlie like he's a cockroach.

"I wouldn't have wanted that one," says Tom. "Not enough men, nor ammo. Not all General Percival's fault, though there'll be those who stab him in the back. The Jap soldiers were better trained for jungle fighting than us and had total command of the air plus their tanks against our armoured cars made it one sided."

Janice toys with a spear. She starts. "How come there's blood on this, Subul?" she whispers.

Subul: "I didn't".

"Ah!" says Janice as she realizes the truth. She drops the spear and the subject. She bottles up her emotions.

"Shona, you'd better join Charlie for a water search. I notice you work well together," says Tom.

Charlie grins and gets to his feet. Shona does the same. They collect all the water bottles. The hum of a distant plane makes everyone freeze, awaiting Tom's orders.

"Relax. They can't see us in a sea of green."

They listen as the plane circles and then fades away.

"What're you going to do when we get home, Tom?" asks Ash, striving to lessen the tension. "Prime Minister?"

Tom laughs. "I might start a demolition firm."

"Or undertakers?" says Ash. They all laugh.

*　　*　　*

Chapter 14

A t the Japanese airfield the Winco's plane approaches, its engine stuttering. Men run out of their tents to watch his approach. The plane comes in to land, its prop wind-milling, the engine silent. Its pilot dives to gain more speed. He straightens out and lands. The men cheer. The Winco slides open his canopy and jumps down.

Minutes later he sits at his desk angrily twisting a pencil in his fingers. Two young pilots in uniform sit bolt upright opposite him. "Right, I understand the cover's too thick. It's a job for the army now. I'll alert all units."

The pilots jump up and salute. He returns their salute as they exit. He snaps the pencil and picks up the phone. "46 unit? You find those saboteurs, whatever it takes. Keep their leader alive for me to question and kill the rest.... Yes, immediately... Damn Intelligence. I only need him." He slams down the phone.

In their jungle clearing Tom's group lie around a fire. It glows but has no smoke. A roasting lizard swings from above from a pyramid of branches.

Charlie and Shona stroll into the clearing with the water bottles. Charlie gives a thumbs up and they hand out the bottles.

"Any sign of people?" ask Tom.

"Not even an alligator," smiles Shona.

Charlie and Shona sit with the others.

"Smells good," says Shona, licking her lips.

"Should do. I caught it," says Ash.

He cuts the vine suspending the lizard and places it across two mess tins. He divides it into seven portions and offers a portion to each of them.

Ash joins Tom, further off from the others. He crouches beside him. They eat in silence. Tom is disturbed. "Is it right putting all you guys at risk? I'm worried about the girls."

"Better than a prison camp, or torture." Ash recognizes Tom's need for support at last. The young officer can't complete his mission on his own.

Tom consoles himself, stemming his self—doubt. "This info is vital. If in time, it could shorten the war."

"Do it. No alternative," says Ash.

Tom nods, more relaxed.

"That wasn't lack of food, was it, Tom?"

Tom is startled for a moment. He says nothing. He can't tell the true story of Kit to explain his scars. Too embarrassing. The event of how fire ravaged the land, when he was tiny, but stopped at the creek was what he tells Ash. It had left an indelible mark on his brain.

"And yet you set fire to all those planes!"

"Yup! Since then, I've been petrified by fire. Don't tell the others. Change the subject." Tom shudders again. Kit's dragging him behind his horse he prefers to keep to himself. It might be taken as weakness.

"Bloody Hell!" Ash thinks to himself, "Poor kid."

On a diet of fish, lizards, bananas and not much else, Tom and gang walk along the beach, bronzed, bearded and in ragged shorts, apart from Tom, who has managed to keep his shirt in one piece, more or less. His face has the odd nick from a blunt bayonet come razor.

A motor launch passes by about a mile out to sea.

"Under the trees, everyone. We don't want tongues wagging."

Janice trips in the sand and Tom helps her up. Her eyes say her thanks and a little more. The man of steel has won her heart but she's scared of appearing forward, and of rejection.

"I wouldn't mind chancing a boat," says Charlie.

"Give us time and the opportunity," says Tom. "It's got to be at night and giving us space to be well away from land at daybreak."

Children play and a dog barks nearby.

"Better hole up till dark?" suggests Ash. He looks at Subul, who is dragging his feet, exhausted.

"Sure. We'll spy out the land. Try for a boat and provisions," says Tom, as they halt sheltered from sea and village by clumps of palms.

"Anything would be a nice change from fish and bananas," says Janice, smiling to take any criticism out of her words. "We'll find a home for Subul."

"No, I want to stay with you. My family now." He links his arm through Janice's.

"Too dangerous," says Tom. "You'll be okay with your own people."

Subul shakes his head. "They aren't my people and they won't want me. What use am I to them?"

They rest in the shade as evening shadows widen. The jungle insects click and monkeys chatter. Village sounds dim.

As darkness falls, Ash slinks along the waterfront, closely followed by Shona. "Why don't I just leave them," she thinks. "Join the natives. I could blend in." Some magnetic attraction keeps her with the group, not just Charlie. They need her as much as she needs them. Tom has saved her life and possibly this is reciprocated.

The moon makes shadows on the shore. Ash stops and points to a motor launch, twenty feet long. It has an inboard motor. "Just what we need," he whispers. They listen. There is no sound of people. They start forward and are brought to an abrupt halt by a low cough. They freeze. Ash signals to Shona to wait there. He stalks forward silently.

A sentry sits by the cabin door, his rifle propped up against it. Ash springs onto him. There is a violent struggle. Ash grunts and folds up as the sentry chops him across his solar plexus.

The sentry grabs his rifle, ready to shoot Ash. Ash swerves so the sentry butts the rifle into his face. Shona leaps onto the sentry and stabs him to his heart with her knife. The rifle falls with a clatter and the sentry lands in the bottom of the boat. Shona checks him for life and then struggles to lift him over the side of the boat. He drifts away in the tide.

Shona lifts Ash's battered face. He smiles through a haze of blood. She washes it off with sea water. "Can you get to your feet?"

Ash nods. They stagger back to the clearing, Shona struggling to prop him up. As they enter the clearing, Tom, shocked stands to help her, and lays Ash gently down, his back against a tree.

Ash smiles at their concern. "Vas you worried about? You ought to see the other guy. Shona, she did a full job on him."

The others relax and Janice takes a professional look at Ash.

"He'll live," she smiles.

In a not so distant concrete block office newly promoted Captain Saito sits at his desk, on the phone, nodding. "We'll be ready . . . . Yes Sir. I'll enjoy that." He replaces the phone and stands.

In the clearing Tom's group listen to his orders. "We'd better leave at first light. They shouldn't discover the body till dawn. Take the launch. It could be dicey finding provisions round here, so a diet of fish till we reach Java."

"How far?" asks Janice.

"Java's about eight hundred miles long so I'd like to sail along it as far as possible. It'll be much quicker."

"What now?" asks Charlie, stifling a yawn.

"Have a nap. Give the locals a chance to sleep. I'll take first watch till ten. Shona and Janice can take the next. Get under cover, just in case."

They scramble under bushes.

*　　*　　*

Chapter 15

anice hears Tom mumbling and draws closer, unseen. She strains her ears and is amazed to hear him reciting the Lord's prayer.

"And forgive us our trespasses as we forgive them that trespass against us. And Lord, keep us safe in our mission."

"Have you got room for me and God?" she asks him.

Tom opens his arms and she falls into them. They kiss and then Tom pushes her away. "You'd better keep watch. Never be caught with you pants down."

Janice giggles and creeps away to join Shona under bushes a shorty distance from the men. Subul has disappeared away on his own.

Greg emerges out of the gloom to re-join the men. Janice watches him with interest. "Where's he been for so long?"

"Call of nature," replies Shona.

Janice is not convinced. "There's something odd about that guy," she thinks to herself. "I'll ask Tom when I get the chance." She is too tired to think. Both girls succumb to their exhaustion and the perfume of jungle flowers eases them into deep sleep.

In a nearby clump of bushes figures circle the men. Bayonets flash in the moonlight. The enemy surround them. Captain Saito kicks Tom awake. "Oh Hell!"

"Up now," says Saito quietly. "Come with us." His words are reinforced by six soldiers prodding them into consciousness.

The four stumble to their feet, waking into a nightmare.

"Okay, okay!" says Tom, hoping the others won't do anything foolish.

"No talking. Where's the rest of you?"

"Only us," says Tom, hoping the girls will avoid discovery. "The rest died of sickness and their wounds."

They are handcuffed and prodded away into the darkness.

The Japanese soldiers search other clumps of bushes, torches illuminating the undergrowth. Fallen leaves swish as heavy boots displace them. Four shadows loom above Janice and Shona. The girls' heavy breathing breaks as weapons are cocked around them and bayonets prod them. One pricks Janice as she wakes with a cry, alerting Shona. Their mouths are bandaged and wrists bound.

"Pigs!" mumbles Shona through her gag. A bayonet tears her sarong and they are marched away.

Tom and the other men are shoved into a small cell. They slump to the cement floor. A bucket in the corner is their only toilet. Moonlight filters through the bars of a small window.

"So much for the girls being on watch," exclaims Charlie.

"Hm! At least they'll be free," says Tom.

The door opens and a soldier enters, rifle at the ready, another behind him, equally on guard. He approaches Tom.

"Come!"

Tom staggers to his feet. He leaves, followed by the soldier, who backs out and locks the door. Tom is prodded down a passage built of concrete blocks.

Tom stands in front of Saito, seated at his desk. The two soldiers point their bayonets at Tom's rear.

"Captain Tom Hartley?" asks Saito.

Tom is amazed. "How the hell . . ."

"Search him," orders Saito.

The sentries rummage through his pockets. They drop his shorts and rip off his tattered shirt. His hat falls to the floor.

"See, I have nothing!" says Tom.

Saito observes Tom's scars but refrains from commenting. He is astonished by Tom's obvious youth. He should be easy to crack. "Co-operate or else!" Saito makes a throat slitting motion.

"Prisoners of war," announces Tom.

"Where's the rest of your group?" growls Saito.

Tom struggles to pulls up his shorts with his wrists handcuffed. Saito watches him with contempt.

"We're all that's left of them. The maps were burnt in the fire when your men destroyed the village."

"Don't lie to me. There must've been many of you to kill that patrol and the airmen. We've found your women."

Tom hesitates. "I'm telling you the truth."

Saito motions to the sentries. One knocks Tom to the ground with his rifle butt. The other kicks him when on the ground. Saito loses all control. He screams: "Don't think you can lie to the Imperial Army. Tell me where the rest of your men are!"

Tom groans on the floor. "Okay, okay. There were another twenty," he fabricates. "Some were killed by the patrol. The rest died off in the jungle. Starvation, disease, malaria."

"You don't seem that skinny." He runs his whip across Tom's ribs.

"We caught fish," offers Tom.

"Where're you heading?"

"We're trying to get home to Australia."

Saito nods to the soldiers, who kick Tom again and beat him with their rifle butts. He groans.

"It's impossible to get from here to Australia. You are spying for the Americans or you were going to sabotage something else."

"I'm telling you the truth."

"We'll see you and your soldiers in the morning. The truth or you die. They first, one by one and the girls. Take him back to his cell."

The soldiers kick Tom again. He passes out. They drag him away.

In the men's cell Ash, Charlie and Greg are shocked to see Tom's bloody state as the soldiers throw him to the floor. They take off his cuffs and throw in his shirt and hat. They drag Greg out. As soon as the door closes, Ash strides over to Tom. He lifts him up carefully, his back against the wall.

Tom shivers and shakes, still unconscious. He murmurs, dreaming. "No Kit! The fire! Oh Gawd!"

"The bastards," explodes Ash.

Tom opens one eye. Ash helps him on with his shirt. He pops Tom's hat on his head.

"They've got the girls," Tom murmurs.

"That's it, then," groans Charlie.

Ash rises and makes for the door. "Water".

"No, don't. They'll use it as an excuse to bash you."

Tom slumps forward. Ash puts his hand on Tom's shoulder. "Stay with us, Tom. Don't let the bastards beat us," says Ash, really concerned.

The girls knock on the wall in the next cell. Charlie knocks back.

"I wonder where Subul got to?" ponders Ash.

"Probably gone and joined the natives," says Greg.

Night sets in. A quarter moon illuminates the camp's concrete featureless buildings. Subul crawls towards the girls' cell, reaching it unnoticed by the sentry. The soldier strolls towards a door on the other side. He checks it is locked. He pauses and walks towards the corner Subul crouches behind, in deep shadow. The sentry rounds the corner, his eyes focused in the distance. Subul freezes. The sentry turns and disappears round the corner. Subul wipes his brow and waits.

In the men's cell the door opens and Greg is thrown in. His face is bloody. The others awake. "Don't worry. They got nothing from me," he says. "If they don't get what they want tomorrow, they're going to shoot us." His glance at Tom is wasted. He is unconscious again.

Outside the girls' cell Subul lets out his breath. He tiptoes near the window. It has no glass; just bars.

"Are you there?" he calls. There is no reply. He picks up some small stones and throws them through the bars. "Janice, Tom?" he calls softly.

"Subul, don't get caught my love," calls Janice.

"See if you can find us a piece of wire," calls Shona.

Janice looks at her, wondering.

"Be back," calls Subul as he crawls off into the dark.

Janice and Shona stretch to see out of the window but it is too high. They turn towards the door.

"We'll never open that lock with wire," says Janice.

"Watch me," whispers Shona.

"He'll never find any wire in the dark," says Janice.

"Wanna bet?"

They settle down for the night, as much as they can on concrete.

Sometime later Subul crawls towards the cell with a piece of lead pipe in one hand. He reaches the window.

"Anyone home?" he calls. There is no answer so he resorts to the pebble trick again.

"Hi," calls Shona.

"No wire. Use this. Catch." He throws the pipe through the bars.

"Christ! You nearly brained me!" exclaims Shona, catching it. "Silly boy. We can't knock down the door with this."

"No. I bring sentry here. You brain him." He slinks off into the darkness.

Shona passes the pipe to Janice, now fully awake. "You'll have to do it. Step up onto my back."

"I can't. I might kill him," says Janice.

"We'll never escape unless you do,"

Shona crouches and holds her hands for Janice to step up. Janice steps up and wobbles on Shona's back with the pipe level with the window. Shona crouches, bracing her hands on her knees.

Subul creeps round the far corner. "Hey!"

The sentry jumps and then chases Subul round to where he stops under the girl's window, letting the sentry catch him. The sentry hauls him to his feet by his hair, twisting it.

"Ow! You're hurting me." Subul is just loud enough to alert the girls.

The sentry slaps Subul. Janice reacts without hesitation, cracking the sentry over the head. He collapses on the ground. Subul retrieves his keys. He checks the sentry is unconscious and runs to the corner. The girls' doorway is in shadow. Subul runs to it and tries the keys without success. Another sentry approaches in no hurry. At last the lock opens. The relief sentry strolls closer. Subul opens the door, closes it and locks it.

"Sh. Sentry." They freeze.

The sentry tries the lock and then moves on to check the men's. "Hito! Where are you?" he calls. He rounds the corner.

Shona seizes the keys from Subul and unlocks the door. They exit and Janice helps her drag the unconscious sentry into the cell. Subul grabs the keys from Shona and locks the door. They sink panting to the floor.

"Hito", calls the new sentry. His footsteps approach. They all tense up. Shona picks up the pipe and waits by the door.

"Open it," whispers Shona.

He does so, to the astonishment of the sentry.

"Water, water," pleads Janice. She mimes as if drinking from a cup.

"Hey!" exclaims the sentry. He does not fall for it and fumbles for his keys.

Subul pushes past him, punching him in the stomach as he passes. The sentry chases after him and they disappear into the dark.

"Quick! The men," bursts Janice.

Shona locks the door on the unconscious sentry and they race to the men's cell. Shona unlocks the door, checking outside first. There is a distant noise of Subul and the other sentry crashing through bushes. The girls enter to find the men snoring. A glimmer of moonlight shines from the window.

Shona and Janice wake the men, putting their hands over their mouths. Janice wilts when she sees Tom's bloody face.

"Bastards!" Her ladylike upbringing has vanished.

The men are incredulous and then delighted as they see Shona and Janice. Charlie hugs Shona. She disengages herself and gestures to the door. "Quick!"

Ash and Charlie hoist Tom to his feet. Tom smiles: "I'll manage."

"Let's go," whispers Ash: "Keys!"

Shona hands them to him. They exit the cell, Ash locking the door behind him. Outside the cell Janice halts and puts her hand up. "Subul, what about him?"

"We can't hunt for him now," says Tom. "He'll join up with his people."

"He got us all out," says Janice. "Tell you later."

They hurry away towards the beach and soon arrive at the spot where they were captured. Shona picks up a rifle from under a bush. Janice and Greg pick up two haversacks and water bottles. They trot towards the launch, Ash and Greg dragging and part carrying Tom between them.

*　　*　　*

Chapter 16

As dawn breaks the sentry enters Saito's office, dragging Subul by the arm. He shuts the door behind him and throws Subul to the ground in front of Saito. The Captain looks up, irritated. "Where did you find him? What use is a small boy?"

"He was with the prisoners, Sir. They've . . ."

"Can't you see he's a native?"

"He was their decoy, Sir. They've escaped."

"What! Get a search party out. Move! Leave the boy here. I might have a use for him."

The sentry doubles out.

"Come here, boy," Saito speaks in Japanese but gestures to make plain his order as the boy clearly does not understand his language.

Subul rises to his feet cautiously, expecting a slap.

"Do you want to live, boy," continues Saito in English.

Subul nods.

"So tell me what you know about the Captain."

"What Captain?"

Saito slaps Subul. "You know who. The one you helped escape?" Saito adjust his pistol.

"I dunno nothing," says Subul, jerking his head out of range.

"Then I'll have to beat it out of you," says Saito getting increasingly frustrated with Subul, whom he grabs and bends over his knee. The first smack descends. Subul grits his teeth and makes no sound,

"I'm not going to be made a fool of by a small boy, so you might as well tell me now as later," says Saito, smacking him harder. But he is met by silence.

Saito continues smacking him, as if he's enjoying it. Subul certainly is not but although tears start to trickle, he shuts his eyes tightly, refusing to give in.

"Am I going to have to beat you to a pulp?" says Saito after ten smacks.

"I don't know nothing," says Subul.

Saito throws him to the floor. "We wage war on men, not children," he snorts, panting from exhaustion. "I have other uses for you, little boy."

On the water front Tom's party jumps into the launch as the sun breaks through an early morning mist. Ash and Charlie lower Tom into the cabin. Janice gives him water to drink and bathes his face with sea water, causing him to start at the pain. Ash's face still sports a black eye while Greg is surprisingly clear of damage.

"Thanks Janice. Paradise," murmurs Tom. She smiles.

"Get the Hell out of here," calls Tom, suddenly rising to the situation.

Ash starts the engine and opens it to full throttle. The launch takes off into the mist, followed by a rifle shot. They all duck.

"As fast as you can go, Ash," calls Tom somewhat unnecessarily.

Another shot splashes wide. The launch smacks down on the waves.

"Can't see who's firing at us," says Charlie, in a low voice.

"So he can't see us," says Ash.

"Subul, a real soldier," says Janice. "I hope he got away."

"They won't kill a kid . . . will they?" says Ash.

"Wouldn't bet on it," says Greg, with feeling. The others look at him in surprise. Has he had close quarter dealings with the Japs? If so, when?

Greg and Charlie take first watch, Greg on the helm and Charlie searching ahead for other vessels. Ash pores over a chart he has found in a locker. Janice gives Tom more water from her own bottle.

"Thanks, Janice, my angel nurse," says Tom gratefully.

"Any time, Tom" She smiles tenderly at him. He reciprocates.

"I guess we've fuel for a couple of hundred miles," says Ash.

"If we don't get attacked again," says Charlie.

"Lighten up, Charlie," says Shona, with a grin.

"Stick with the fishing fleet and slow up. We don't want to attract attention," says Tom. "We'll hide out on an island for a day or so."

They stop their chatter and think their own thoughts.

"How the Hell did we get out of that one?" thinks Tom. His body feels more mobile, thanks to Janice's attention.

"What's become of Subul?" thinks Ash. He has become fond of the boy and is full of admiration when Shona tells him the story of his part in their escape.

The launch putters round the edge of the fishing fleet and drifts further away. A small island filters through the mist, half a mile distant.

"We need to put that island between us and the fleet. Then they won't see where we head for next," says Tom.

"I wonder where Subul is now?" says Shona.

"He'd only get in the road," says Greg, brutally.

"He saved your life, Greg," reveals Charlie.

"You're kidding," says Greg. "The spear!" blurts Janice. "Bloody."

* * *

CHAPTER 17

The launch's engine gives a splutter and fades. Ash opens the throttle but it dies. They rise and fall in a greasy swell.

"Water in the petrol. How did it get there?" Ash looks accusing Greg.

"Don't ask me."

"I saw you returning from somewhere the night we were captured," says Shona, her eyes slicing Greg.

"Having a leak," he explains.

"Must've been a long one!" Shona's sarcasm bites.

Tom is steely eyed. "It's time you told us what you've been up to, Greg. It had to be you at the airfield, trying to alert the sentries."

Greg is shaken. As Ash drains the petrol tank, Greg thinks back to a jungle clearing. In front of a rough army tent sits a Japanese officer on a canvas chair. Before him on the ground lies Greg, his cheeks smeared with blood. Two Japanese infantrymen flank him with bayonets on their rifles poking him. He gasps from pain. Tied to a tree leans his brother, Bernie. He has been badly beaten.

"You will work for us or your brother dies," says the officer, pulling out his pistol and pointing it at Bernie's head.

"Okay, okay, whatever you want," says Greg."

Greg fades back to the present. He rises, steadying himself against the mast and whips out a pistol covering them all.

"So you went through my pack. I thought it was you," says Tom. "And your Jap mates searched my pockets so you know I'm not carrying anything."

"You've committed it to memory, or your hat! No one thought to check your hat," accuses Greg.

Ash clenches his fist. "Traitor!"

"What would you have done in my position," says Greg. "The Japs have my brother. If I don't bring you back, they'll kill him. I hate the bastards. Killed enough of them haven't I?"

"You might have let us know," explodes Tom.

"And risk losing my brother?"

"We'd have thought something up."

"They know about you, Tom. I rang them in Singapore."

Charlie nods, remembering the phone ping in the shop.

"So what do you aim to do now?" asks Tom. "Manage this boat on your own?"

"No, you're going to take it back to the Japanese patrol boats and give yourselves up."

"Like Hell!" says Tom.

Greg waves his pistol towards Tom. "First, you're going to tell me what you know about the code books." Greg cocks the pistol.

Their mutual hate bounces off him. Janice shrugs, as if: "What's the use?" She pulls out a fishing rod and dangles the hook in the water.

"You've got the right idea Janice," says Greg. "Ash, the far jerry-can has clean petrol."

Ash scowls at him. He picks up the can and fills the tank. He replaces the cap and tries the engine. It splutters and then catches.

Janice winks at Ash out of Greg's vision. She stands, blocking Greg's view and pretends to concentrate on fishing. Ash nods. Janice sits as Ash guns the engine, pulling hard at the tiller at the same time. The launch lurches in a new direction. Greg stumbles off balance. Janice whips him across the face with the rod. He backs away and lurches over the side, dropping his pistol. He swims after the boat, yelling: "You can't leave me."

"Better pick him up," says Tom.

Janice is surprised by Tom's sudden humanity.

"Not bloody likely," says Ash, gunning the engine flat out.

Greg yells but they leave him swimming after them. He evaporates in the mist.

Shona shouts: "Swim back to your Jap friends."

"You shouldn't have left him, Ash," says Tom, to their astonishment.

"Feed the sharks," says Ash. "He'd have no trouble in shooting any of us."

In Saito's office he studies a map of islands at his desk. A sergeant stands beside him. "You take the north, Sergeant Hogo will search the south. I'll co-ordinate the sea search. These men are making fools of us. Their capture is of national importance."

"Yes Sir," replies the sergeant, hiding a smile.

"Go!"

The sergeant salutes and exits. Saito walks over to inspect the shoes Subul is cleaning. They shine brightly. Saito ruffles Subul's hair and says in a friendly voice: "I've got a son like you."

"You killed my mum!"

"It wasn't me. I don't kill women."

"It was one of you."

"That's war."

Subul keeps deadpan, bottling up his hatred. Saito shrugs and returns to his map.

The launch surges through the water between two little islands. Tom and Ash are one stage more healed and looking cheerful.

"They may have better things to do than chase us," offers Ash.

"Like go back to their wives," says Shona, with a smile.

"Yeah. Be gone by morning," says Ash.

Tom looks doubtful. "That was a brave thing you did, Janice. He might've shot you."

Janice smiles and keeps quiet.

Not far away near the fishing fleet a motor torpedo boat putters to a halt. Two sailors board a fishing vessel and search it. A heavy machine gunner covers the vessel. Saito paces the deck, stopping every so often to peer through the mist. Two spotter planes pass overhead in the direction of the small islands. Captain Saito searches the horizon with binoculars, muttering to himself. He swears in frustration.

Tom's launch emerges from the silhouette of an island, out of the mist. Charlie kneels on top of the cabin, searching for other craft. Tom whispers: "See anything, Charlie?"

"No, too fuckin' thick."

On Saito's MTB an anchor is lowered. "Keep your eyes open. I can almost feel they're not far away. When you see them, don't sink them. I want the Captain alive."

"Sir," replies the gunner, clicking to attention. Saito controls his irritation at the noise.

On their launch Charlie still peers through the mist. Ash has the launch at Slow Ahead. There is no other sound but the soft putter of the engine. Occasionally they pass the silhouette of another vessel, ghost-like. Janice lies on a roll of canvas. Tom peers along one side and Shona on the other. Charlie stiffens. He points ahead to the right. "Boss, there's something out there. Not moving. No lights."

"Dead quiet everyone," whispers Tom through whirls of mist.

Ash turns the tiller so they head away from the other vessel. He reduces the engine noise. They drift, each face tense.

A powerful engine starts up.

"What now?" asks Ash.

"Got a white flag? Anything'll do."

Janice rips off her blouse and hands it to Tom. He passes it up to Charlie. "When you see them, wave this and keep waving it."

"I'd rather die than fall into their hands," whispers Shona.

"We might not. Give me your water bottles everyone, quick. Take a drink first. Then empty them."

They obey, emptying them over the side. The MTB engine throbs closer. "Bloody Hell! It's an MTB. We've had it," breathes Charlie.

On Saito's MTB he cleans the binoculars and peers through the blanket of mist. There is the ghost of a boat. "It might not be them. Wait."

He spots the launch and clenches his fist. He gestures towards it to his machine gunner. The man nods and fires a burst, clipping the launch's bow. Saito picks up a loud hailer. "You in the launch, we're coming aboard."

On top of the cabin, Charlie waves his flag vigorously. Ash slows the engine to a murmur. Hidden behind the cabin the girls help Tom fill the bottles with petrol. He takes his time, avoiding spilling the explosive liquid. Shona tears small rags from her sarong with her knife. Tom "corks" each bottle with a piece of rag.

"Charlie, tell me when they're twenty yards away."

Charlie nods. Tom lines up the bottles on the seat nearest the MTB so they are concealed by the edge of the boat. Tom, "A match, a lighter?"

There is a deathly silence apart from the water lapping the boat and the MTB's engine's dull throbbing.

Charlie is resigned to capture.

Shona: "Oh no!"

Ash: "Give me a piece of rag, now!"

Shona hands Ash one. He soaks one end in petrol. He points to an engine spark plug. Tom nods, understanding the plan.

Charlie makes a vigorous sign behind his back. The MTB edges alongside, throwing its engine into reverse. It bumps them, nudging Tom off balance.

Ash lights the rag for Tom from the spark plug. He hands the burning rag to Tom, keeping the lit end away from him and the bottles. A bottle cork drops on the deck.

On the MTB six sailors are poised to jump onto the launch, their weapons at the ready. Captain Saito: "Steady, wait." He recognizes Charlie's tattered uniform, "Got them!"

Charlie jumps down into the launch. A sailor lands on the launch's cabin. Four water bottle bombs fly through the air, fuses burning. They land on the deck of the MTB, bursting into flames and explode.

Ash guns the engine. The launch shoots forward throwing everyone onto their knees or bruising elbows. The sailor rolls into the water.

"Bloody male driver," calls Shona.

"Duck everyone," shouts Tom.

The MTB explodes with a giant blast. Tom and group cover their heads with their hands from falling debris. They hold onto each other and the edge of the launch, which Ash has at top speed. Pieces of MTB shower into the sea. No other vessels can be seen through the mist. Sharks circle round where the sailor hit the water. He swims, yelling.

"Save him?" queries Ash, recognizing Tom's humanitarian streak.

"Try."

Ash pulls the rudder round and the launch swerves in a tight curve back towards the sailor, who throws up his hands and disappears with an agonizing scream beneath the surface.

*   *   *

Chapter 18

All are shocked for a moment.

"Sorry boss," says Ash thinking, "One problem the less."

"Look," calls Janice. A small body floats in the water, draped over a piece of debris. It is motionless. Ash slows the boat by the body as a shark cruises by. Shona reaches out and pulls the body into the launch. Charlie holds onto her thighs.

Tom carries Subul into the cabin.

"Subul! Is he dead?" queries Janice.

"I guess so," says Tom sadly, as he lays the body tenderly on a bunk.

Janice pushes past Tom and blows into the child's mouth. Then she pushes his chest. Water trickles out of this mouth but there is no sign of life. Just more water. Janice repeats time after time but nothing happens.

"Sorry, love. He's a gonner," consoles Tom.

In her emotion, Janice fails to notice the unconscious endearment. She keeps on pumping and blowing, frantically, ignoring Tom watching hopelessly. It seems to no avail.

Suddenly an eye opens. Janice: "Oh Subul!" She burst into tears as she hugs him.

Tom, "He's alive!"

Subul opens both eyes and smiles. "Big bang," he rolls over and sleeps. Janice rises to her feet. Tom pulls off his shirt and lays it over Subul. Janice hugs Tom, thrilled. She suddenly thinks: "I could do this again," as she feels the warmth of his body.

It is evening and the mist has lifted. Tom is spelling Ash at the helm. The engine throbs at full bore and the sail is down. The others sit on the bench seats looking relaxed now their chief enemy is no more. Subul sleeps as his body repairs from the shock of the explosion. Ash checks the engine.

"We're almost out of fuel," he announces.

Tom nods, unperturbed. Charlie sits in front of the cabin with binoculars. He points at a distant town.

"We'll cut in behind the town as it gets dark," says Tom. "Make it look as if we're passing by."

"I wonder how the war's going?" says Janice.

"The Yanks should make a difference," says Ash. Best thing the Japs could have done, bombing Pearl Harbour, bringing them into the war." He flashes a glance at Tom, who ignores the remark.

"How could you say that? We'd be in a right mess without them," says Janice.

Tom cuts the engine. A motorboat approaches to pass with ample room. "Fishing lines out. Girls hide. Subul, stay inside."

The boy was just about to leave the cabin and see what was happening. Charlie jumps down to pick up a line. Ash and Tom already have theirs trailing. The boat passes and Tom waves idly. A man in native costume waves back. They are all so brown they must appear like natives.

"Phew!" exclaims Janice.

"He could be just a local out for a joy ride or fishing trip, or a Jap spy," says Tom. "No need to get local tongues wagging. Girls don't fish around these parts."

"I might just be fishing," grins Janice to herself, thinking of Tom.

"Can we sit up now?" asks Shona.

"Yes, he's well on. We'll try for a clothes change tonight."

"Shona would look cute in a new sarong," says Charlie.

"So would you," she returns and they all laugh.

In the evening, as dusk falls fast, they tie up the launch in a row of other boats. Subul sleeps in the cabin while Ash lurks beside him with a rifle on the seat. "He'd make a good playmate with my boy," thinks Ash, looking at his relaxed features.

In the township of Parangtritis, Tom and Janice flit from one clump of trees to another. They cruise the rear of the houses. Janice points to a washing line with clothes left on it. Tom nods and grins. She darts to the line while Tom keeps watch. She grabs clothes off the line. A dog barks making her jump. She grabs one more item and runs to join Tom at the fence. A large mastiff chases after her. As she reaches the fence, Tom opens the gate letting her out. The dog follows, ripping off her remaining clothes, leaving her stark naked. Tom gives the dog a mighty kick and it runs off howling. He closes the gate. "We're not here!" They race along the deserted lane and dash into an alley. Janice hands a flowery shirt and dark pants to Tom. She steps into an attractive sarong, while Tom squeezes into pants several sizes too small.

"Can't leave them here," he says.

She conceals Tom's rags inside her sarong and gives him a quick hug. "You could have done that a minute ago," he laughs.

"He really is human," she decides.

In another part of town, Shona and Charlie have already changed into local costume, gained in a similar way. They blend with local people in the street. Marching feet approach. "Japs," whispers Charlie, his guts twisting.

A woman in sarong points to a door. She opens it and gestures Shona and Charlie inside. She shuts and locks it behind them. The soldiers march past.

"Are we that obvious?" asks Charlie, alarmed.

"Your hair's too light and you smell different. I'm Malam."

"Thanks. You saved our lives," says Charlie.

"Go now. They'll search houses if they know you here."

"You very kind, Malam," says Shona. "Do you know where we can find food, tinned or fresh?"

"You have no money, have you?" asks Malam. She smiles at their despair and strides to a cupboard. "Lucky I shop yesterday. Take these." She throws a dozen varied tins including a large baked beans tin marked "Heinz" into a little sack. As an afterthought she adds a bunch of bananas.

"You're a good woman," says Shona. "After the war I'll repay you."

"Tell your countrymen to hurry up and rid us of these terrible Japanese. Go . . . I check." Malam opens the door slowly and peeps out. She beckons them outside. "Good luck." She closes the door softly behind them.

On the quayside Ash has his rifle at the ready as footsteps can be heard. He waves Subul into the cabin. Tom, Charlie, Shona and Janice stagger along. The men carry two jerry cans each, the girls one and Shona has the sack of provisions over her shoulder. They quietly stow their gear away in the launch and sit exhausted. Ash makes for the engine. Tom puts his hand up for silence. No one is about. He nods to Ash, who starts the engine and they putter seawards.

*   *   *

CHAPTER 19

D ays later they are only just in sight of land. Subul trails his hand in the water.

"I wouldn't do that, Subul if I were you. A hungry shark might fancy a bite," says Tom. Subul jerks his hand out to their amusement. Fishing lines trail behind without a bite. A heavy bank of cloud threatens ahead and the waves heighten.

"Good to have Java behind us. I reckon we'll be in Darwin in a week or two," says Tom, trying to lift their spirits.

"Getting low on fuel again," says Ash.

Tom points to the cloud thickening. Janice looks frightened. "Will the launch take a storm?"

"Need to keep her head into the waves," says Ash.

"Just enough revs and no more," says Tom.

The boat rises and thuds down. The sky darkens and waves tower. Water comes aboard. Charlie bales flat out with the empty bean tin. Tom uses a metal bucket with better effect, panting. Janice takes over from Tom. He slumps. Shona snatches the tin from Charlie and bails like mad. Charlie is exhausted. The wind worsens.

"At least the Jap planes won't see us in this," says Charlie.

"The first positive thing he's said so far," thinks Janice.

"They won't need to if it gets any worse," says Tom. "After all we've been through, Nature is pretty unkind," he thinks.

"Isn't that an island?" asks Janice, standing up to get a better view. The boat lurches and she is thrown overboard.

Tom throws his hat into the bottom of the boat and dives after her. The gap between the boat and the struggling swimmers widens. Ash puts the boat into reverse. Tom closes on Janice. She throws up her hands and sinks. He grabs her and puts his arm under her neck.

The engine splutters and dies. "No!" exclaims Shona.

Tom kicks out for the boat but they get no closer. Tom tires and they drift further away.

"They'll never make it," cries Shona.

Ash swings out an oar towards them. "Grab it Tom!" he yells.

Shona places the other oar in the far rowlock and wiggles it in the water. The boat drifts closer to Tom by degrees. He grabs at Ash's oar and misses. Ash leans out so far the boat is in danger of capsizing. Charlie leans the other way and stabilizes the boat. Tom manages to grasp the oar with his fingertips. Ash pulls them alongside the boat.

"Help them in, Charlie," cries Shona.

He drags Janice aboard after a struggle and Tom clambers aboard with Ash's help. Tom and Janice lie panting in the bottom of the boat. Water swishes around them.

"Thanks mate. Keep baling," says Tom.

Charlie and Shona windmill their oars to keep the boat into the waves. Ash bales for his life while Subul uses the bean tin. Janice holds the tiller. Tom lays empty jerry cans on their sides so they fill and them empties them over the side.

"We're closer to the island," observes Janice, and indeed she is right. In their struggle for survival they have drifted unnoticed within two hundred yards from an island.

"We'll take the oars, Charlie." Tom seizes one and Charlie the other. They row like mad and manage to turn the launch into the waves.

A larger wave approaches.

"Hold tight, everyone and prepare to swim," shouts Ash, grabbing Subul.

"Can't swim that far," gasps Subul.

The wave hits them, overturning the boat. They are spilt into the water, spluttering and striking out for life.

Janice swims strongly with Tom shadowing her. Ash is on his back, towing Subul by one shoulder and threatened to be dragged under by successive waves. "Only a little way now, mate," says Ash to the waterlogged boy, quite incapable of taking in anything.

"Help!" splutters Shona as a wave beats her in the face.

Charlie swims to her side and together they make it to the beach. Janice and Tom stand in the surf and drag Ash and Subul onto the sand.

"I guess that's as far as she'll take us," gasps Ash as the boat splinters on rocks.

"I don't want any more sea voyages," says Charlie, surveying the jungle edged sand.

Subul lies on his back with a wide smile. "Ash is my dad now," he says. "He saved my life."

Ash lies exhausted and wordless, wiping could it be a tear from his face?

"I hope there are no Japs on this island," says Tom. "That'd be the last straw. When you guys've got your breath back, we'd better check it out."

Sometime later Tom and Janice struggle through dense vegetation. With no machetes, they make heavy weather of it. Tom stops. "Listen!" They hold their breath and hear tinkling water."

"Sounds pretty good to me," says Janice.

"Come on," says Tom and he leads, tearing creepers out of their way. They break through beside a little rocky outcrop. A spring tinkles into a little pool of crystal clear water. Palms shade them from the sun. They cup their hands and drink. Tom pauses. "Champagne." He mouths a kiss to Janice. She sends one back.

"So peaceful," she sighs.

A parrot shatters the peace and they both laugh. The magic of the place brings them closer together. Janice starts to say something. Tom seals her lips with his finger. He holds her by the shoulders for a moment. They kiss, then longer and deeper. Eventually Tom pulls away. "Better find the others. Business as usual," he warns.

They climb to the highest rocks of the island and scan around. There is no sign of any others, not a tell-tale plume of smoke. "We've got it to ourselves," Tom announces.

"Hmm," says Janice sexily.

Tom shakes his head. Janice looks at him, all coy. He laughs, relaxed at last.

Under a crescent of palms, Ash, Charlie and Shona sit on a log as Tom and Janice break into the clearing.

They slump to the ground. Tom checks their faces. "No Japs?" He drops his hat on the sand and wipes away sweat from his face. They all shake their heads. "Us neither."

Janice picks up Tom's hat, tracing the outline of a thin booklet under the sweat-skin with her finger. "What's this?"

"That's the code book and battle plans the Japs were after. Got to get it back to Aus. It could alter the war."

A wave of realization passes over the others. So that's what drives Tom.

"That's why you always wear it," says Shona.

"A spy," says Charlie, and then bites his lip, wishing he hadn't said it.

"My job was to find out the Burma invasion troop numbers and routes, explains Tom," smiling indulgently at Charlie.

"We may never get off this island," says Janice, eying Tom. She smiles to herself. "Now I've got him."

"Great. We can live off coconuts and fish and sit out the rest of the war," says Charlie.

"You'll have to walk on water to leave here," says Ash.

"How far are we from Aus. now?" asks Janice.

"Could be as little as two hundred miles," says Tom.

"A long swim," says Ash.

They smile, apart from Tom. He has his head in his hands. "So near and yet so far."

"Got an idea," says Janice.

The others look at her with amusement.

"Shoot," says Tom.

"We need to attract the Japs here."

"Better than festering on here for years. The war could be over and we'd never know," says Ash.

"We'll do it," says Tom, perking up. "Come on Charlie. Help me collect firewood."

Charlie is anything but enthusiastic. "Fall into Japanese hands," he thinks. "Tom's lost his head. Or he soon will."

*   *   *

Chapter 20

They make for the highest point of the island. Tom and Charlie drag firewood from the jungle. Shona and Janice collect dry grass, aided by Subul. Charlie lights it with matches from the native woman. Tom puts damp grass on it to create smoke.

Days later they have made a crude shelter from branches and large leaves. They sit round a fire with a wild turkey suspended over it. Subul kneels by it, turning the turkey with a stick.

"A week without a sign of the enemy or friends," says Ash, despondently.

"Just be patient. They'll come," says Tom, hiding his own impatience.

"Not too soon, I hope," says Janice." She fondles Tom's arm.

He places his hand on her other arm. The others grin.

Shona crashes through the undergrowth to join them, breathless.

Tom stands quickly. "Who?"

"An MTB, coming close over there." She points to the north of the island. They all jump up.

"And Charlie?" asks Tom.

"He'll be down when he's sure they've landed, they're the enemy and which way they're going."

Ash starts to trample out the fire.

"Great. Wait till dusk, another hour or so. We need to create diversions to slow them down and stop them from returning to the MTB," says Tom.

"Such as?" asks Janice.

"Another fire the opposite side of the island. Draw them away from their vessel."

Charlie arrives, gasping for breath. "They've landed about six hundred yards that away." He points to the north.

"Come. Good luck Ash," says Tom.

"What's he . . . ?" starts Charlie.

"Later," says Tom, leading off towards the boat.

Ash arrives by his piled fire with a glowing ember. He looks around . . . No Japanese. He throws the ember onto the fire. Subul blows the sparks to life. It blazes after an initial splutter. Ash throws more branches onto the fire and they take off into the jungle.

On the shore a sliver of moon illuminates a large rubber dinghy on the beach. A sentry sits on its upper rim, his rifle propped between his knees. Tom and the others arrive between the trees.

Charlie whispers: "How do we get to him? He'll see us."

"Think you can swim round from that point, come up behind him from the sea?" asks Tom.

"Not sure about that," says Charlie, hesitantly.

"I'll do it," says Tom, disappearing into the trees.

On the top of the island, six Japanese arrive at the fire. They approach cautiously and stand by it, jabbering.

Back on the beach the sentry gets to his feet and walks up and down.

"Bloody Hell!" says Charlie. "Tom's lost his chance."

Tom appears in the sea behind the dinghy. He ducks as the sentry walks back towards it. The sentry sits down, facing the trees. Tom rises from the water, crouched almost as low as the dinghy. The sentry slaps at a mosquito. Tom freezes, reaching the rear of the vessel. The sentry turns towards Tom. Charlie growls from the jungle. The sentry raises his rifle towards the noise. Tom springs onto his back. His forearm closes on the sentry's throat. His other arm presses on the sentry's neck. Tom breaks his neck. The sentry crumples. Tom drags him into the water, holding him down till the air leaves his clothes. He floats away just below the surface.

Charlie, Shona and Janice run to the dinghy. Charlie picks up the rifle. They drag the boat into the sea and get in.

"Where the Hell's Ash and Subul?"

"We'd have heard if the Japs had found them. Nice one, Charlie," says Tom.

"Can't look for them in the dark," says Janice.

"How long will you give them?" asks Charlie.

"A couple of minutes more," says Tom.

They wait in silence, listening. Ash runs out of the trees towards the boat, Subul close behind. They hop in.

"Paddle," orders Tom.

They approach the MTB from the sea side, where they will be least expected. On board three Japanese lean on the shore side rail, looking towards the island. They smoke and chat.

On the beach the patrol arrives back and search for their missing dinghy. The sergeant shouts to those on the MTB,

"Where's our dinghy?"

There is no reply as Tom and Shona drag two unconscious bodies to the other side, aided by Janice and Subul. There are splashes as the bodies hit the water. Charlie struggles with a big sailor, who forces Charlie's knife out of his hand. He lifts Charlie above his head to throw him overboard. Tom chops the sailor with the side of his hand in the kidneys. He drops Charlie. Charlie grabs the rail and hangs there above the sea. Tom kicks the sailor in the belly. He folds up. Tom chops him on the back of the neck. He falls unconscious. Shona leans over the rail and holds onto Charlie's wrist. Tom slides the sailor to the rail and struggles to lift him over it. Subul appears from hiding behind the deck-house and helps Tom with the legs. The sailor slips into the sea.

There are shouts from the shore. A bleary eyed lieutenant stumbles up the companionway to deck to investigate the noise. Ash chops him on the neck and helps Tom slide him overboard.

"Help," shouts Shona as Charlie is slipping from her grasp.

Tom runs to her side and helps Charlie back on deck.

"Thanks mate. How many more?"

Tom, unsure, shows ten fingers. He shrugs.

Four more Japanese climb onto deck, each armed with a rifle or light machine gun. As each comes through the narrow door, Ash or Charlie chops or knifes him. Tom and Shona slide them over the side. Janice and Subul collect weapons. Shouts increase in volume from the shore.

Charlie stands back from the door to the companionway holding a captured automatic at the ready. Ash runs to the engine and starts it up. Shona takes the helm. Tom stands behind the heavy machine gun. He checks the ammo belt. He cocks it, aiming at the figures on the shore. He sweeps them with rapid fire. They all fall like dominoes. Tom swings the gun round to cover the door. It swings open and six Japanese come out firing. They have no chance and are mowed down in seconds. Charlie pulls the bodies out of the way. Ash helps throw them overboard. Tom looks at the bodies with disbelief.

"My God! We've done it," says Janice, with a gun in her hands.

A hatchway opens just beyond Tom. A weapon points at him. Janice fires through the hatchway. The man screams and the hatchway slams shut. For a moment Tom stares at her, aghast at his brush with certain death. Janice stands open mouthed in astonishment at what she's done.

"You beaut," exclaims Tom.

"I did it!" shouts Janice.

"Charlie and Ash, check below. Be careful," instructs Tom.

They descend, weapons at the ready. Tom continues to hold his weapon steady on the door.

"It's all ours," shouts Ash after a few moments. Just one wounded.

Charlie appears at the door, dripping blood.

Shona screams, rushing to him. "No!"

Charlie: "It's okay, girl. Not mine. I had a tight embrace with the cook." He grins.

Shona: "You bastard! How could you!" They form a clinch, hugging.

Ash appears at the door, supporting a very young Japanese sailor. Blood drips from his shoulder. He looks terrified.

"Kill him? asks Ash.

"Enough killing. Patch him up and give him the dinghy to the island," says Tom.

Ash smothers his surprise.

"Yeah, and we're sinking. Someone's shot out a ruddy great hole in the bottom of the boat," says Ash.

*   *   *

Chapter 21

T om looks, "Hell! What have I done?"

Ash disappears behind the deck-house with his captive.

Tom swings the gun away and uncocks it.

"A ship!" calls Shona.

"Where?" asks Tom.

Shona points to the rain blurred horizon.

Tom's stomach sinks. After all they've been through, to become a prisoner of war and his mission unaccomplished. This is the end. "Hell, not a prison camp after all this!"

"It's not an MTB. Looks bigger," says Tom, inwardly praying.

Janice watches the water rising up the companionway in horror. "Get out, quick!"

"It must be a Jap vessel. Our mob won't be this far from home," says Tom, despondently.

"It's a Bathurst class corvette, 80 crew, one of ours," exclaims Charlie in delight.

The corvette speeds towards them. They all cheer.

"Get ready to swim for it, guys," calls Tom.

"Becoming a habit," says Charlie, optimistic for once.

Ash tries to keep the MTB's bow into the waves with an oar. The boat fills with water. They must sink before the corvette reaches them. The corvette looms out of the murk. A large meshed scrambling net hangs from its side.

A lieutenant calls out, "Climb into the net, everyone. Hold on tight."

The sea seems a little calmer in the lea of the vessel's side. Their boat is full of water and is sinking beneath their feet.

"Girls jump," calls Tom.

"I can't," says Janice frozen by her recent drowning experience.

Tom takes her shoulders and Ash her legs. Tom: "One, two three." They throw her towards the net. She hooks an arm through it.

Shona jumps, landing close to Janice. Janice's hand slips by degrees from the rope. Shona hauls her further into the net.

Ash grabs Subul and jumps. Tom follows. The net is hauled up the side of the vessel with them resembling a fish catch. At the top they roll out of the net onto the deck to be greeted by a tall lieutenant and the guns of a suspicious crew.

"And who the Hell are you?" asks the Lieutenant, waving away the guns as he takes in the girls and young Subul.

Captain Tom Hartley and in need to get vital information to the Australian army," says Tom. "And thank for saving our lives."

He grins his relief and offers his hand.

"Lieutenant Paul Jones, Australian navy," says their host, squeezing his hand . . . "We'd better get you below. Shower and a change of clothes."

In their cabin below Janice and Shona towel their hair dry. They wear naval ratings tunics and trousers. They stop their actions and hug each other spontaneously.

"Safe from the terrible sea, at last," says Janice.

"Surely we're on our last leg home."

"Your home," laughs Shona, her face glowing.

"Welcome to my place and we'll get you set up," returns Janice, anticipating civilization, proper meals and Safety. There is also a big question mark about Tom? Is he really hers, or will he be whisked away to another theatre of operations, or even once things return to normal, will he still care for her?

In another cabin Ash and Charlie lie on their bunks, Subul is curled up asleep like a kitten on his, while Tom sits on a chair facing them. All are shaved and like the girls, wear Naval tunics and trousers.

Tom rises and paces up and down, frustrated.

"At least we're heading for Darwin," says Ash, attempting to reduce his tension.

"The stupid, brainless lieutenant won't even let me use the radio. By the time we land, it could be too late."

"He doesn't want to attract enemy attention?" queries Ash, reasonably.

Tom nods. "Can't this tub go any faster?"

"Corvettes' max speeds are only fifteen miles per hour," says Charlie. "Still we're not Jap prisoners."

"How do you know all this, Charlie?" asks Ash.

"My uncle's on a corvette minesweeper."

"You've come a long way from the defeatist I first met, Charlie," says Tom, smiling and relaxing.

Charlie is suitably pleased and embarrassed.

A week later Tom and his group wait on a bench outside the General's office. The men are in smart pressed uniforms. The girls wear new dresses and have had their hair shaped. Subul wears shorts and a T-shirt and glows.

Tom rises and walks up and down. Ash glances at Charlie, amused. Tom approaches the door and is poised to knock when it opens and a secretary, Carol smiles at him. "The General will see you now, Captain Hartley."

The others make to rise. "The Captain only," she stresses.

The others slump back, disappointed.

Tom charges into the General's office. The General, enthroned at a large antique desk with In and Out trays and two phones, rises and shakes Tom's hand, while Carol sifts documents at a smaller desk.

"General Robert Ashton. Good to meet you Captain Hartley. I hear you have survived an epic journey."

"Yes, Sir," says Tom, bursting to learn the news.

"I've looked at your maps and code book with interest. The code book is of course out of date by now and I'm afraid you're too late for the Japs' push to India. A pity. Knowing their numbers and proposed routes would have saved many British lives."

Tom is devastated.

The General continues, "However you'll be pleased to hear the British have held them and are driving them back in places."

"All for nothing," says Tom, striking his fist into the palm of his other hand.

The General smiles, "Not quite. Will you call the others in now, Carol."

She rises, opens the door and waves the others in. She indicates they should stand in a row, next to Tom.

The General stands. "I want to congratulate you all on a wonderful effort. Captain Tom Hartley will be in for a medal in due course and maybe others of you too."

Tom is still gutted.

The General continues: "Although you failed to make any impact on the enemy's India campaign, not for want of trying, I am delighted to inform you your heroic wiping out of the airfield saved Darwin from a much worse bombing."

All, including Tom, are delighted.

The General salutes them. "Your country salutes you all as heroes. Even you, young man," He leans forward and embraces Subul, who shrinks, shyly. "I'll have a quiet word with your friend and protector." He smiles at Ash.

A little later they relax in a park. Tom embraces Janice. A little further on, Charlie embraces Shona, while Ash feeds ducks on a pond with Subul.

"Where do I go?" Subul asks Ash nervously.

"Would you like to come and live with me and my son?" asks Ash. "You'd be good company for him."

Subul says nothing. Tears glisten in his eyes as he rushes to hug Ash.

Charlie looks at Shona for a moment, wondering if this is the right time and place. "You'll hang your hat with me?"

"Does that mean what I think it means?" asks Shona, not quite believing it.

Charlie holds her shoulders for a moment, gazing into her eyes and smiling. "It means, will you marry me, like stay with me forever?"

"Of yes, forever." Shona kisses him long, like forever.

They pull apart like a cork coming out of a bottle, wave to the others, arms round each other's shoulders and amble away.

Janice and Tom laugh, wave back and to Ash, who is strolling away with Subul, looking up at him like an adoring puppy.

"That just leaves us," says Janice. "You won't have to go back and fight again, will you?"

Her concern touches Tom. He waits to answer, amused by her tension. "And leave you? The General's asked me to stay here on his staff and lead the Intelligence."

"And?" asks Janice, delighted.

"Will you marry me?"

"Too right I will. Wild horses won't pull us apart."

They kiss, break for air and kiss again.

*   *   *

SEQUEL: CLEANING UP

CHAPTER 1

Six months later they were all awarded medals and there was a big splash in the paper, but Tom was not mentioned by name. Something to do with Security.

Charlie was wrapped up with Coastal Defences on Tom's recommendation and Shona had a bulging tummy. Subul learnt to drive Ash's tractor and competed with his son as to who could plough an acre the fastest. Ash was listed as essential manpower, feeding the nation. He had a funny feeling Tom had something to do with it.

Tom worked all hours but still found time to build a cot, while Janice nursed till her pregnancy dictated otherwise.

The war dragged on and many brave Allied troops lost their lives or returned home physically or mentally scarred.

When will Mankind learn that Peace is preferable to War?

As war drew to a close, with the two atom bombs dropped on Japan, who otherwise would have continued fighting till hundreds of thousands more on both sides had been killed or wounded, Tom was allowed home, one of the first to be demobbed. He and Janice were married in a registry office with no fuss or expense.

As Tom and Janice drew up at the homestead in a rented car, they were delighted to see that it had rained enough for Greg and Dick to expand the herd. There must have been near a thousand head of cattle they passed along the drive paddocks.

It was with mutual relief that father met son, both alive and well. Greg and then Dick met Janice, each summing up the other.

"You've got good taste my boy," said Greg, with a delighted smile as he shook Janice's hand tenderly.

"I know," laughed Tom, as he swept her into the new wing that Greg had the foresight and firm belief that Tom would return, to build. It was clinker built like the rest of the house but very sturdily made, with long, low windows, each with its own shutters.

"Before you get too used to my being here," warned Tom, "I've a final assignment, no not with the army, that must be completed."

"No," said Greg and Janice together.

"It shouldn't take long, if my suspicions are correct. I have a clue where Granger, the bank manager who stole over £50,000 of our money may be lurking."

"Is it worth it, Tom?" asked Greg. "We've got enough to live off. Even with our impending addition." He looked at Janice's bulge. Something might happen to you. It would be terrible."

"Nothing worse will happen to me than what I've been through at war and here," said Tom, determinedly. "I reckon he's skulking in Hawkes Bay, New Zealand," and he explained why.

He might get the drop on you," said Janice, and what will you do to him? There's been enough killing."

"Don't worry my love. I won't kill him. Either hand him in to the police or I'll find a way of making him pay for the lives he's damaged. Don't forget, some of the people he robbed of all their money took their own lives, being destitute, all because of him."

"I can see you're set on it," said Greg, but you might wait till the baby is born."

"I want it over and done with well before that. Give me a week and if you don't hear from me in a month, Dick can come looking for me."

"Too right I will," said Dick. "How about I come with you now?"

"No, you're needed to run this place, thanks all the same," said Tom. And that was that.

Next day, Tom took a bus to Brisbane from town and from there he hitched a ride in a mail plane to Auckland. After a night in a B & B, he hired a car and set off for Hawkes Bay, via Lake Taupo.

*   *   *

Chapter 2

Granger, by one of those strange quirks of fate, saw in the Auckland Weekly News an article about Australian and New Zealand troops returning from the war. His mother, after Tom's visit, had written to him warning him that Tom was possibly on his trail. She had seen Tom peer into her drawer and had not been fooled by his re-arranging the dropped flowers. His early departure had confirmed her fears. At the foot of the news column it had mentioned the exploits of Tom's group and though not providing his name, there was a photo of him with two pretty girls and the rest of his party.

Granger was in a quandary. If he stayed in Auckland, Tom would not have much chance of finding him, but should Tom go hunting him in Hawkes Bay, it would only be a question of time before he discovered the absent landlord's property and then he might trace him back from there.

In any case, while Tom was alive, he would always live in fear of discovery and a long jail sentence. If he hid out in his sheep station, he could ambush Tom and kill him. There would be plenty of space to bury or burn his body. His man, Brian was out there, dependent upon him for his secure job, till he died and would follow any instructions he gave him. Granger had cultivated a relationship with him, and they were very close. As he thought more about the body disposal, he remembered an old hut up in the foothills, with its own well. The body could be dropped down the well and then there were plenty of large rocks to fill it in. No one would ever discover Tom.

The more he thought about it, the more he liked it. He could always claim that Tom had never found him and so must have come to his end perhaps in the sea. That was a good idea. He could leave his clothes on a beach, just above high tide, to be discovered eventually.

Granger anticipated a little torture just the pleasure of it, before finishing off his victim. How about setting the Dobermanns on Tom, naked, weapon-less, starved, so weak, in a hunt up the mountain, so he would be running towards the hut. Very convenient. He licked his lips with the thought of the chase. Don't feed them too well till Tom appeared, as Granger thought he would inevitably. He was so excited by the prospect that he could hardly wait for Tom to find him. The trap would be set and waiting.

Tom drove past Taupo, with its hot pools and good fishing, stopping for a fish and chips, where a host of tourists had also stopped. While he waited his turn in the queue, he wondered how best to trace the thief? The estate agents were an obvious source. Before long he was in Napier with a standard list of questions: What large properties in and out of town had been sold during the summer of 1941? Their address and the name of the purchaser? He pretended he was doing an historic survey of the important people of Hawkes Bay, who had risen from nothing to riches during and since the war.

Napier was a wash-out and likewise, Hastings. They were pleasant towns with a comfortable atmosphere and friendly people only too ready to help, but very few properties fitted into that category. The Depression only ceased during the war and there wasn't much money around to buy large properties. Anyone who did would stick out like a sore thumb, which suited Tom very well.

Next, Tom went to Waipukurau, a tiny one street market town in South Hawkes Bay. There were only two real estate firms so he went to the biggest with several windows of properties. He had a gut feeling that he might be getting warm. There was a nice young girl in the office on her own. She said, "I wasn't here back then but you're welcome to look through our records. We're bound by law to keep them for ten years so you may find some interesting property sales."

Tom searched hundreds of sales, putting on one side everything over £20,000 for a start. He tried putting himself in Granger's shoes. He would want a remote property, not an apple orchard, with all those pickers, and off the beaten track. He spent the afternoon leafing through the records until he came to a couple of sheep stations that looked promising. He decided to try the furthest from town that evening, as he was too excited to wait till morning. He thanked the girl, not mentioning the properties. He did not want her phoning them in good faith so they might have a meal ready for him. He said he would go on to the next town as his searches proved futile.

He set off in the car, a dented old Ford, and followed his map into the back-blocks. He kicked himself he hadn't stopped for a meal, and checking his petrol reckoned he would have just enough to get there and back to a service station he had noticed on his way out of town.

As he neared the property and the sun started to sink behind the mountains, he reckoned he would park the car a bit down the road and jog to a position where he could observe the house and its owner's activities. If Granger was there, he might have company, which is exactly what Tom wanted to avoid. He wanted the man on his own, so he could force him to give him access to his funds and discover where all the other unfortunates' funds were hidden or invested.

He saw from the map that there was an outbuilding, ideal for hiding behind to observe. He left his car behind a stand of willow trees and checked it was safe from an inquisitive bunch of cattle beyond a five wire fence. He noted that the cattle were in excellent condition and so was the fence.

It was nearly dark as Tom jogged down the drive and then forked off towards the barn. He slowed to creep up to the corner and peer round it at the house. It was a well—built house and had its own power supply, as he could see from the bright lights in the windows. They were curtained so he could not see inside.

Frustrated, he decided to creep up to the house and listen for voices, or perhaps Granger was on his own.

*　　*　　*

Chapter 3

Tom stepped round the corner of the barn and suddenly felt himself falling, not far. It was too dark to see what he was in and he wondered if it was the start of a well. He felt around the walls. They were of crumbly soil with no purchase, and too high to climb out. Suddenly he felt vulnerable. He was in some sort of pit, unable to get out. There was no moon and everything was black. If this was Granger's place, he could not call for help. God knows what the man would do with him if he recognized him after five years. And there was only one contact he had made in Waipukurau with departing words that he would be moving on. So no one knew where he was.

Tom decided to get some sleep and hope that with light dawning, he might find a way out of the pit. He was soon in dreamland and that was how Granger found him next morning.

"Ah, who have we here?" said a voice as Tom woke, wondering where he was. "Good God! We've trapped a young man. Yes, I recognize you. You're Tom Hartley. Come to find your money, Tom? You've come to the right place," he gloated.

Tom looked around him and realized to his horror that he could never get out of the pit on his own.

"Quite a clever device, isn't it? We thought you might come visiting and prepared this trap for you. It was the obvious place you'd spy on my house from. So here you are."

"Hell! There's more than one of them," thought Tom. "Even when I get out of here, it won't be easy to overcome two." He saw the other man peering at him, his scarred face studying him coldly.

"So what now Mr. Granger?"

"I could leave you there and let you die of starvation but you might be found if one day someone thinks it's a good place for a slurry pit or something. Besides it would be so dull."

"Great!" thought Tom. "They're going to get me out of here." His hopes were soon dashed.

"Since you are entirely at my mercy, you will do exactly as I say."

"Yes," replied Tom, thinking back to when as a boy he had been at Kit's mercy. Well he had got out of that one.

"First, remove your clothes down to your underpants."

"Eh?"

"No one is as dangerous without their clothes, and I know you can be a force to be reckoned with. A war hero. Well we'll see how low the hero can be driven. Off with them now!"

Tom took off his clothes as instructed, immediately feeling more vulnerable. "He's planned this out. I'm in trouble," thought Tom.

"Now hold your hands together, fingers intertwined above your head."

Tom had no option but to obey. A lasso was dropped down and tightened on his wrists, held by Brian.

"Now stick out a leg at right angles in front of you."

Tom did so and another lasso was snared round that leg, tightened and hauled so he was upside down, his other leg trailing. He was hauled up out of the pit, stretched between the two men, helpless.

They bound him up like a turkey trussed for dinner. Then Brian fetched a ute truck and they humped Tom onto its tray.

He wondered what was coming next. It wouldn't be pleasant, he was sure.

They hauled him inside the house and through a door, first moving a concealing dresser, into a windowless room. Four rings had been set in the walls. They tied one limb to each ring so he could move but only so far.

"There's a bucket for your toilet and you can sleep on the floor. This is the beginning of your weakening process. We will give you just water for the first week and then see how you feel. Brian and I will take your vehicle for a ride to where it will never be found."

"What are you going to do with me?" asked Tom nervously. Never had he felt so helpless.

"We can't let you go, ever," said Granger. "That must be obvious to you. We'll have a little sport with you before you disappear. Two hungry dobermanns await you outside. We'll give you a start up the mountain and then let them chase you. You'll do wonders for their appetites. They're being kept short of food for the time being. Just to make it a quick end, you can tell me who knows you are here?"

"I phoned home last night from Waipukurau, saying where I was going today. They'll come looking for me if I'm not in touch tomorrow. They'll alert the local police. You'll be in prison in no time for kidnapping," blurted Tom, thinking up his escape story.

"Where did you phone from, Tom?"

"The public coin box by the car park."

"There you've made your final mistake, young man. That phone box hasn't worked for months. No one knows where you are and they're not likely to discover, are they?"

What a mistake! One that may have sealed his fate. Tom cursed himself. Now he really was up the creek.

Granger grinned in triumph as he saw the truth on Tom's face.

"So I'll leave you to your hunger and dreams, of what might have been if you hadn't charged in here in the dark, eager for revenge. Brian will bring you a mug of water before we go to bed. We can't let you die and spoil our sport."

Granger, and Brian, who had been listening to all this with admiration for his employer, left Tom to his thoughts in the dark. The moment they had gone he tried pulling on his rings, but they had been set in concrete and there was no give. He was there till they released him for his death chase. How he wished he had brought Dick with him. Or even just filled up his car at Waipukurau. At least there would have been a trail to follow. All this might not have happened if he had waited till daylight and not charged in so full of confidence. His thoughts faded till after what seemed like many hours, Brian brought in an enamel mug of water, which he drank thankfully.

"Thanks, mate. You don't want to be hanged for murder do you?"

"What murder? You don't exist. 'Sides, I wouldn't miss the sport for anything. Sleep well." Brian left, shutting and locking the heavy door behind him, with a chuckle.

Tom eventually fell asleep, in spite of his naked body on the cold concrete floor, mentally exhausted.

*　　*　　*

Chapter 4

Back on the property, Janice was cheerfully preparing their dinner. All seemed perfect here. Greg was delighted with the mother of his grandchild to be. Dick enjoyed not having to do his house duties and Greg and he enjoyed her sparkling company. As they sat down to their meal, Greg said, "I hope Tom's found the louse. He'll get our money back and then put him behind bars, I'm sure."

"He won't have trouble with an ex bank manager" said Janice. "You should have seen him in the war. Unstoppable! I expect he'll have found Granger by the end of a week, and we can expect him home soon after that. Just a few weeks for the magistrate to get into gear."

"Funny he hasn't rung us' said Greg. "It would be good to know he has arrived safely."

"The Kiwi phone service isn't always that reliable," said Dick. "I know. I've been there."

They continued with the Good Life, happily ignorant that they would not see Tom again.

Tom woke several times through the night, desperately uncomfortable. He had dreamed of life on his property watching their young child grow and blossom. Waking to reality was a shock. Think as he might, he could not come up with any escape plan. Even if he managed to shed his bonds, impossible in the circumstances, the heavy door was between him and freedom. He had heard the bolt slide across the other side, an omen of doom. Then there were the dogs. Dobermans could be killers and these sounded as if they were. He had a glimpse of a pistol on a table as he was hustled into his cell.

Gradually Tom slumped into hopeless depression, waiting for his next drink of water.

When it came, Granger brought it to him, leaving the door open behind him . . .

"Enjoyed our hospitality, did you?"

Tom groaned.

"So you cocky young fool, you underestimated a mere bank manager. Right into the trap. Snap!"

Tom said nothing, knowing it to be true.

"Suppose I let you go, what would you do?" Granger enjoyed toying with him.

Tom grasped at the only straw he had. "Whatever you see fit. I've got enough money to live off and I would guarantee to remain silent if you let me go. After all"—he paused for inspiration—"I would not like to admit that I had been made such a fool."

Granger pretended to be interested and continued fishing.

"And suppose I took a photo of you as you are now, you wouldn't like that in the national papers?"

"No way," acted Tom hotly. "Please don't do that. I'd do anything to avoid that. Anything you want."

"Lick my boots," said Granger.

"What, now?"

"Yes, now."

Tom had nothing to lose. He bent down and licked Granger's muddy boots, spitting out the filth. As he did so, Brian had slipped in silently and taken a flash photo.

Tom wondered what was coming next.

Granger laughed. "It's so good seeing the war hero grovel, and now I have proof of how low you'll sink. My obedient victim."

Tom held in his rising anger. Granger would love to see him pulling at his bonds.

"That's all for now. By tomorrow your mind will be steadily sinking and that fine young body will be one shade weaker. An interesting scientific experiment. A pity we can't share it." Granger strode to the door, beckoning Brian out and they left the cell, chuckling.

Tom's mind was already as low as he could imagine he could sink. All he had done to survive the war and what for? He nearly wept with frustration. He was left alone all day with his thoughts. He wished they would come again, for the company, foul though it might be. At least it passed the time and gave him something to think of. Just sitting or standing was driving him mad.

By the end of the first week, with no food or exercise, Tom could hardly stand. He was amazed how his muscles had already softened.

Granger entered in the morning and looked at him speculatively. "You'll be easy meat for the dogs in a day or two."

Tom shuddered. "How will you sleep at night with murder on your hands?"

"Murder? No way. I just let the dogs out on hearing an intruder, not that I will ever need to offer a defence. Should you survive, highly unlikely, I'll finish you off with this." Granger pointed to his pistol in his belt, which Tom had been too blurry to notice. "So you see, in two days' time you can say goodbye to this world. I can already see the dogs tearing you apart. Rather like in the Roman Emperor Nero's time. Yes I'm a cultured man. I know my literature." Granger smiled evilly.

"You're twisted," said Tom, just managing to fight back a little. "You ought to be locked up."

"Save your breath. You're the one who's locked up, in case you haven't noticed. Ah, how wonderful to have the power of life and death over a fellow mortal. Prepare for the next world, Tom." Granger made for the door, pushing past Brian, who had been listening and enjoying it all.

*   *   *

Chapter 5

The next forty eight hours passed all too quickly for Tom, as he spent it flexing what muscles he had left, in preparation for his last race. The morning came and Granger arrived with Brian, who cut his bonds, while Granger kept his hand on his pistol, just in case.

They helped Tom stumbling out of his cell and through the back door. It was one of those misty mornings with the sun just breaking through in places. Tom looked at the dogs straining at their leashes, eager to get at him.

"We'll give you ten minutes' start, otherwise it'll be over in a trice—boring. You will run towards the ruin up there and I will be in at the kill with Brian. Fifteen minutes of life, I reckon at best. Goodbye Tom. The enjoyment will stay with me for ever. Go!"

Tom stumbled off in the direction he had been directed. He did not want to die even earlier from a pistol shot. After a few strides he felt his legs gaining strength. If only he could reach those rocks. It seemed no time at all when he heard the dogs giving tongue as they were released. It gave his legs a new burst of energy but too soon they felt increasingly as if tied to lead weights. He looked back over his shoulder to see the dogs' mouths open closing the gap fast. The first rocks were not big enough to climb up from their reach, but he had another faint hope. He reached them seconds before the dogs were leaping at him.

Tom lifted a rock and smashed it on the head of the first dog but as it fell dead, he felt the second biting his thigh. He drove his fingers into its eyes and it let go, yelping. He seized its mouth and yanked it apart, breaking the jaw. It could not even yelp. He could see out of the corner of his eye, the two men closing. Granger was furious but Brian more so.

"You've killed my dogs. I'll pull you apart."

Granger could not fire for fear of hitting Brian, and Tom scrambled up the remaining rocks towards the ruin. His arms felt so weak as he climbed and his legs were close to giving way.

"It's okay Brian. That's where we want him. Now we've got him." Tom had collapsed beside the building some thirty yards away and close to the well, he knew nothing of. Granger fired at him missing but a chip of rock cut his cheek.

"Ah ha," shouted Granger in delight. "First blood to us," as blood trickled down Tom's cheek.

"We'll joint him in revenge for my dogs," said Brian, still in front and holding out his skinning knife. As he reached Tom's feet, Tom pulled them up, looking terrified. Brian came on, ready for the kill. Tom did a classic foot in stomach throw and Brian arced through the air to land headfirst down the well.

Granger stopped, aghast for a moment, then took deliberate aim from twenty feet away and fired just as Tom rolled out of sight round the corner. "Stuff him!" exclaimed Granger. "Right."

He approached the corner of the building cautiously.

Round the corner Tom had found a dirty old rag, part of a shirt, and he placed a small rock in the sleeve and whirled it round his head. As Granger fired without looking round the corner, missing Tom by a mile, the rest of his body appeared and Tom let fly. The rock hit Granger in the head and he collapsed on the ground with a surprised look, semi-conscious.

On his way down the hill, dragging Granger by his feet, Tom put the wounded dog out of its misery with a shot from the would-be murderer's pistol. It was a long drag down and Tom was tired out of his mind. It did Granger no good at all.

Tom took great delight, once he had regained his clothes, tying up Granger in the cell. He gradually gained consciousness and was terrified.

Tom left him there to await his fate and helped himself to the best meal in his life even before he cleaned the blood off his cheek and bound up his leg. He never remembered later what it consisted of, but it was Food!

With the door firmly bolted on Granger, Tom suddenly felt safe but totally spent. He fell asleep in an easy chair and slept a full ten hours.

When he awoke, he heard faint cries from Granger. He grinned when he saw the man had wet himself. He collected a bucket of water and threw it over his would-be murderer.

"Give me some water," begged Granger.

"In time," said Tom. "I'll have my breakfast first. Bacon and eggs sound about right. A pity they are the last in the fridge. By the way, if you want water, and not to be left to stew in here for good, tell me where all that money you stole is now."

Granger was cracking up and quickly divulged that the share certificates for half a million pounds worth were hidden in a secret drawer in his desk. He always took them with him when he left Auckland.

Quickly Tom rushed to the desk and pressing the right knob, was faced with a folder thick with certificates, including some in an Australian Gold Mine. He could hardly contain his excitement.

Crikey, was he enjoying this!

He suddenly realized Janice and Greg would be wondering about him. He phoned them and was put straight through.

"Mission accomplished," he announced to Janice's obvious relief.

"You might have phoned sooner," she complained.

"Sorry. I was a little tied up. Tell you all about it on return. I'll have a week or so with the police explaining a body and a crook. 'Bye darling."

*   *   *

Chapter 6

T om had a shower and found some of Brian's clothes fitted him, while his were drying. He allowed a bruised and frightened Granger to clean himself up, always with the "borrowed" pistol in his belt. Then he tied his wrists and took him in his car to Waipukurau police station, delivering this stranger to a puzzled sergeant. He got the policeman to ring the bank at Kilacoy and confirm that Granger was wanted for large scale fraud. Then with his previous tormentor in a cell, he went back to the property with the sergeant. He showed him the bonds with which he had been bound. He took him up to where the dogs still lay and showed him the well with Brian's body stuck half-way down. I'll let you work out how you get him out of that," said Tom to the astonished sergeant.

The policeman made him write a full statement of the course of events, having been shown the trap that led to his confinement.

Tom showed where the pistol had been fired when it cut his cheek, and bared his stomach to show how he had been starved.

Before they returned to town, he cooked them a good meal, courtesy of Granger's deep freeze and the sergeant asked about some of his war exploits.

"Do you reckon I'll have to wait for the court hearing or will my written statement be sufficient?" asked Tom, when they had returned to Waipukurau. He explained he had a wife due to give birth before long.

The sergeant considered all he had heard and witnessed and then decided that Tom could go home but to be on call, if needed back to give evidence in person. Tom heaved a sigh of relief and having explained to the car firm the circumstances in which their vehicle had disappeared, over the phone, he took the first bus to Palmerston North and then another to Auckland. He slept the night having eaten fully once more, treating himself to a hotel.

In the excitement of it all, he had almost forgotten the other purpose of his trip. He had hidden the share certificates under his mattress and nearly left them there.

Greg and Janice were at the bus stop in Kilacoy to welcome the conquering hero home. Dick had resumed domestic duties just this once and they sat down to a roast beef dinner.

A couple of weeks later Tom drove Janice into town to await the baby's arrival. Share certificates were returned to their rightful owners through the bank and Tom and Greg received theirs now worth £70,000, a fortune. They turned half into cash, just in case of another slump.

After all the stresses of his young life, Tom and Janice were rewarded by a bouncing baby boy, Andrew, who soon had a halo of golden curls.

Some years later Greg died and already the new Andrew Hartley was a fine rider, aged ten, and an expert with a lasso. He found one day, in the back of a drawer a medal. "What's this, Dad?" he asked.

"That's a long story, Andy. When you're a little older, I'll tell you—some of it."

THE END